MACHO!

Victor Villaseñor

Arte Publico Press
Houston
Texas
1991

Acknowledgement

First, I'd like to thank Febronio, Jesús, Jorge, Tomás, all the men that I grew up with on the ranch in San Diego, California, and who taught me about Mexico and the conditions of working in the fields. Also, I'd like to thank José Antonio Villarreal and Américo Paredes, our two fathers of Chicano literature—a literature that's just beginning and has a long and rich future. *Gracias.* Keep writing. Also I'd like to acknowledge Terry Watson, Ann Lichten, Margaret Bemis—who all helped me so much in those early years of learning to read and write. (1973)

Arte Publico Press
University of Houston
Houston, Texas 7204-2090

Previously published September, 1973
by Bantam Books

Cover design by Mark Piñón
Original painting by Frank Romero:
"¡Méjico, Mexico!" Copyright © 1984
Photograph by Rick Meyer

Villaseñor, Victor Edmundo.
Macho! / Victor Edmundo Villaseñor.
p. cm.
ISBN 1-55885-027-9 (alk. paper)
I. Title.
[PS3571.I384M33 1991]
813'.54—dc20 91-14914
CIP

The paper used in this publication meets the requirements of the American National Standard for Permanence of Paper for Printed Library Materials Z39.48-1984. ∞

Second Printing 1992

Printed in the United States of America

To my parents,

SALVADOR and LUPE VILLASEÑOR,

after ten years of writing and 260 rejections—my first one!

Thank you, Papá and Mamá!

Author's Note

In re-reading *Macho!*, I found out that I'm not the same person who wrote that book twenty years ago. I thought of rewriting parts of it—feeling almost ashamed of some sections. But then I got to thinking, hell, the 60's were the 60's and that's who I was then, so I'm not going to change it. It's rough and sometimes sings as badly off key as Bob Dylan—he was no Joan Baez, believe me—but what it says is still important.

Thank you.

Con gusto,

Victor Villaseñor

MACHO!

Macho: *m*. Sledge-hammer; anvil bank; square anvil. || *adj*. Masculine, vigorous, robust; || *m*. Jack, male animal; he-mule, he-goat; masculine plant, rice seed with husk. (Commonly used in reference to a hardworking man who's responsible and keeps his word no matter how difficult.)

BOOK ONE

All around, the ground was warm, almost hot, even in the cool of the night. It was the time before the earth-trembling birth of a volcano.

In 1943 in the flat cornfield of a Tarascan Indian, some smoke began rising. A spiraling column. The Indian and his son and their team of oxen watched. The ground shook, and a great explosion erupted. They ran in fright to the local priest. The priest and many locals came, and they began to pray for forgiveness. But still the exploding fire continued, and the lava came glowing red and yellow like molasses . . . and was later measured at 1994 degrees Fahrenheit at one mile from the erupting volcano.

The locals dug a ditch and prayed some more but still the slow heavy lava came. They moved back, dug again, and prayed again. But still the lava came, and in one week formed a cone five hundred feet high and covered an area of five square miles. The volcano was named el monstruo *and forced four thousand Tarascan Indians from their homes. And, with the wind, it sent a cloud of black ashes to another valley one hundred miles away. And in this other valley, the people witnessed the day turn dark with falling snow of blackness, and they ran to the church and remained inside for days, praying and mourning the end of the world.*

Later, when their priest got word of this new volcano, he explained in terms they might understand and the people believed . . . and went out and found their valley black and smooth and shiny as water. They didn't know what to do; this had been their valley for farming, and now it was covered with blackness. They began having hunger.

Years later a first son was born, and he knew nothing of the now-dying volcano. He knew nothing of the scientists and tourists who came to the area of Paricutín—now the volcano's official name—one hundred miles away. He knew nothing about the new roads put in by the Mexican federal government. He knew nothing about the new power plant and scientific experiments being done in Mexico by the USA. He was a Tarascan, born one hundred miles away, and all he knew was that in the valley there was a lake of evil where children were not allowed to play.

Then one day his father came home all excited. That black, evil lake was God-sent! An old man had found out the volcanic ashes enriched the earth. The boy watched his father and mother; they were so happy, and that night they ate much. Even a little meat.

Now the boy was big . . . and the ashes had long ago been plowed under, and those wondrously-rich crops of the valley were gone. And for the last few years, strange clouds had been coming in the wind. Man-made. Invisible. Down the valley from the experimental grounds. And now there was famine. Not just hunger. These man-made clouds did not enrich. They killed—bugs and birds and water; and now, children die and fathers cough much, get drunk, and mothers pray, and a few, but very few, try harder than ever before ... to survive.

Nearby stands the peak of Mount Tancítaro, 12,014 feet, and there it holds ... giving witness to the last part of the twentieth century.

CHAPTER ONE

They, the family, lived in a house with the walls made of sticks. The sticks were tall and thin and were tightly tied, one right next to the other with clay slapped between them. The roof was of palm leaves, and the roof and the walls were good—good against the wind and rain. In this mountainous area of Michoacán, Mexico, such a house was called a *jacal.*

The eldest son awoke. He slept on the ground in the small third room with his seven younger brothers and sisters. He lay by the outside wall where the clay had eroded from between the sticks and the wind blew in and the light shone through. He looked out the long crooked crack and saw that the *arado*—the plow, the group of stars called the Dipper—said it was time to get up and go to work.

He got up, already dressed, picked up his sombrero, *huaraches*, heavy poncho, and went out to the overhang of the roof. There, with no walls, was the kitchen. He saw his mother, squat and dark and old before her time, and she was busy with the fire. He put on his heavy raw wool poncho and nodded to her, not saying a word, and went out behind to the chickens and goats. He got his father's one-eyed horse. He talked to the big sorrel gelding as he saddled him with the old wood saddle, and the horse knew him and was well at ease. Then he tied down the cinch, made of wide grass rope, and checked everything over and hoped the saddle would last a few more rides. At one time this had been quite a good saddle, but now most of the leather strappings were gone and it was falling apart—falling apart like this big hut that had three rooms and at one time had been the envy of all the poor people of the pueblo. Three rooms. Almost unheard of. One big supply room for the family's *maíz, frijol, calabaza*, garbanzo and chile. Another room for his father and mother. And a third room for the children. And then lastly a lean-to for an open-room kitchen had been added by his father, who at that time had acquired fame for being a workman.

He led his father's big red horse around to the front of the once-proud *jacal.* He went under the lean-to and said, "And Papa?"

"He is sick," said his mother, handing her son, Roberto, a *jarro de canela* and a plate of *galletas,* which had lately become very popular in the pueblo. "He came home late and is very sick. He will not be able to go with you now."

The young boy looked at his mother, said nothing, and nodded. Then he squatted to drink his boiled cinnamon bark from the *jarro* and eat his crude animal cookies. He asked nothing more about his father. His mother grew nervous.

"Roberto?" she said. "He will meet you in the fields when the sun is chest-high. He will. I'm sure. It's just that he is sick right now."

He continued to say nothing, and finished his *jarro de canela* and animal *galletas,* then stood up. He was a head taller than his mother. And, because his father was so often sick from drinking, for nearly a year Roberto, not yet eighteen, had supported the home.

His mother, Jesusita, handed him his hollowed squash for water, a *guaje,* and three tacos made with beans,then wrapped in leaves of corn husks: She kissed him and said, "Take care and go now . . . you are the eldest."

He nodded—he'd been hearing this story all his life—and he went out and mounted the big one-eyed gelding and rode through the little pueblo of houses with gardens and chickens and pigs and goats, and was out of the valley and in the foothills by the mountain before the first cock crowed.

The pueblo was a village of the old style and the young were to respect their elders no matter what. In fact, if a man hit a neighbor's boy and this boy was foolish enough to go tell his father, his father would whip him once again and go thank his neighbor.

And so last month when Roberto was made foreman, with older men under him, the men under him not only began to hate him, but also rumors began throughout the pueblo that Roberto had sold his soul to the devil, and that was why he was getting ahead.

CHAPTER TWO

There on the mountain Roberto began his work. His work of hunting the oxen that he had put to pasture the night before. He found them and called them each by name.

"Hey! White pigeon! Hey! you, Billy-goat! Hey! you, Blackbird! Come, you no-good lazies! It is time!"

The *bueyes* understood who it was, so they obeyed and began their daily walk down the mountain to the fields to go to work. And, in the valley, there were two new water channels. The federal government had put them in to bring water from a small brother-river of the great father-river of the Lerma. These channels were wide and deep, and the men of the pueblo had put logs with clay slapped between them to make bridges. Roberto now moved the *bueyes* toward one of these bridges. The *bueyes* didn't like it, but Roberto pushed them and called their names, and they trusted him and so they crossed. One, then two, then all the others. Twenty head in total.

Roberto lifted his sombrero and looked to the sun was just becoming visible. He was on time.

The bridge rattled. Then one log moved a little, and the clay broke from between the logs. Roberto's horse shied and off the bridge they went. Roberto hit the flat hard water with a scream of pain and went under with the one-eyed horse on top. Roberto fought and pushed, but couldn't get free. He pushed down deeper, then away to the side and strained upward. He broke the surface and breathed. Deeply. He felt a stab of pain in his side but saw his horse struggling; so he forgot his own pain and swam to the big gelding. He grabbed him by the bridle and worked him up right. He put his own heavy-wet poncho over the horse's head and made him completely blind. He mounted, and began swimming him down the channel.

He was wet and cold and had no poncho, but he never once thought about his own discomfort. He felt it, yes, of course, but he didn't think about it. No, he just mumbled prayers instinctively and thought about the oxen and the ten men who waited for him so they could start work. He swam the horse until he found a place where the steep walls lessened. He unblinded the horse, got off, climbed the bank, and pulled the horse up. The horse leaped and fought and fell three times. Finally he made it up.

Roberto looked at the sun. It was chest-high off the ground. He was late. He mounted quickly and began to run. He was on the wrong side. He would have to cross the bridge once again. At the bridge, he turned the horse away and blinded him, then saying a few quick prayers he turned to the bridge and bolted him across. He unblinded the big gelding and took off running and in moments was with the oxen. There were only sixteen. Two teams were missing. In each team one of the oxen was green, unbroken. Roberto made his hand into a fist and raised it to the heavens.

"*¡Cabro-oo-ón!*"

But then he realized this was no help, so he began to think and not pray or curse and decided to get these sixteen to the workmen, get those men working, then return and find the two other teams. For he had tied each green steer, horn to horn, with one of the strongest and best trained of his older *bueyes*, so there was not too much that could go wrong. He pushed the sixteen on and, at the field that they were working, he found the two missing teams already there and ready to work.

He smiled. He had not been shamed. He had thought ahead well, and the big mature *bueyes* had done their job. He, Roberto, was still one of the finest *vaqueros* of *bueyes* in the whole valley.

The men, nine of them, with large sombreros were sitting around a small fire. One, tall and light-complexioned, stood up, held his hand horizontally to the rising sun, and greeted him.

"You are late. One finger of sun."

Another man, old and squat, saw that Roberto was soaking wet and said, "Come. You better come by the fire and dry off."

The first one smiled, glanced about at the other men, and asked, "What happened? Eh, *muchacho*?"

"*Nada,*" Roberto answered, and remained mounted. "Nothing."

This smiling man looked at Roberto, then grinned and glanced about at the men. "Hear him talk? Ah? Nothing happened." And he laughed lightly. "And your papa? Eh? Is he not coming? Or is he sick with a *cruda* again?"

"I owe you no explanation about my father's doings," snapped Roberto. "You don't pay the wages!"

"Boy! Were you not taught to respect your elders?"

"Yes! I was taught so. But I was also taught that we make no money with talk."

"Oh? Are you then telling me to shut up?" The man was warming his hands over the fire and was about thirty-five, big and strong, and well-known for his Saturday-night *parrandas*. "Ah? Are you telling me to hold my tongue and go to work?"

"No," said Roberto and held back ... He knew he had to go easy. He was the foreman. He was the smarter. He was responsible if anything went wrong. No, he would not be angered like his father. "Of course, I am not telling you anything. No one tells you anything. You are your own man, your own boss. We all know that. But ... to get paid ... we have to work ... ."

"Oh? Is that so? How about that! You are very wise, a wise-ass little boy!" The man was raging-angry. Roberto glanced at the man's machete by the fire, then at his own in his saddle, and he remained quiet but ready as the man said, "You disrespectful *muchacho mocoso*! All you young ones of today think you know so much!" The man reached for his machete.

Roberto sat still, not reaching for his, and said very evenly, "You have family, you have mouths to feed, remember them. And also ... I have not given you reason to fight. We are honorable men of work; let us be careful not to provoke each other. The weather is upon us, and we are all very tired. Yes, if you must know, I fell in the channel with my horse!"

All the men laughed. The angry man didn't reach for his machete. And Roberto didn't say anything more.

The squat old man stood up. He was the eldest of the group and he was wide and very strong, and last month he had been foreman. In fact, he'd been the one who'd recommended to the owner that Roberto be made foreman. As he now stood up, he was happy. He'd made the right recommendation. All the men were tired and nervous, always at each other's throats, and yet Roberto had been able to handle the situation. He picked up his *guaje* and drank. "Come ... it's growing late, and the boy is right. Let us not provoke each other. We are just tired. We work hard, harder than ten years back, and yet each year we get less of a crop. Come, let us work before the sun grows strong and drains away our strength."

Saying this, the squat old man and the other workmen went off toward the oxen, and as they went they called the names of their different teams. Their calling-words sounded like song. The teams responded and got up from where they lay resting, and each man ushered his team of oxen along with his *otate*, a long bamboo shaft, to where they had left their great oak yokes the night before. The *bueyes* moved slow and easy. As always, since before the ancient Egyptians, the oxen positioned themselves automatically to their own yoke. Each man put the yoke to them and cross-tied it to their long horns with the leather straps called *callundas*, or *aperos*, depending on the local village custom. Then they sang more songs to their team of *bueyes*, picked up the *arado* and began moving the *bueyes* along with the *otate* in one hand and the *arado* in the other. Now and then, they held both hands on the *arado* and the *otate* under their armpit. The sun came, and the sweat began to ooze from both men and beasts.

The boy, Roberto, sat on his horse and watched in case some *buey* broke away. None did. So he dismounted, and unsaddled and hobbled his horse. He sat by the fire to dry off and took out a taco made of *frijol*. It was soaking wet. He put it in the coals, then rolled it to and fro. He ate, and drank water from his *guaje*. He looked at the sun. He now knew his father was not going to come. He glanced across the flat field to where his father's team of *bueyes* lay on the ground waiting and chewing their cud. They had only ten or twelve more days to plant this field of garbanzo and he, a boy, had been made foreman and promised a bonus of food supply if he could do it and ... he would do it. He had to. His family didn't have enough food for the coming winter. And, if he could get the bonus in food and not money, then his father couldn't waste it on drink and they would have enough food supply.

He began taking off his father's *callundas* from the saddle. He would now plow, use the *arado*, the tool that had been handed down to his people from the stars above. The formation of stars that in English is called the Dipper, his people called the *arado*, and believed the design of these stars had given their ancestors the vision of the plow. Through God, naturally. And so that was good.

He crossed the field with his *otate* and his father's *callundas*. The oxen awaited, as always, chewing their cuds, and this was good. He began his labor as he mumbled prayers for strength, for protection, for fortitude against the great hot sun. Soon the sweat began and ... this, too, was good.

Since the division of land after the revolution of 1910 and the new constitution of 1917, there are legally very few large landowners in the Republic of Mexico.

Legally the larger ones do not own more than the average little farmers. Roberto's patrón *had a little extra land and he hired some of the village men to help him farm. But only during the garbanzo season, the second crop; after that the small farmers, finished with their own first crop,* maíz, *the staff of life.*

And the patrón, *Don Carlos Villanueva, was old and carried a silver-headed cane and was basically a good man, so not too many people hated him, even though he had a little money.*

CHAPTER THREE

The sun, *la cobija de los pobres*, was now warm, and Don Carlos Villanueva arrived in an old run-down Chevy. He carried a cane and walked out into the field. He was old and tall, gaunt and bony, and he waved his cane about when he talked. It was well known that it had a long sword within it and that no man walked on his shadow. He owned three deaths, and owned them justly. The *patrón* bent over and picked up a handful of dirt. He rubbed it in his hand and smelled it. He threw it back down and tilted back his Texan hat as he looked out across the field. He called his chauffeur.

"Boy! *¡Muchacho!*"

"*¡Sí, señor!*"

" ... go and call Roberto. I wish to see him. I'll be over there by the shade of that mesquite tree."

The young man walked off.

"Don't walk. Run! We have other places to go!"

The young man began to run. He found Roberto two fields away. He informed Roberto and started back at a slow walk. Roberto stopped his *bueyes*, put them to rest, and at first he ran. It was a half-mile distance. Halfway there he stopped. He gripped his side where the horse and saddle had fallen on him in the channel. He looked up at the great hot sun, then went on at a good trot. The old man was sitting on a log in the shade of the mesquite tree.

"*Sí*, Don Carlos," he addressed his *patrón*. very formally. "I am at your service."

Señor Villanueva said nothing and looked at Roberto for such a long time without saying anything that Roberto grew nervous.

"Roberto," said the old one, motioning him near with his silver-headed cane, "come close."

Roberto moved closer.

"Why did you stop halfway across the field to grip your side? Are you hurt?"

"Oh, no, *señor*! I am not. I am fine. I can work!"

"Good," said the owner. "Good." He stood up. He was half a head taller than Roberto. His skin was much lighter, and his eyes were blue. "Now, tell me ... why are you working the *arado*? I do not want my foreman plowing. Tell me ... have you gone for the garbanzo seed today?"

"No. I was going to go at noon when the men and *bueyes* rest."

"Oh. And you ... you weren't planning to rest, the heat of day as I like all my help to do?"

"No, Don Carlos, I am sorry if that is wrong but ... I was not planning to do that."

"I see." The old man breathed and eyed the boy, then began to cough. He took out a white handkerchief and coughed so much that his entire skinny body jumped with each cough.

"Water. Please. A cup of water."

Roberto ran to the car where the young chauffeur sat listening to rock music from the car radio. Roberto yelled, "Turn off that music and get the hell over here with some water!"

"What did you say?" said the chauffeur.

"You heard me!"

Roberto jerked the car door open, and the boy yelled, "Okay, okay," and picked up a canteen of water and took it to the boss at a run.

"*¿Sí?*" said Roberto after the old man had drunk and stopped coughing. "How may I serve you?"

The old one sat down. He looked at Roberto a long time. He truly liked this young man. He was courteous and formal and honorable. "Listen," he said, "this is for your future. Each year the air gets worse. For years, every year I find it harder to breathe." He took off his hat, wiped his forehead and the band of his hat, then glanced to the far mountains. "When I was a young man, one could see over that range to the tall peak of Tancítaro, but we can no longer see that far. Except after a hard rain." He coughed. "I don't want you plowing, Roberto. You are responsible for much more. Now tell me ... where is your father?"

Roberto bowed his head. Humbly. "He is sick."

"He is sick, ah? Sick of what?"

Roberto glanced up. "*Patrón*, please, do not ask me that. It is not proper for a son to talk badly of his father."

"I see," said the old man. He nodded and put on his hat and reached out and patted Roberto on the shoulder. "You are a good son to your father. A good son. I like that ... I have two sons but they are ... .Oh, well, I'll tell you what. I don't want you coming down sick on me, trying to do your father's work and your own also. So ... I'm prepared to make you a deal. Are you game?"

"*Sí*, Don Carlos! Of course."

"Good. This is my offer. I'll give you your own wages plus your father's wages, but not in money. I'll give his to you in food supply along with the bonus I've promised you if ... " He began to cough terribly. " ... get this crop in! Understand?" And he stood up and began waving his cane. "In the cities they are already dying by the thousands. I tell you, each day they are dying ... oh, let me not confuse you with an old man's knowledge." He calmed down. "Here. Come here. Breathe. Breathe deeply." The old man put his hand to Roberto's chest. "See how it hurts a little."

The young man felt no pain, but didn't want to disagree with his *patrón*, so he nodded yes.

"Good. In the mornings ... even before the sun ... work hard! Real hard! And rest the midday. Then in the late afternoon work a while again and believe me, in one month's time you will feel better and find you accomplish more work. Now, go. Get the garbanzo seed. BUT NEVER DO YOUR FATHER'S WORK AGAIN. You rest at noon when you work for me." He picked up some dirt. "Maybe it has not got to the soil yet. The air, it's gone. Birds are dying, and many other birds are not coming any more. Oh, God ... please, not the soil. Maybe we can still have a good harvest." He was quiet. Remembering. "Like the ten years after the snowstorm of blackness ... and I, Carlos Villanueva, was the first one to realize it was good for the soil." He turned, talking to himself. "Maybe ... I can think of something again. Oh, God, help us!" And the old man went to his car. "*Ve con Dios*, Roberto, and recall my words about resting and breathing and ... about our deal. I think it best to tell no one. Understand? Not even your father."

"*Sí, cómo no*," answered Roberto and he watched him go in the old Chevy. Roberto wondered but could not understand about the breathing and hurting and dying of birds and people; so he decided, like his *patrón* had said, that he would not confuse his mind with what he did not need to know, and he turned, running to what he did need to know; the *bueyes* had to be unyoked so he could saddle up and go to town for the seed. Yes, the seed—that was needed, and that he did know well. It was food. It was bonus. And he would not tell his father. He would keep it secret between his *patrón* and himself so there would be food for the family for the whole winter.

He ran, gripping the pain on his side.

Norteños *are men that return from the United States with money to BURN!*

And they always come back with a new Texan hat, a tejana, *and two new pairs of Levi's and one beautiful suede jacket from a Mexican border town. Most important of all they bring with them a .45 automatic with two extra clips, and call themselves* NORTEÑOS*!*

They contract the local music for themselves and stand at the cantina doors TEN FEET TALL in their hats and pants, guns and holsters, and now and then buy drinks for their old friends who do not have the nerve, the tanates *to go up north and break through the wall of electric fences and enter the land of plenty, the U.S. of A., a land so rich that what garbage they throw away in one day could feed entire pueblos. Or ... so these* norteños *say, and laugh and laugh and burn more money.*

CHAPTER FOUR

He mounted his father's horse and rode the four kilometers into town. He passed by the plaza with the tall shady Tabachin trees and heard music and men laughing. He rode by the cantina and saw that the *norteños* were still there, and he shook his head, hardly able to believe it. They had been back one month and they were still going strong. This was really something. The group of five that had come a few months back had run out of money in a week. One of them had come to work for his old boss with the *bueyes* but had quit in two days, saying that they were stupid fools to be working for so little. That in California, picking fruit, a good man could make in one week what they did not make in a whole year down here. A week later he was killed in a cantina for calling the wrong man stupid. Roberto now reined up in front of the open door of the cantina. There were three *norteños* and four musicians and many other men and ... one man was his father.

Roberto's jaw tightened.

Quickly he reined the one-eyed horse up the street toward the feed store. He didn't want his father to see him. He got the garbanzo seed and put the sack on his horse and secured it. Then he led the gelding by the reins, going around the other side of the plaza so he wouldn't pass by the cantina. But it didn't help him avoid his father. There they now were, out in mid-plaza in the shade of the tall green trees. They were listening to music and drinking and eating and dedicating songs to different women in town. He saw his father. He felt shame for him. He tried to pass on by quietly.

But then he heard one of the *norteños*, the one called Juan Aguilar, say, "*Oye,* Tomás, isn't that your little Roberto?"

"Why, yes!" said his father. "And he's got my one-eyed horse. The fastest horse in the territory once upon a time, but now ... you know, he is old like me. Old and tired."

"Call your son over. I've heard that old man Don Skinny Shot-up Leg has made him foreman." His father called Roberto over. "Hey, boy!" said the *norteño*. He was an older man, in his mid or late thirties, like Roberto's own father. "Once, years ago, way before you were born, old man Villanueva made me foreman too. Come, let us have a taco and beer together. As foreman to foreman!"

"No, thank you," said Roberto, and looked at the small barbecued goat they had on the public pit for public feasts, and his stomach growled with hunger. "I just had lunch. I'm full and I have to get back to the fields with the seed."

"Oh?" said Juan Aguilar. He was an old-time *norteño* and had a dangerous reputation. When he talked men trembled. He owned many deaths. And not all justly, either. "You are too busy! Ah? Too important! Too big to have a taco and beer with me, ah?"

Roberto looked at him curiously, but said nothing. He couldn't figure out why such a man would get upset so easily. "Oh, no, *señor*," he said. "It's not that. It's just that I'm behind in my work. I meant no offense. How could I? I'm just a humble boy." And he stopped and said no more.

Juan Aguilar eyed him, trying to figure if this boy was playing games with him or not. But before anything could come of either man's eyeing, they were interrupted.

"Stop that!" yelled Roberto's father. "And come eat! Do not be insolent to my friend, or I'll thrash you!"

Roberto's father then lifted his beer to drink. Roberto watched, and his face hardened at the thought of his father eating and drinking, and then bringing home nothing for the family.

The *norteño* Juan Aguilar saw, looking from father to son. "Come," he said, changing his tone of voice and speaking kindly. "And please ... do not give me polite formalities about being too full to eat. Have a couple of tacos and a beer with me and then ... go. Get back to work."

His father belched. "Yes, do what he says! Show your upbringing."

"Yes, Father," said Roberto, his voice thick. He tied up the big gelding. He ate. He drank. He laughed at their jokes. He ate some more. And the big *norteño*, who had invited him to come and eat as foreman to foreman, now came close with beer in hand and said, "How are you doing with Don Skinny Shot-up Leg?"

"Good. He pays me."

"Oh? How much does he pay you?"

"Enough. In fact, today he offered me ... " He stopped himself, glancing at his father. He didn't want his father to know of their private deal. As it was, his father picked up both of their wages every week. For he was still a boy, and this village maintained the old custom, and boys—just like women—could not handle money. Only men could handle money. He and his *patrón*, by making a secret deal without his father's knowledge, had been very daring. They were going against traditional custom.

"Oh, I see," said the old *norteño*, guessing at the boy's situation. "Good!" He slapped Roberto on the shoulder and changed the subject. "Tell me ... how strong are you? Ah? Can you lift that sack of seed to that horse without trouble? Could you do that all day long?"

"I've lifted them."

"Good! And the sun, the heat, does it bother you?"

"It never has."

"And the cold and wet season? Do you get sick then?"

"I've never been sick."

"Wonderful! Just like I used to be. Come after work today, I want to see you." He smiled and stood up.

Roberto figured that he was being dismissed, so he stood up and said he had to go back to work and gave his many thanks.

"It's nothing," said the *norteño*. "*Nada*. With the money we make up north, this is all nothing. Here, take a piece of barbecue to your *mamá*."

"Oh, no thank you," said Roberto. "We have plenty at home."

"Boy, don't you get polite with me! I know you. You are a good boy, of the old style. I like that. So no more games. Let me help you, please. It is my honor as foreman to foreman. Now, take the meat home. And go to work."

"Thank you, *señor*."

"Do not thank me. Come tonight. I have business to discuss with you." And the man began to cough. Cough real hard, like Roberto's *patrón*, and Roberto wondered about this coughing but said nothing. The man stopped coughing. "Tonight!"

"*Sí, señor*. Of course. After work. Tonight."

And as Roberto turned to go, he noticed his father had laid down in the grass and was asleep, mouth open. He was beginning to snore in a liquored stupor. Roberto looked at him for a moment. Then he left quickly, taking the meat, and then going out to the fields.

Two men were not working. They awaited the seed. He gave it to them and bit his tongue with self-anger, but gave the men no explanation. He did his other errands quickly, then put his father's team of *bueyes* to the yoke and worked hard. And when the sun went down and the day grew dark and the others had all gone home, he finally unyoked his father's team.

Then he resaddled his horse to take the twenty head of *bueyes* up the mountain. The other men's work was done, but he still had much to do. At the bridge he blinded his horse and passed with no trouble, going on out of the valley, into the foothills, and up the mountain. Now it was completely dark except for the half-moon, and he had to find a good place for the oxen with plenty of food and water so they would eat and drink and lie down and not drift far in the night. That way he could find them easily in the morning. If this was not done properly, in the morning it would be very difficult to locate them, and the men would lose the cool of the morning, when most of the work had to be done.

He rode on, driving the twenty head of huge animals. Once his one-eyed horse stumbled. He petted the horse, talked to him, and the big gelding trusted him, and all was well and they went on. They found a good place and he said good night to his *bueyes* and headed for home. Going down in the dark was bad; much worse than the coming up. Finally, he mumbled a few prayers without even being aware of it, and led the horse until they made it to the valley. He remounted. In front of him he could see the lights of the pueblo.

When you and your woman, or a close relative if you are not married, baptize another couple's child in the Holy Catholic Church, you then become not only the child's godparents, but you, as a man, become the other man's dearest friend, his compadre. *For life! Two men bonded together and willing to defend the other's honor as his own. And if your* compadre *happens to be quite a bit older than you, then he is almost like a father and a brother and a best friend all wrapped up in one.*

A few months earlier, Roberto had baptized, along with his fifteen-year-old sister, the child of an older man in the Holy Catholic Church and footed the bill of the fiesta *as is the custom. And then he bought extra tequila for his* compadre *and himself, and they got drunk together and talked of the boy's future and became very close. The best of friends. For LIFE! And to be RESPECTED, no matter what!*

CHAPTER FIVE

It was late at night when Roberto got home, and he was hungry and tired and barely had the energy to put the horse up before going under the lean-to in order to eat. Getting there, he found his *compadre*, and his mother said, "Your *compadre*, a wonderful man, has been waiting for you so you can eat dinner together."

"Oh," said Roberto, seeing that his *compadre* had brought along his two biggest children, and not the little one he had baptized a few months back. "Have you been waiting long, *compadre*?"

"Not too long," said his *compadre*, I have been here waiting for you, only since sunset. That is all. I don't mind."

"I am glad you don't mind." said Roberto as he washed his hands and sat down on the log bench by the warmth of the fire.

"No. Of course not. We are *compadres*!"

"Yes. We are. Tell me ... how are you passing it these days? Are you doing all right?"

"Well," he said, and shrugged, "you know how it is. There's no work now that we got our own personal crop in."

"Work? I can use another plower of *bueyes*."

"*¿Bueyes?* Oh, no *gracias, compadre*. I am not so good with them. And the sun. I get sick out in those treeless fields."

"Oh. I see. Tell me ... have you and your children had dinner?"

"Why, no, *compadre*. Of course not! That would have been rude. Your kind, wonderful, and most gracious mother invited me to join her and the family, but I declined. I wanted to wait for you!"

"Oh," said Roberto. "That is very thoughtful of you." His mother was now bringing plates of barbecue and *frijoles* and a stack of tortillas. She set these on the two old wooden crates that had the faded imprint of Cutty Sark Scotch and a sailing ship. Where Roberto's father had found these boxes, no one knew. But they were good boxes to eat out of,and Roberto and his family, felt proud to own such boxes with a sailing ship. They figured fish had come in these wood boxes; fish from the sea that was supposedly over there. Far far away. Roberto nodded and begged for his *compadre* to start first and watched, taking note of how much his *compadre* served himself. Then he, began to serve himself and he said, "Mamá? This is a lot of barbecue. Did you not eat some yourself?"

She grew nervous and said, "Yes! Of course!"

"No, she didn't!" said one of Roberto's smallest brothers. "We had none. She saved it all for you."

Roberto froze. He glanced at his mother. She was all nerves. He glanced at his *compadre* and saw how he kept eating and quickly feeding his two kids, acting as though he had not heard. Roberto said nothing. He just got up and handed his plate of food to his little brother and saw how he and three others came to it like hungry little dogs. "*Compadre* ... my dearest *compadre*," he said, wiping his hands.

"Yes?"

"You came to eat with me yesterday. Did you not?"

"Well ... I came to visit, and it happened that ... you know ... you, invited me to your most gracious table."

"It happened, ah? Just happened that you arrived at about dinnertime. Well, LISTEN! my dearest *compadre*. Tonight, eat! I can see that you and your children are hungry. So enjoy our food! And I feel good and honored to have you as a guest. but, unless you show up for work tomorrow morning and start inviting me to YOUR TABLE ... " And on these last two words his voice thickened and his eyes narrowed small and mad and his jaw muscles quivered. "Never come here again and just HAPPEN to get invited to our table." He stopped. He breathed and added, "I speak clearly, do I not?"

"Yes. You speak clearly ... and ... and for one who's so young and a *compadre*! God forbid! I'll attend church for you tomorrow. I'll ... I'll ... " And he stopped talking, ate quickly, finished his plate, and got up. "Come, children. Finish up and let is go!" And he, the *compadre* for life in the Holy Catholic Church, left in a big hurry. "Never will I shadow your path as long as I breathe!"

"Good!" yelled Roberto. "Good!"

Roberto's mother began scolding him, telling him that the rumors were true. He indeed had lost all respect and sold his soul to *el diablo*, and that was why he was doing so well. And one thousand times one thousand she would rather have them poor and hungry than to have him, her firstborn, condemned to hell forever and ever. His father, Tomás, would hear of this. He would know what to do with a *muchacho* who talked disrespectfully to his elders and ... my god! to a *compadre* on top of that! She began to pray, and Roberto ignored her and watched his young brothers and sisters eat. Then he turned, saying that he was going to the plaza to see about some business.

His mother, old and squat, and yet not even thirty-three years old, called, "Please ... don't go! Please! Oh, my God! ?What have we done wrong?" And she told her eldest daughter to run after him. "For the sake of God!"

The oldest daughter, Esperanza, ran out to the street and caught up her with brother. "Roberto?"

He heard his sister's voice and stopped. "Yes." If it had been anyone else he would have kept going, but Esperanza, was different from most girls. She had argued her way out of the house, out of the traditional job of the eldest daughter being like a second mother to all the younger children, and she had gone to school. Which was fantastic. For no eldest daughter in the village had ever done so. "What do you want?"

"Nothing. I just came to say you did the right thing. That damn freeloader!" And she raised her hand in a fist. "If I were a man, I would have hit him!"

Roberto smiled. His sister was thin and dark and had huge brown eyes, and when she used words like "damn" her face became so strong and righteous that he couldn't think of her as a girl. She was so different from other girls. She was smart and quick, and he liked her as a person, a friend, someone to talk to. Almost like another man.

"Thank you," he said. "Thank you. Now, go on home. Take care of Mamá. I have business."

"With the *norteños*?"

He eyed her. "How'd you know?"

She shrugged. "How do we know anything in this small town?"

He looked at his sister, and there she stood, dark and arrogant, and he knew what she meant. She read books, and she was always complaining about this being a small town. He nodded. Her reading seemed to do nothing but make her more and more unhappy. But he said nothing. They had argued about this before, and it had never helped. She was a dreamer. She was always confusing her mind with faraway things and forgetting the immediate. He nodded, patting her on the head.

"Yes. I'm going to see the *norteños*. But don't worry ... I won't go north."

"Why not? If I were a man ... hell, I would have left this lousy place years ago!"

He stiffened. "Esperanza, I forbid you to talk this way. God made you a woman. You are not to question. Have respect! Is it not bad enough that I broke customs tonight?"

She smiled, and her eyes went large and brown and full of fun and mischief. "If I were a man," she repeated, "I'd break all the customs every day!"

Roberto began to speak, to anger, but then he stopped ... and held, saying nothing. His sister was so un-girl-like. It was hopeless. Boys didn't even call on her because of her infamous sharp tongue.

She smiled and took his hand and spoke as if she knew his thoughts. "Don't worry about me. I just talk tough to you. After all, you're the only one I can talk to." She blew him a kiss and turned, running down the rock-laid street in graceful bounds.

He watched until she was within their *jacal*; then he turned, going into the night. Poor thing ... she was hopeless. She would never get a husband the way she behaved. Hell, she was already sixteen and still single.

It is said that in Mexico it is impossible to take a census. The birth rate is so high and the death rate so fantastic that only a rough approximation is at all possible.

And, in the State of Michoacán, with more Indians per capita than most states, even this rough approximation is impossible. For a lot of men attempt to go to the United States, and many never return. In fact, of the few who do return, only one of fifteen comes back with money to burn!

The others who return, return with very little or broke and lost and hungry, and tell everyone that my God, it is so hard, so impossible with all those damn gringos!

And the one in fifteen, who does return with money to burn, agrees and calls himself lucky and muy macho. *And these* muy machos, *who know the ropes of the legal and illegal red tape, go north year after year until their power of youth leaves them, and then they take up with a young strong man of good heart whom they can control and use to their advantage; they take him and show him the ways of things, and for this, if they are good men, they take a fourth or so of his wages. But if they are bad men, they kill him or desert him and come back with both wages and tell the pueblo that the youth was taken by the* americanos, *the dirty gringos and shot for being a wetback. The people of the pueblo believe them, and the census—it continues to be unreliable.*

CHAPTER SIX

He, Roberto García, now walked into the cantina and looked around until he spotted the Texan hats of the *norteños*, and then he went toward them, looking at their expensive hats, looking at their beautiful suede jackets, looking at their Levi's and western boots, and then finally he saw their guns. Their guns and holsters, and he felt very small and very weak. He wore homemade clothes made of coarse cotton sacks and *huaraches* made of bad leather. He stopped.

One of these *norteños* he had never seen before. This one wore a bright red shirt with white thin stripes, and he was playing with a small box as Tomás crossed the room in a big hurry. Tomás carried a tray of glasses and a bottle of tequila, rushing to the *norteños*. He bumped into the shoulder of *norteño*'s with the bright fancy shirt. The *norteño* turned savagely.

"You stupid fool! If you dirtied my shirt, I'll shoot you!"

Roberto's father, a tall lean man in comparison to most of the men in the cantina, cowered and began apologizing and trying to clean the man's shirt with the sleeve of his homemade shirt.

"Don't, you fool! Your shirt is filthy! Get away!"

"But ... but my drink?"

Roberto stood still ... breathing in until his chest was huge. And then, still holding his breath, he heard his father continue to beg, and he felt like screaming, raging, drawing his machete and cutting that *norteño* from throat to balls in one swift motion. But he didn't move. He breathed out, and his vision blurred. How could his father have deteriorated to this? At one time his father had been a famous workman. And a good provider, but then, two or three years back, he began slowing down. Always being tired. As if he got up in the morning already exhausted. Why? What had happened? *El Don*, his boss, said that it was common, that it had to do with something or other that came down the valley in the wind that caused men to grow old and tired before their time.

Roberto now stopped and looked at his father and saw that the dark fancy *norteño* was still belittling him. Roberto nodded, feeling far away, alone, and committed. Yes, he would most definitely have to take revenge on this *norteño*. After all, this was the code.

Roberto now felt a calmness, so he sighed, tired-good, and walked across the room, forgetting his dress, his weakness, his whole immediate person, and came up to this table with these men with guns and took up ground. Tall. Heavy. And good in self.

Juan Aguilar saw him and smiled. "Come. Join us. Your father was just getting ready to join us."

Roberto looked at his father. His father was drunk and looked worn out.

"No," his father said. "Just give me my drink, and I'll get back to my card game."

"Okay," said Juan Aguilar, and turned to the fancy *norteño*. "Pedro, give Roberto's father a big glass of tequila."

"What?" said Pedro. Pedro was short and dark and wide of cheek, and he looked all Indian and very much like Roberto except for his eyes. His eyes were small, and Roberto's were large. He looked up and down Roberto. "Give what to who?" he asked.

"You heard me," said Aguilar, and he smiled and just sat there. So calmly. He was tall, and his eyes were blue, and he was very good-looking. "Do as I say, *compadre*." And he winked. Handsomely. "Ah, *amigo*? Give Roberto's father a big glass of tequila. For ... this is my boy." He smiled.

Pedro smiled back, tight-lipped, and looked from Aguilar to Roberto. A typical peasant boy carrying a machete, like any other Indian peasant. Pedro said, "what, you mean ... this one's father?"

"Yes," said Aguilar. "I mean this one's father."

"Oh, is that so? Well, listen," he said to Roberto. "If you're so special, you must know what this is. Do you?" And he raised up the small box he held on his lap.

Roberto looked at the box. It was a transistor radio. But he'd never seen such, so he shook his head no. The man with the fancy shirt laughed.

"It's a radio," he said. "A radio! And if I had new batteries, I could turn this knob and it would play music! Do you hear me? *¡Música! ¡Mariachis!*" He laughed. "I bet you don't believe it. I bet you're as stupid as everyone else in this backward village and don't even comprehend what I say!" He stopped, looking at Roberto. And he saw much of his old Indian past in the boy, and he didn't like it. For now, ten years after having gone north, he didn't consider himself Indian, and he didn't like reminders. It hurt. So he now yelled, "Answer me! Do you comprehend what I say, or don't you?"

"I comprehend," said Roberto.

"Oh," said Pedro. "You do, do you?"

"Yes." Roberto nodded.

"Well, then, explain."

"It's a radio like the radio in my *patrón*'s car. But it doesn't work, because its power is dead."

Pedro's eyes opened wide, and all the *norteños* burst out laughing and began teasing Pedro. And he, Pedro, had to take it. For all night he had been playing his transistor and explaining its miraculous batteries to the different townsmen and calling them stupid when they didn't understand.

He, Pedro, now viewed Roberto fully and saw beyond the Indian face and peasant dress, and he knew why Aguilar had picked this boy. This Indian boy was well-fed. Well-nourished. And he had a wide frame and a powerful neck and a solid bossness about him like the boys of old. Like the Indians from Pedro's own village before the roads came in and brought the tourists. There was no fear in this boy as he stood before five *norteños*, men of America. No bowing of his head, no dropping of his shoulders. Hell, there was no smallness, no begging, no huge admiration, and so he, Pedro, felt like cutting this ancient Indian pride out of Roberto's gut. But he couldn't. Roberto was Aguilar's boy, and Aguilar was his *compadre*, his true fellow *norteño* with whom he had struggled for ten years back and forth across *la frontera de los Estados Unidos*, and that was that.

He turned to his drink. Aguilar patted him on the back and brought out a cigar. "The glass of tequila for his father," he repeated, and struck a big Mexican match.

Pedro said nothing.

"*Amigo*," said Aguilar, "be a sport. All night you've teased and pushed the knife into people's bellies so, what the hell. It was your turn to get a little sticking."

Pedro eyed his old friend, and then he drank his drink and said, "Don't push it, *amigo*."

Aguilar laughed. "Oh, well, an Indian is always an Indian-without-reason." And he calmly reached across the table and served Roberto's father a big glass of tequila and never turned to see how Pedro, his friend of so many years, took these words of insult. What the hell. He too wore a .45, and with him nobody fooled around. He was tall, big-boned, and half-white with a heavy beard that needed shaving every day, and these beardless Indians were small-time to him. He was originally from over the mountains in the State of Jalisco. He was big-time. He gave the glass of tequila to Roberto's father and smiled handsomely, and Roberto watched and felt much warmth toward Juan Aguilar. He asked himself: why couldn't his father have been like Juan Aguilar? So calm. So strong. So respected. And he, Roberto, breathed ... and said yes, within his being. Yes, he would go north. His sister was right. This was a small town.

Aguilar had eyes that saw and said, "Come. Sit down. And let us drink as foreman to foreman. Bartender! Bring my young friend a beer!" The *norteños* were drinking tequila and beer chasers. Aguilar drank off his beer. "Make that two! Bring down two of your best!" Then to Roberto, "Tell me, you hungry?"

"Well," said Roberto as he sat down, "not really. I ate at home."

"A taco won't hurt you. Or maybe a little *menudo*? Eh? What do you say?"

Roberto felt his stomach move. *Menudo*, soup made of tripe—that sounded wonderful. So he began to say yes when he saw his father. He stopped. His father was over there playing cards with other men in homemade clothes, and he and those men looked so ... so nothing.

Aguilar saw and said, "Your father ... do not worry. He has no more money to lose, so nothing more can happen to him." He called to the barman. "Service! We want food!"

"Not for me," said Roberto, "I'm fine." He breathed. He would come right to the point. It was making him nervous sitting here with these men with their boots and pants and guns. He cleared his throat. "Now, getting to this business ... Why are you being so good to me?"

Aguilar turned, very surprised. Roberto's eyes saw, but he went on. Quickly.

"You said it was business. So tell me, what is it you called me for?" He swallowed and waited quietly. Such directness to an adult by a boy his age was bad. He was breaking custom. He glanced about the table. All the *norteños* were watching and smiling. Pedro laughed.

"Hey, Juan! You picked a very fast-with-the-mouth boy."

Roberto flinched but held ... this was not the proper time to take revenge. He ignored Pedro and turned to Aguilar. Aguilar, the biggest of these four *norteños*, was not smiling. He brought out a match and relit his cigar. He smoked. He drank. He looked at

Roberto. Heavily.

"I'd heard you were forward," said Aguilar. "But I had not imagined to what degree. You play no games. I like that. That is the American way. Come right to the head of the nail and"—banged his fist on the table—"get it done! *¡Pronto!*" He drew close to Roberto. "Listen, this is my business. I'm inviting you to join our group of four experienced *norteños* and to be my personal boy and come north with us."

Roberto nodded but did not say anything. He would not act too hungry. It was bad manners and usually cost money. He said, "I appreciate your offer, but I can't. I have no money for the voyage, and ... I am responsible for a crop, and I have a home to feed."

"Oh ... I see," said Aguilar, sitting back and raising up his *tejana* and pushing back his beautifully fringed suede jacket. He put his thumbs in his gunbelt. His Levi's were new, not yet washed. His shirt was khaki and looked very expensive, like a soldier's shirt. He nodded; and the other three *norteños* joked and laughed and drank their tequila and beer. Roberto ignored the other *norteños* and wiped the mouth of his bottle with the palm of his hand, as was the custom, and drank. He felt nervous but didn't wish to show it. "Tell me," said Juan Aguilar, "if those things were taken care of, would you like to go? Eh? Go up north to make big money?"

Roberto nodded yes, but then shook his head. He began to explain about his responsibilities once again but the big *norteño* cut him off.

"Listen, boy, I don't think you understand! Dozens! No, hundreds of young men would give their right eye to go with me, because I know the ropes! I've been going up north whenever I feel like it for fifteen years. And my knowledge is pure treasure!"

"*¿Señor?*" said Roberto slowly, trying to figure what to say. He had to be careful. This was a touchy situation. Pedro and the other *norteños* were laughing at Aguilar, and Aguilar was getting mad. "I do not doubt your knowledge or your worth. You come back with money often. So this is self-evidence of your worth. And also, I agree, many young men would give much to go with you. Yes, of course." And he went on talking, being diplomatic, and he was amazed with his own soundness of mind. Where had it come from? He didn't know. All he knew was that there was much hunger in this village, and yet he was able to feed his own family a little every day, and he had to keep doing whatever it took to bring food home. "... but these other boys who are so willing to go," said he, bringing matters to a head, "are usually not doing very well here. And I, myself, do well here, so why should I go?"

Pedro and the other two *norteños* burst out laughing, and Aguilar, the big man, held. He was outraged. In the last three years of recruiting boys he had never been asked any questions. He drank and breathed, then began to cough. Roberto kept very quiet and watched him. Aguilar took out a white handkerchief. He coughed a few more times, then stopped coughing and looked at Roberto a long, long time. Then said, "Come. You are not a dumb or greedy one. You are bull-solid in the head. You and I must talk straight. Okay?"

"Okay."

They went outside. Alone. And the night was cold. They breathed, smelling the green of the trees, the plants, the fields, and Roberto thought: how many boys have gone with this man? And how many have never returned? And he, Roberto, didn't know the answer to this question, but, having realized the question, he was alert and forewarned.

"You see," Juan Aguilar began, "going north for me is not that hard. I know the ropes well ... but I now have a cough and cannot work like I used to, and I need a young man to make a deal with. A smart strong young man who does well down here where it is almost impossible. Hell, up there such a young man would make thousands of American dollars. Not pesos. But dollars, the gods of this earth. Do you understand?"

Roberto nodded, but then shrugged. He would show no need to this man. None. Absolutely.

"Listen. Now my deal is this ... BUT TELL NO MAN! UNDERSTAND?" And he yelled these last few words in Roberto's face, but Roberto didn't take fright. He simply looked at him curiously. The big man looked back, then lowered his voice once more. He had picked the right boy. This one stood solid. He continued, and Roberto listened. "You see, I need a good young man, like yourself, not like the soft lazy ones that I can get a hundred for a dime. But one like you. A foreman. Who can produce. And with my knowledge, I will put such a boy where there is work, and we will both work, and I will take only one-fourth of his pay." Roberto began to speak. "No, let me finish! One-fourth is very fair. Because normally a boy who goes up there and does not know the ropes will end up being robbed by *coyotes*. By lying lawyers with promises of legal papers. By filthy *pochos* who charge to get you across the *frontera*. By innumerable crooks who live off the innocence of you-know-nothing *braceros*.

"But with me ... none of this will happen, and in one year, with the fruit picking, the truck loading, and then the hiding out at chicken ranches, this boy, that knows how to produce and deals with me, will come home after all expenses with anywhere between one thousand American dollars and two thousand. Believe me! Because I know the ropes, and we will spend very little of our earnings. Very little. Hell, my poker games will cover our expenses for the trip and living of the entire year." Roberto's eyes went large. Aguilar laughed. "This talk of thousands is confusing you! Hell, I bet you don't even know how much one thousand American dollars is here in Mexico?"

"I don't."

"It's one hundred and twenty thousand pesos! Or maybe it's only twelve thousand pesos. Oh, well," laughed the *norteño*, teasing the boy further, "that doesn't matter. Eh? Either way, it's so far beyond your comprehension that you cannot believe it, and you will stay here and rot like all the others."

"And your fourth, eh? Does it come out of that twelve thousand pesos? Or did you mean I'll clear that even after I give you one-fourth?"

The big *norteño* leaned back, thumbs in gunbelt, and he smiled. He had this boy, he had him good, and so he said, "That is clear! For you to bring to your *mamacita* and not have to turn over to your father like you now have to, because you'll be coming back *un macho* and no one will be your father."

And hearing these words—"no one will be your father"—gave Roberto a jolt. A bigger jolt than the money itself, and he stood up, feeling so strange. And his sister's words came to mind: "If I were a man, I'd break all the customs every day!" And he wondered ... such sacrilege. Such terrible thinking. But maybe ... maybe? But then he stopped. Juan Aguilar was still talking.

"One thousand American dollars is either one hundred twenty thousand pesos or twelve thousand pesos, but either way, it is so much that you will be able to buy your *mamá una casa. Una casa blanca con teja* and have a milk cow and a few head of cattle for meat and sale. Believe me ... look at my place. I have a good *casa* for my *mamá*, and this trip will to so well, if I deal with the right boy, that I will be coming back to marry and retire, and the boy I teach the ropes to will be able to go back on his own year after year. How about that? Big money! Beyond your highest expectations."

Roberto nodded. Nodded again. "Tell me ... you say a thousand dollars is so many pesos. But if I could eat meat every day, could I not work like five men and maybe bring two thousand or three thousand or ... Oh, my Lord Christ from above! It hurts my head to imagine. When do we go?"

"Then it's a deal?"

Roberto nodded. "Yes!"

"Give me your hand."

They shook hands.

"It is then done!" said the big man in the Texan hat and the Levi's and the .45 pistol and suede jacket. "It is done! *¡A lo macho!*" And he squeezed Roberto's hand and said, "Squeeze back! No more of these soft humble Indian handshakes! You are going to be *un bracero*! And when you return, you will be un *norteño*! Like me! With money to burn! squeeze!"

Roberto squeezed, and the big man laughed, and Roberto squeezed as never before in all his life, and the big man, a half head taller, took note of the strength of this young one, and he jerked him forward, knocking Roberto off balance so he would not squeeze any more. Then, having the advantage, he laughed.

"Come," he said, slapping Roberto on the back, "and let us go have a beer. And talk out the details. You'll need a little money. You'll need a letter from the local mayor. You'll need a letter from the priest. Can you read and write?"

"I went two years to school. I know enough."

"Good. Good. And you might as well get a letter of your foremanship from Don Skinny-Bones. Yeah, the old Don is a bastard like all owners, but he is not so bad. Years back he gave me a letter and lent me my first stake to go north over the electric fences. Two hundred and fifty pesos. Maybe he will lend you some money. If not, I'll lend you. Hell, two hundred and fifty is only twenty dollars in gringo money. Half a day's work at overtime in the harvest season up in California. When can you leave?"

"I need four or five days to finish my responsibilities."

"Five days . . . that's cutting it short, but for you I'll wait. You're a good man. So now let's drink! Foreman to foreman! To the future!"

And so it was settled. Roberto would be leaving his village for the first time in his life. Over the mountain and to the north and across electric fences to the land of plenty, the U.S. of A., where so many go but so few are ever heard of again.

Mexico is very mountainous. It has more snow-covered mountains closer to the equator than any other country. It has many eternally ice-capped peaks of over 17,000 feet. And, being so high and yet so close to the equator, it often has both tropical and mountainous vegetation in the same area. A fantastically versatile land. In fact, the story goes that when Cortez, the Spanish conquistador, returned to Spain and was asked to describe the country he had just conquered, he was so lost for words that he finally picked up a sheet of paper and made it into a ball, then flattened it out a little and said, "There is Mexico!"

That may be only a story, but the idea is correct, and all through history it has happened time and again that in such a land the people of each village become isolated. And especially if there is little education. So in Mexico it is very common for people to live in isolation. Knowing no one over the mountain, but everybody knowing everybody in their own village, until finally they are one people and they develop a code of law between themselves so strong that they never go to the law for help. In fact, killings are never even reported. They attend to them by their own code. And thus, with most of the twentieth century gone, Mexico is still the leading nation of violent deaths. Of course, this does not include the nations that think they are at war.

CHAPTER SEVEN

As always, the next morning Roberto awoke before daylight and looked out the crack of the wall between the two tied-together sticks and saw the *arado* and knew it was time to get up, but he didn't. He lay there and thought. His whole life was going to change. In a few days he would be going north to *los Estados Unidos*, and yet it seemed so impossible. Truly unbelievable. His mother called. He answered her and jumped up and picked up his sombrero and *huaraches* and poncho and went out to the kitchen without walls. He looked at his mother. She was busy with the fire. He nodded and went out behind to get his father's one-eyed horse, but stopped. His father was already there, and he was saddling up. Roberto watched, not saying anything, then went over by the goats and took his morning leak and came back and said, "*Buenos días*. Will you be going with me?"

"Do not get insolent with me! I know what is going on."

"What?"

"I said, I know what is going on!"

"Papá? What are you talking about?"

"Boy! Do you want a thrashing?" And he reached out and slapped Roberto across the face. Roberto held still between rage and confusion, but then only bowed his head respectfully. This was the custom. This was what a son should do. "You've made me into the laughingstock of the town. And you did it on purpose! I know!" His father stopped talking and led the big gelding around to the front of the house. Roberto followed. "So Don Skinny will give you my wages even if I don't work. Eh? Are you denying that? You can say nothing! Because it is the truth! The chauffeur overheard and told everyone, and now everyone is laughing at me." He slapped Roberto again. "I should give you a good whipping. But I don't have time or patience. Come! Let's eat, and we will see about him giving you my wages in food supply. You stupid kid! Food supply costs him nothing. And you believed he was doing you a favor by not giving you my wages in money. What a fool you are!" They sat down, and Roberto's mother brought them plates with *frijoles* and tortillas. This morning Roberto ate what his father liked. He didn't get his *jarro de canela* and *galletas*. "Hell, when I was your age I worked like five men! I worked hard and would yet come home and do more work. Look at this house, I built with my own two hands. Look at the corrals ... " And his father went on and on, and then they were off to work. His father riding the horse, and he, the son, at a trot afoot.

And like that they went through the pueblo out of the valley, and into the foothills. At the mountain his father reined up. "Where did you pasture the *bueyes* last night?" Roberto told him. "Okay. Run up and get them. It is not good to take a horse up there in the dark. Too easy to get the horse hurt. Right?" Roberto nodded. "Don't you dare nod at me like a dumb Indian! Answer up with words! You're not *un indio*!"

"Yes, Father. You are right. Most certainly."

"Go, then!"

Roberto took off afoot, and in half an hour was back with the *bueyes*. All twenty head. And they, father and son, one on horseback and the other afoot, drove them down the foothills and into the valley. And when they got to the bridge at the channel, Roberto called to his father to blind the horse. His father told him to shut up and drove the oxen across and began crossing himself. The horse bolted to his blind side and went off the bridge and into the water. His father screamed. Roberto ran to the bank. He saw the horse fighting the water, but couldn't see his father. He waited some more and then saw bubbles. He dived into the channel and in moments had his father on the bank. Roberto left him there to rest and took the horse and swam with him downstream like the morning before. Blind. Then about two kilometers down he got off and pulled the horse up the bank. The big gelding finally made it. He mounted and ran up the valley along the channel. His father was gone. He looked about. Then, after much pounding of heart, he made out a human form in the early-morning mist. Walking toward town. And he knew it was his father, and he felt bad. For truly, he had shamed his father again. He had made a fool out of him even more badly than the man in the bar. He cleared his throat.

"Papá!" he called. "Papá!" And he began to go after him, but he stopped. He couldn't go after him. He had responsibilities. And that was that. He blinded the big one-eyed horse, bolted him across the bridge, and caught up with the oxen. The sun was already visible on the horizon, and there was much work to do before the day grew too hot and drained the strength of both men and beasts.

That night when he got home, the house was quiet. He stabled the horse and washed up and found his older sister. She told him their mother had heard that he had made a deal with a *norteño* to go up north and that their mother was terrified. She was sure he would go and never come back, like so many that were never heard of again. He told Esperanza to stop this foolishness, to help their mother understand. She could do it. She read books. Then he asked where his mother was.

"She's at church," said Esperanza. "Lighting candles and giving away our last few pennies. Where else would she be?"

"And Papá?"

"At the cantina. Begging drinks. Where else?"

Roberto stiffened. He nodded. He looked at his sister. And there she stood, looking straight back at him, offering nothing. Like a man. *Un macho.* With a proud arrogance.

"Tell me," said he, after a long silence, "when I make money up north, can I send it to you? And you take care of it so Papá won't drink it all?"

She nodded. "Sure. Why not? I'm a woman, so I've got nothing better to do."

He exploded. "Esperanza, this is important! Do not create more problems! I swear, you are a devil of self-importance. That is sinful! And it does not help our problems at hand."

"What do you want me to do? Eh, big brother? Make the sign of the cross and swear yes yes yes yes in the name of the Holy Church!" She turned and walked away, head high and strong. "Come. I have dinner for you. Jose, your little brother, waited to eat with you. He likes you. Dumb kid." She began going into the kitchen and then said, "Sure, why not? I'll guard the money. I'll make out a list of how much we need for each thing." And she went on talking and acting bored, but in truth she was thrilled. She would now get to be the boss. Yes, she would do it.

Roberto, tired and hungry and weak, sat down with his little brother, Jose. He was three years old. Esperanza brought them plates of *frijoles* and tortillas and a cake of goat cheese. He ate in silence. My God, he was so hungry. This would only stop the growling of his stomach. He gave the cheese to his brother and said he had business and left. He went by the church and glanced in and saw his mother. He breathed. Then he went in and knelt down beside her, and she saw him, and her eyes lit up but her face remained sad and mournful like she believed the custom for praying and she prayed on and on as he made the sign of the cross but didn't pray. Later they went out and she talked, asked and begged, but finally he said, "No, Mother ... do not worry. Please, all will go well, and next year I'll buy you a house. A house with a kitchen inside and a big tank of water and room full of food supply. Believe me."

She said she wanted no such things. They were for the rich, and he would have to sell his soul again and again to acquire such. He shook his head and looked at his mother a long, long time. It was a half-moon night, and they were standing before the Holy Catholic Church. He kissed her on the forehead and said good night. He had business. He'd be home late.

"Please," she said, "do not go to the cantina. You know how those *norteños* always get wild before going north. Please. Come home with me. I beg of you!"

"No. Understand. The supply room is empty and we need food. Good night."

He went off into the night, and dogs barked as he walked across the plaza, and there, among trees, he stopped and saw the dim lights of the cantina and heard the loud noise of the *norteños*. Every now and then they'd speak a few words in a strange language. Supposedly it was English. They explained that they had to practice their English before going north. He breathed and glanced about. He had not left yet, but already ... this town, this village, this pueblo felt different. It felt small. So very small indeed.

He crossed the cobblestone street and went to the cantina. The *norteños* were dedicating songs to different girls in town. He thought this was not good. Such openness to girls in this small pueblo could bring trouble from a father or a brother. It was the code. But he let it go and went into the cantina and was received well, and that night they ate plenty of meat and drank beer and threw bones to the local dogs and cats. And when one cat refused the bone he was tossed, the *norteño* Pedro, who was sitting next to Juan Aguilar, drew his .45 and shot the cat, and everyone laughed and laughed and they then shot two or three more dogs and cats, and it all seemed normal to them. Roberto was then taught his first words of English.

"H-hhhh-eellllooooo!"

"No, no," laughed Aguilar, gripping Roberto's mouth. "Your tongue must always be outside your mouth when you speak the gringo 'hhhelllooo'!" Roberto was happy and drunkish, and he tried to say "hello" with his tongue all out. "There!" said Aguilar. "That's the way! Now repeat the whole thing. Remember? This is the proper way to ask a young American secretary for the location of the bathroom."

"Hhe-lllooo! Where is theee shithouse!" Roberto smiled proudly and all the *norteños* laughed and said that was wonderful. He could speak the most important English words in the whole gringo language.

Roberto smiled, glancing around and feeling very fine. That night he went home singing loose and happy and proud. No more humble Indian peasant. No more weak-handed handshakes. He was going to be a *norteño*! And nearing home, when a watchdog barked at him he didn't call out to the dog; no, he picked up a rock and hit him. Hard! And then laughed and laughed as the dog ran off. Hell, no more weak-handed Indian-peasant handshakes! He was a man! *¡Un macho! ¡Un norteño!* And the next night it was the same after work. He went to the cantina to his friends who were *norteños*—ten feet tall in their hats and pants, guns and jackets, and no man walked their shadow! They had money to burn! Hell, they could even dedicate songs to the different girls of the town, and no one could say a thing.

Inside he went over to the table of his new partner, Juan Aguilar, and was greeted well. Juan was not sitting with the *norteños*. He was with several of the poor local peasants. He was buying them drinks and telling them good-bye. They were old friends. Friends who didn't have the nerve to go north. And in a day or two they, the *machos*, would go north. At the next table were the other *norteños*, and they too were drinking their good-byes and dedicating songs to different girls in town. Roberto sat down next to Aguilar. He was so happy. In a few days they would catch the bus on the highway seven miles out of town and go to Guadalajara, the second largest city in the Republic of Mexico, and there transfer to a modern bus. A type they called in the United States "Greyhound", running dog, and go on in this modern dog bus all the way north, past Tequila, Tepic, Mazatlan, Los Mochis, and up to Guaymas. Or more exactly, just a little south of the great city of Guaymas to Empalme. To the huge American building to see if legal crossing to work was possible. And if it wasn't, then they would go *a la brava*! The brave way! Slang for going into *los Estados Unidos* in a brave and illegal manner.

Juan Aguilar laughed, and began telling Roberto many stories about events which he had witnessed himself. Gringo stories of injustice and dishonor to the Mexicans, to *la Raza*, to the family of the Holy Catholic people, and so they would have to be very, very careful.

Roberto drank and listened and had a strange feeling: these men drank and fooled around too much. Last night he, himself, had even started to act a little like them. Something was wrong. He sipped and watched Juan Aguilar's lips making words like justice, and honor, and truth, and he, Roberto, had a feeling that this was all just story and not truth. Because they were going up there to work. Not to conquer gringo women and to prove honor. And he wondered: why all this money-making talk. Hell, if men like these did well up there, then he, if he kept his head, should make double what they made. And he nodded in self-agreement.

In the background, the dedication of songs to local girls continued, but Roberto didn't take note. He was too high on beer and tequila and dreaming of the future. And up there, in the future, he was ten feet tall and confidently drunk on this new feeling of freedom, of power, of destiny, and of the unexpected. For he now knew to the bone that he could pocket this town and walk away with it without ever even noticing.

He drank some more.

So their code of arms is beyond all logic. It is bred in their bones and is more honored and respected than any law.

For example, just across the state border of Michoacán in the State of Jalisco there was a horse race between two pueblos in the mid-1960's and all the people of the two villages came and made their bets and drank tequila and ate tacos and had a few friendly cocks fight to the death. Then the match race between the two fine horses commenced and everyone watched, and the race was so close that each side said it had won, and one man, more tequila-happy and cock-fight-inspired than most, drew his .45 automatic and shot another. And then someone shot this first man, and then everybody started shooting everybody. The women and children ran, and the men, happy and loud, shot some more, and in moments there were eleven men dead. Two dead children. One dead woman. And fifty-seven wounded.

The federal troops came in, but no one informed on anyone. The government passed a law that federal troops would have to be present at every race from then on. The mountain people said yes, of course, but then ignored the government and continued their sports in the good old-fashioned style. Horse races! Cock-fights! Bull-fights! All a lo macho*!*

Every man protecting his own horse, his own home, and his own women. And if he fails, but gets killed in honor, he can rest in peace, for his relatives—brothers and cousins—will carry on and see honor kept ALIVE unto death.

CHAPTER EIGHT

A man's voice bellowed. Everyone turned. *Norteños* and peasants alike. And there in the doorway was an old man. Roberto's ex-foreman. The old one who called to his *bueyes* so softly that it sounded like song but now he was bellowing.

"Here stands a man!" He was dressed in simple peasant clothes, but he seemed to have no fear or big impression of these *norteños* with their rich fancy clothes. "And this *hombre* wants to eat! And drink! And then . . . " He smiled grandly. "This old man wants to put his mount against anyone's mount." His eyes were ablaze. "This old man wants to take from you your gringo money before you return to *los Estados Unidos*!" He came walking up. Proud and happy and altogether king of his own universe. "Roberto! Come stand with me and let us take bets and lessen the weight of their purses!"

Roberto stood up. Juan Aguilar, cigar in mouth, stood up also. Aguilar's eyes smiled, and he yelled to the old man.

"May I join you also? I like your style. And, if you allow it, I'll back your bets."

"Well," said the old man, "I'll consider it." He was playing hard-to-get. But actually, he had no money, and he had gambled for his own self-great-style to bring this about. "Come, have a drink with me. I'll buy, and we'll discuss it, *a lo macho*!"

Aguilar's eyes danced. This old one was no shy *indio*. He was a fine open soul of, a true man. His balls hung well. He was the living example *que lo cortés no quita lo valiente; ni lo valiente quita lo cortés*.

Pedro leaped up. "I'll bet against you, old man. Hell, I think you have no money, no horse, no nothing, and have managed to trick my friend Don Juan Aguilar; and I'd enjoy taking money from my great *amigo*!"

The old one turned to Pedro. Calmly. "I'm no bar fly. So don't waste words of fear on me. Put your money where your mouth is, child."

Men burst out laughing. Pedro glanced about and then angrily drew out a wad of money. "Here, old man! Now, you draw yours!"

"At the race. Tomorrow morning. At sunrise. I'll draw. Not now." And his eyes twinkled. "I hope you've got a mount. I know you yourself are very capable, but even a man of your ability needs something between his legs."

Pedro reached for his *tanates*. "I got plenty between my legs, and I can still get it up! Can you?"

"At sunrise." The old man twinkled. "At sunrise."

And so the date of the duel of horses was set up, and all night men drank, ate, talked, and prepared for the duel of horses.

Horses! The spirit of the gods. For in this part of Mexico all *machos* see God mounted on a great dark stud, racing through the heavens, with a huge sombrero on his head, and tomorrow at sunrise, God would be put here on earth. Among real *machos*.

The night retreated; and the sun came in long and full like a cock to a womb, and all was lovely.

Lovely.

The men of town were all up. They didn't go to work. They all were meeting outside of town where the river widened and ran so smooth and quiet and tall and dark. Mesquite trees grew along the bank and there, by the trees on the side away from the river, was a *carril*. A permanent soft dirt road for the traditional dueling of men's mounts. Every village had its own *carril*, and every village dueled, and every village lost many lives every year through the spirit of God on horseback.

Then, at daybreak, no one could find the old man.

He, *el viejo panzón*, had disappeared a few hours before. Many men began laughing and joking. Aguilar got angry. He asked Roberto if this old man was what he presented himself to be or not.

"He is the best of men," said Roberto.

"Good," said Aguilar.

Pedro came over. "Well, amigo, I've got these brothers, the Reyes, and they got two horses ready to run. One not so good, and the other pretty good." He smiled. "They're the owners of the famous Charro Diablo, the undefeated horse of all these parts, but . . . I told them not to bring out their best. I explained to them that you and I are *compadres*, and I didn't wish to shame you. Only to get the best of you." He laughed. "But hell, to have brought any horse seems to shame you! You've got nothing to run!"

"Listen, *amigo*," said Aguilar softly. "The old man will be along shortly. In the meantime, let us have some foot races. Ah? I'll race my boy, Roberto, against any boy you can find."

Pedro smiled and looked Roberto over, and Roberto showed him nothing. Absolutely.

"Hell, I'll race against him myself!"

"You're on," said Aguilar. "Pick your distance. You're a little old, so you should have that advantage."

"Old?" His face twisted and he pounded his chest. "Me!"

"Yes, you are old so you—"

"I'll go fifty *varas* against any man alive!"

And so the foot race was set up, and Roberto, stripped down to his pants, was rubbing his bare feet in the soft earth and exercising his toes and feeling good and ready, when a shout came from behind and everyone turned, and there was Antonio, *el viejo panzón*.

"I've come to race!" yelled Antonio. He was mounted on a big white jackass. No, it wasn't a jackass. It was a huge rawboned mule, and on each side of the mule was an enormous aluminum can of ten or fifteen gallons. They were milk tanks. The big mule was truly weighted down. "Come! Who will dare race his mount against mine."

Roberto looked at Antonio and his mule. Oh, God, they were going to be made fools of. This mule looked all bones and dried-up skin. Roberto glanced at Aguilar. Juan Aguilar was glaring at him. Roberto swallowed.

"Money," Antonio was saying as he got off his old white mule, "is no trouble. Aguilar here, from *los Estados Unidos*, is my partner." He winked at Aguilar. Juan's eyes narrowed. Undauntedly the old one came close to Roberto and Aguilar. "Stick with me. We'll show them." He turned to the people. "And to race ... well, there he is, Blanco! The fastest mule in the whole world, and he will best any horse for one hundred *varas*! Eh, Aguilar? We will take all bets."

Aguilar removed his cigar and said quietly, "I gave my word, so, yes. But ... if we lose ... " He patted his .45. "That's that."

"Don't worry," said the old one. "We got it in the bag. I'll ride, and no horse has a chance against this mule."

"You ride?" Juan's eyes went huge. "You weigh too much, and they've got a young thin boy on the mare they wish to race."

"Sssssh! I got to ride. I'm the only one that knows how to hold this old mule back so we don't win by too much."

"Oh," said Aguilar, and he nodded and figured ... bye, bye, money. This old Antonio had gone *loco en la cabeza*, and indeed, he himself was a fool, as Pedro had so well said.

The old one took the milk cans off the mule, and they lined up the two animals. The mare was black and looked nice. The white mule looked awful. The people got off the *carril.* A team of officials were put at the starting point and the finishing point. The old man was riding his mule with a great heavy work saddle plus his weight. The black mare was ridden by a young Reyes brother bareback.

A shot was fired, and the race was on.

The old man shot off with a great scream and a blast of farts. The mule's tail was spinning as the old man dug spurs and the mule farted and farted and farted. Blasting, echoing explosions. A continuous sound of *pedos.* And the old white mule won by a neck. Not too much, for the black mare had been gaining on the mule very quickly in the last few yards.

Men cursed! Paid off their bets and wanted another race. Pronto! This goddamn Aguilar with his gringo money could not take them. They were men of honor, and God should be riding his great horse of spirit on their side.

The old one got down off his mule. "Well," he said as he rubbed his back. "I can't do it again. I hurt my back, but if you don't mind, maybe partner Roberto or his brother Juanito can ride." Juanito, Roberto's brother of eleven, had just come up on the one-eyed horse.

Men yelled, sure, of course! They didn't care who rode. Only they had to make the distance half a length longer. One hundred and fifty *varas.*

"Okay," said the old man, and winked at Roberto and Aguilar. "We cover all bets." And he called Aguilar over and told him to bet heavy. This might be their last race, because they'd win by too much. Aguilar nodded in fantastic wonder. Hell, at this point he'd believe anything. Then the old one explained to Juanito how to ride, how to spur, and he added, "Remember, the most important thing with this old mule is to make him fart. The more *pedos* you get out of him, the faster he goes.

"He's like me. Eats a lot, works hard, and farts it out. It keeps the system clean." He made a fist. "Big farts! Strong ones from the gut."

And so the race broke out again, and the mule burst out with a stream of continuous *pedos* that sounded like jet-propelled power, and the black mare with the bare-back rider never had a chance.

Now men were really mad. They wanted a better horse to put up against this goddamn farting machine. Another Reyes brother came up. He was in his twenties, and he said, "How about our great horse, El Charro Diablo!"

Antonio shook his head. "No. That horse is too great. Only my *patrón*'s mare, La Niña Linda, would have a chance with such caliber of stud. I am no fool. I know my limitations." He was speaking very humbly. He was hustling in the best of ways. Roberto and Aguilar were watching. They were truly proud of their partner. "I cannot run against the best. You are way too good for me. But ... " And his eyes twinkled. "I'll run my old mule for twenty-five *varas* against your great black stallion."

Pablo came up. Pablo was the eldest of the Reyes brothers. There were thirteen brothers, and he was the boss. The father was rumored to have gone soft in the head. "No, you won't! That stud runs for no less than one hundred thousand pesos! What do you take us for, fools? That mule couldn't run against the ass-smell of our great Charro Diablo!" He spat to the ground. He wore a .45, cocked and ready.

"Well," said the old man very humbly. He was dressed in work clothes and was being very meek. "Not in a race of distance, but ... for twenty-five paces, my mule will outblast even a tiger. I'll make a race with you. Why not?" And he pounded his chest. "I'm alive, and breathing, and the whole world is for the winning!"

Pablo's face turned red, and he took up ground. Six or seven brothers came around him. All armed. They were not too wealthy, but still they were a very powerful family. They didn't need to go north for riches. They owned land. "Old man," he said in a ridiculing tone of voice, "you are a fool to try to mix with us. We are out of your class. We own property and we are *hombres de estaca! ¡Puros machos!* We don't hang around with gutless, shiftless *norteños*!" Aguilar flinched. The other *norteños* flinched also. "All you and these nothings wish to do is upset our great horse so he won't race against your boss's horse some day. Don Skinny Money Pants sent you to try to play us for fools! I say you and Don Skinny are a bunch of ... "

A cane tapped Pablo on the shoulder. Pablo turned. And there stood ... *el Don.* And he was dressed in full *charro* dress with a great huge expensive sombrero and he wore two guns, .45's. And they were cocked, holstered in silver, and he looked carved out of history. Tall. Thin. Proud. A truly magnificent Don Quixote with white hair, and a large moustache, and glistening dress of traditional *charro*. His blue eyes now twinkled. He removed his thin *cigarrillo*. He smiled.

Roberto and Antonio moved to his side. Aguilar saw but didn't move up. This wasn't his fight. Pedro smiled and stepped away. The other people scattered.

"Señor Reyes ... please, when you wish to talk about me ... talk. Here. To my old face. For, believe me, I am old and ready to die, and so, to take a disrespectful mouth with me would be pure honor."

He smiled. He smoked. He knew that Pablo Reyes, not a completely stupid man, would stand here and take this in the daylight hours, for the vigilantes, a group of honest men, would be here any moment. He, *el Don*, was in charge of the vigilantes.

"The money," he continued, "anytime your family has enough money, and, yes, enough guts, I will be most happy to bring my mare out and race against your great stallion, but until that day, be more a man of your position."

Pablo smirked. "My family will bet you one hundred thousand pesos anytime."

"In what? Pigs? Rocks? Worn-out land? Oh, no, my friend, I wish to see cash. Cold, hard cash."

And he, *el Don*, backed away, and all around the *Don* now came a group of men with homemade shotguns. *Retrocargas*. And they were doing the vigilante thing and trying to see if a day of horse races could happen without bloodshed. And so it came to be. The races were done, and no one was killed, and the day marched on until she, the night, came and covered all with her warm, sweet body. Deeply. As always. Yes. And so it was night, and men were so up high, in an almost religious state, that women were now needed. For their code of honor unto death had not been realized, and the taste for blood had not been fulfilled. And in this moment, in the female quiet of this mystic night, it was easy to see why the Virgin Mary had come to be Our Lady de Guadalupe in Mexico. For only a virgin's blood could subdue man in such high free feelings of God on earth.

BOOK TWO

The earth shook, and a trembling roar exploded as fire leaped to the sky and lava oozed across the earth ... forming another mountain ... also to-be-spoken-to.

Mexico is so close to the equator and yet so high up in the air that the blood boils, the mind goes light, and the heart beats strong. And yet, not all of Mexico is so drastic as it is here in the mountains of the southwest. These mountains around Jalisco, with Michoacán to the south and Zacatecas to the north, are famous for their machismo. They are famous for the best tequila, for the finest horses, and for men who carry expensive guns and have an insane orgullo *to uphold their own personal law. In fact, this area is said to have no children or women. For all people here are machos—alive in the brave, wild, and free style in which man was born to live.* Corridos *have it that men from this area never manage to live long on the border between Mexico and* los Estados Unidos. *Because they aren't used to the shadow of law, Mexican or American. So the first time a man raises his voice at them, gringo foreman or* pocho *American, they kill them. Now. Pronto. And then they either make a stand and die or run back to their beloved mountains, where no man walks another's shadow; and men don't owe a death, men own a death.*

Also, it is true that in this rugged land no one is too very rich and no one is too very poor, because the land is so hard that each must work his own. And a native son can hide out and know that not even the federales *will come after him. For mountain people take care of their own.* Nunca se rajan. *So when men leave this area to go north to the United States they are blind, out of place, and that is why so many get lost or killed and never return.*

Also, there's a standard joke in this part of Mexico. They say, "Thank God I have no sisters." For it is true, a man with no sisters is pretty sure of not ever needing to get involved in the people's code of honor unto death. But a man with many sisters has real problems and so he learns to sleep with both eyes open.

CHAPTER ONE

The *norteños* were in the bar dedicating songs to Pablo Reyes' sister with the moustache. The songs were funny, and the *norteños* were having a fine time when suddenly a gunshot echoed. A scream of swear words rang, and two *norteños* heard their names called. They leaped away, drawing their .45's, but it was too late. Two men stood in the open doorway of the cantina shooting their homemade *retrocargas*.

Roberto, sitting beside Juan Aguilar, felt several hits of pain. He dropped to the floor. Aguilar was beside him, squirming and bleeding. And all around, people were screaming, dodging, and then shooting back. The lights went out. Roberto took hold of Aguilar. He found the back door. He dragged Juan out. He heard horses coming. He helped Aguilar to a *cerca*, a fence made of rock, and tried getting him over it. But Juan was hit bad and couldn't make it.

Horses were coming, they were coming closer. Roberto knocked some rocks down and picked up the big heavy man and tossed him over the *cerca* and into the pig pen, then leaped in himself. The big man yelped with pain and wrestled among the pigs, who thought it was feeding time and were trying to eat him. Roberto kicked the starving pigs away, and Aguilar stopped yelping.

"Who's coming?" asked Aguilar.

"I don't know." The pigs were making noise, and the men inside the cantina were screeching in pain and shooting their .45's and now and then being answered with the huge blasting sound of a single-shot homemade *retrocarga*.

Still the riders came, pounding hooves over cobblestones. And now Roberto and Juan heard them say: "I killed one bastard! I'm sure!"

"Well, I don't know about that. But I sure gave lead to that big *hombre* who was sitting with Roberto García."

"You didn't hit Roberto, did you?"

"Who cares? Hell, he's one of them now."

"Yes. I guess you're right."

Roberto got angry. He now knew who they were. They were two of the younger Reyes brothers and they had been good friends of his until a few weeks ago when he had to fire one of them for being lazy. He picked up a rock and pushed a pig away and made himself ready to leap on the *cerca*, when suddenly he heard a roaring blast and felt the lightning flash of Juan Aguilar's big .45 right by his ear. He gripped his ear in terrible pain and heard another, and another, and the night cracked open in his head like dawn as he dropped the rock and gripped his head in echoing blasts of pain. Both riders fell from their horses and the horses burst out racing in fright. Aguilar then leaped the fence and, seeing one of the brothers still twitching, he shot him again and the man's head leaped and came down in messy pieces.

Roberto trembled, and glanced around to see if anyone had witnessed this last shot. This was bad. To shoot someone was all right; it was the code. But to walk up and kill him when he was helpless—that was not correct.

Now Juan Aguilar wobbled and began to fall, but didn't, and went to the *cerca* and sat down, rock wall to his back. He put in a new fully loaded clip of .45 shells and held ready. Now there were people coming from everywhere, and the two dead bodies would be identified, and word would be sent to their home, and before daybreak the father, with sons and cousins, would be coming, and Juan Aguilar and all his friends would be hunted. *A la prueba.* Unto death. Roberto swallowed.

Two hours later, with the *arado* saying it was past midnight, Roberto's father led the blind horse out of town. Aguilar was strapped on the horse. Roberto was gripping the horse's tail. They, all the survivors, were going north. Two *norteños* had been killed. Juan and another *norteño* were wounded. Pedro had not been wounded. And so in the moonlight a group of seven men and one blind horse were now making their way out of town, on the road, along the little brother-river of the great father-river of the Lerma.

And there came Roberto's mother on the other side of the river. Crying, and shouting, and praying, and bellowing like a cow with calf. She loved him. And she wanted him to stay home. To please, for the mercy of God, not go. Because he'd never return. She just knew it. And for two kilometers she followed on the other side of the moon-bright river, crying her love and fear and heartbreaking sorrow. Roberto began to cry and told her to please go home. But still she came, rosary in hand, bellowing her love. Finally she fell. Exhausted. And Roberto's father said, "No, *mi hijito*, don't cross the river to her. Let us go on. It will only make it worse, and besides ... if the Reyes catch you, they will kill you. They are a big family. Thirteen sons. And eight of age to handle a gun."

Roberto called to his mother and said he would be back. He would return with money and buy her a house. And he began to cry and wobble. His father told him to grip the horse's tail with both hands, and led them on. On and on. The ten kilometers to the highway where the bus stopped under a big tree to pick up the country people. They had to hurry and catch the bus and go into Guadalajara, four hours away, and get Juan to a doctor, or he would die. Roberto, he would live. He had only been hit in the shoulder and face.

The bus came over the hill shortly after daybreak, and Roberto's father said, "*Hijo*, here comes your bus and ... truly, I didn't want you to go. Too many never return. But now you have to go. So listen and, believe me, if you think there is hunger here ... wait until you get to the camp of legalization. I went there once when I was young, and people ... they come from everywhere, trying to legalize themselves to *los Estados Unidos*, and they die like flies." He breathed. "Son ... come here." They walked off to a private distance. "Listen, now you must go, we both know this, so I'll tell you what I know. In a small town everyone must be honest because everyone knows everyone, but where you are going, no one knows no one ... so no one is honest. Your best friend might some night cut your throat for a few pennies while you sleep." Roberto began to protest. "Shut up! And believe me, trust no one. And especially not these experienced *norteños*. It is rumored that on the other side, once you boys have made your money, that they abandon you or kill you and take your wages and blame it on the gringos. Be careful. Come home to us. I love you. You are my first and eldest son!" He embraced Roberto. "Now, go! And take care and keep your eyes open ... especially if you ever get money.

"Oh, and one more thing ... if you get scared and break down after a few days out, don't feel ashamed to come back. Many men do. I did."

Roberto held, looking at his father a long, long time, and he felt love, honest and raw, for the first time in years, and he started to speak, but his voice choked up and so he just nodded. Then turned. Going. Going quickly. He got in the bus and waved to his father and to the land where he had been born and raised, and which he had never left before. He thought he would cry.

He felt a poke in the ribs. It was Juan Aguilar. He was handing Roberto a small bottle of tequila and saying, "Drink. I know how it is the first time. Drink. And try to go to sleep. Keep it all a dream for a while, or the reality will bring tears and ... men like us, shot and bleeding, must never cry again! We are *braceros*! *¡Norteños!* And even the devil himself must step aside!"

Roberto smiled and drank and listened to the motor of the old bus and glanced about at the ranch people with cages of chickens and pigeons, and over there one man with a turkey and a woman with a little pig, and there ... two full-blooded Tarascan Indians, much like himself, with piles of blankets and figures carved of wood. He drank. And felt good that his bleeding had stopped, and he looked out and gave true witness to the morning, the land, the vegetation; then he saw two *burros* loaded with sticks of firewood and a man afoot driving them, and he smiled ... so familiar a sight ... then in a field he saw two *bueyes* starting their work before the sun became too hot and drained both man and beast of strength, and he breathed, wondering about his own *bueyes*, and he held back tears and drank again and mumbled some memorized prayers for God to help his family and also help him, Roberto, to not get lost, or killed, or fall off the end of the world. He had to live. He had to find work and earn money, or they, his family, would starve.

Empalme is south of the U.S border several hundred miles, and in the late 1950's and early 1960's a temporary camp for the legalization of labor to los Estados Unidos *was set up in Empalme alongside the Sea of Cortez. The Americans put up offices in a huge warehouse, and they processed a labor force of thousands of* braceros *to work in the U.S. Men came in from all over Mexico, and this little town of a couple of shacks grew overnight into a desperate anthill of fifty thousand. Men were processed by the thousands every day, but still more came, and the little community grew into a carnival of temporary structures, restaurants, con men, whores, and it was a nightmare.*

Men, hungry and lost. And in the heat of the day, well over a hundred degrees, they stood in lines by tens of thousands. And soon they began suffocating each other and passing out by the hundreds, and as one fell, quickly another would pick his pocket and disappear into the mass of men who didn't know each other . . . and the fallen one was trampled as they moved on, exhausted and sweaty, like starving dogs trying to get contracted into the land of plenty.

And how could they do anything else? They'd been in line for weeks, months, and they were waiting for no man. They'd borrowed, stolen, and begged to get the money to get this far, and they had to do it! They had family depending on them back home.

CHAPTER TWO

In Guadalajara, the other *norteños* went ahead and left Aguilar and the other wounded *norteño* under a doctor's care. Roberto walked about the city looking up at all the tall buildings and almost got hit by a car. So he quit looking and went back to the house where they rented a room from a friend of Juan Aguilar's.

The next day the other *norteño* died, and that was that. So Aguilar took his jacket and boots and told Roberto to try them. Roberto didn't want to, but ... he'd never had store clothes. He put them on in a rush. They fit wonderfully. Hell, anything would have fit wonderfully. And that afternoon they left on the bus, a big modern bus with no chickens or turkeys, and they traveled fast up to the north, too. Roberto took off his boots and held them lovingly against his suede jacket and watched the country, the mountains, the valleys, the towns, and they traveled fast like that for one night and one day, and now there were no mountains. All was flat and so hot and humid that Roberto felt his body oozing wet, and he could hardly breathe. It all smelled so close and full of strange powerful odors that he didn't like it. Where he was from, high in the mountains, it had always smelled thin and clean. Even in the midday with the sun so very hot. Later that night a woman passed out and fell off her seat. No one helped her. Roberto went to her. He tried putting her back in her seat. She was dead. He went back to his seat and for a while watched the bouncy body of the dead woman. It all seemed so far away. Later, the bus stopped and they got out. They were in Empalme. And there were men everywhere. But no women. Just men. By the tens of thousands. And they seemed to have nothing to do, and they just stared from under their sombreros and said nothing. Roberto shuddered. They all seemed dead. Like they had no faces. No expressions. Just dark and tired masks of desperate want.

Juan Aguilar said, "Follow me and don't talk to no one. I think I know where to find our friends."

Pedro and the others, who were not wounded, had come on ahead. Juan and Roberto and the other wounded *norteño*, Miguel Sánchez, were to have come together. But Miguel had died. Now only his pants and boots, hat and jacket, came along. They walked through the mass of men. The terrain was flat and sandy with a few scattered palms. A truck drove by with a huge voice. A bullhorn. And it gave information on which Mexican state was now being taken first in the American line.

Men raced! Others cursed!

Roberto saw and said nothing and stayed close to Juan Aguilar. There were men all over. Bunched together like hungry chickens in a cage. And Roberto could tell by their dress that they didn't come from his pueblo area. Many wore city clothes. Pants and shirts made in stores. Roberto remembered his old mountain clothes made of coarse cotton sack, and he noticed that there were a few dressed like that. But not many. They walked on, and as he went he came to realize that he was taller than some. Just a little taller, but truly much wider of shoulder and hip. He looked well-fed and powerful compared to most. But still he held close to Juan. He felt fear as they moved among this mob of men and no women, and so he, Roberto, kept his hands over his front pockets where he had his hundred pesos—eight dollars—all his money in the world. He was terrified.

Finally, about three kilometers away from the bus stop, they found some old rotten train cars, and there, with lots of other men, they found their other townsmen, and Roberto felt a strangeness. He had never liked these men back home. In fact, he was planning on killing one of them, and yet, out here among all these no-man faces, he was suddenly filled with such affection to see his townsmen that it was a foreign feeling to him. Completely. And they all smiled and embraced, talking and getting the facts of the immediate situation, when Pedro yelled, "Hey, wait! Is this jacket and hat not Miguel Sánchez's? Eh? Answer up, you no-good kid!" And he drew a switchblade and came at Roberto. Roberto leaped away. He slashed at Roberto.

"Don't!" shouted Aguilar. "Miguel died of his wounds, and I gave . . . "

But Pedro didn't hear Aguilar's words. He was short and lean and well-known for his knife, and even though he was nearly forty, he didn't have one gray hair. He was pure lethal Indian and hard of body and mind, and at the present, his entire focus of being was on this boy, Roberto.

Juan Aguilar laughed and tried to make light of the situation. "*Compadre* ... please. He is my boy. Listen to me. Miguel, on his dying bed, gave the clothes to this boy."

"He what?" asked Pedro. "I don't believe it!"

"But, *compadre*, it's the Virgin Mother truth. He gave him his clothes and said, 'Roberto, take my clothes and go up north. And take from the dirty gringos! Take in my name!' You knew Miguel, you know how he was. It's the truth, believe me."

Pedro nodded. "Okay. That sounds like old Miguel. I believe. But you,"—and he pushed the blade to Roberto's throat—"had best take! And take plenty! In memory of Miguel!"

Roberto swallowed, moved the knife away with one finger slowly, and said, "Don't worry. I'll take."

"Good! And don't forget!"

Roberto nodded. Nodded and swallowed and held his rage within and said nothing. Absolutely. This one was the one who had shamed his father and ... he would pay. He would. Later. And so Roberto kept his hand over his pocket with his money as the men talked on. Finally one of the other young men realized what Roberto was doing. He laughed and laughed and told everyone, and Juan Aguilar snapped at Roberto to stop that. My God, people would think he had ten times more money than he had, and someone would cut his throat before sundown.

Roberto turned dark red with embarrassment and took his hands away, and the *norteños* and the other young men laughed and made jokes and agreed that for sure Roberto was *el más indio*, the dumbest Indian, among them.

Roberto said nothing and just kept listening and looking and taking everything in. For truly, he was beginning to agree with them: he was very stupid and naïve.

A truck came by. It was calling on a big bullhorn that this Mexican state was now up with three hundred men to be legalized, and if they had their papers already in, they had better get up there in the American line fast. Men leaped and ran, and others cried out with pains of hunger, wanting strength to get up and go but unable to make it. And so they cursed and threatened, but that was that. They couldn't make it. They were drained, all sweated out of life. Others who were not called screamed at the heavens and begged to be called before they were too weak to pass the American physical. Lately, many who were called were rejected. They had been waiting here in this nightmare for so long without proper food and shelter that they had become physically unfit to be laborers.

One old man, over there in the corner of the boxcar, had his eyes closed and was grinding his teeth and yelping, "They give me nothing! *¡Nada! ¡Nada! ¡Nada!* That is what I need! The more I want, the less I get, so I can be sent *a la chingada* once and for all!" And he would laugh, an awful sickish laugh, and keep his eyes closed to all the world and repeat this over and over. Old weathered face, eyes shut, mouth laughing, and yelps of pain, and all around him men smiled. It was funny. It was awful. It was rawbone humor and it was truth. Mexican style. *¡Viva la vida!*

Others, who had been across to the land of plenty time and again kept quiet, very quiet, not wasting their energy. Once they were called they would get in line and hold tall so as not to be trampled. So many, after finally getting into the last line-up, were trampled to death because they had no strength left to fight the mob and hold their own ground. So these experienced ones rested. Rested so they could get their papers processed and pass the physical. That's all it took. After that, the Americans, those great gringo dirty bastards, would take care of them from there on. First, the Americans would give them a room to bathe in. A room that rained. And then would give them orange juice—cold! no kidding!—a big paper cup of cold orange juice which was said to taste like honey, and then one or two sandwiches. A thing made with bread on the outside and meat and cheese and lettuce on the inside, and then, bathed and fed, they would be put on trains with seats, wonderful seats, at no cost and shipped north to the land of plenty, where they would work all their bodies could stand and they would not only get paid but fed and bathed and paid some more!

Fantastic! These gringos!

And it all began when a gringo finished inspecting your ass, then said in English, "Okay!"

Okay! That was the great word. The one which got you cold orange juice that tasted like honey.

¡Car-rrrr-amba! The wealth and organization of these dirty bastard gringos was incredible. Fantastic!

Okay!

Yes, okay! That was the magic American word: OKAY!

Then, to the anthill of men, came the coyotes, slang for sharp legal-sounding crooks, and they came with promises to get papers processed in eight days' time.

Eight days! For they were attorneys and knew how to deal with these gringos and get things done the American way. And so men got in line by the hundreds and gave their money to these men in suits in the shade of a big beautiful umbrella with the Mexican flag on one side and the American flag on the other side. And these attorneys took three hundred pesos from each single man as fast as they could all day long and into the night for six straight days, and then, on the seventh day, they didn't come back. And grown men with callused hands and knives in their belts fell down and cried, weeping like children. Broken and ashamed. Then began, by the thousands, the long journey home.

Home, afoot, to where children cried of hunger and women prayed and men got drunk, but still there was more there than here.

Others, who didn't go home but were broke and hungry, began stealing and fighting and killing, and the local police were helpless. There were just five policemen, so what the hell could they do against thousands of desperate men?

CHAPTER THREE

Roberto was taught this fantastic word, "okay" and to say it loudly with his tongue all out, and then he and the other young men were put in the line. Or more precisely, put in the mob who awaited in the barbed-wired field in front of the remodeled warehouse of the Americans. The norteños took turns, one at a time, and stayed with the youths as the other two rested in the shade of the boxcar and fought, fist and knife, to keep a place for them all to sleep at night.

One week passed, another week passed, and still they waited in line; then Juan Aguilar gave a mordida, a bribe, of one hundred and fifty pesos to a guard to find out about their papers, and the guard found out that their papers had never been submitted. Juan Aguilar raged! That goddamn coyote lawyer from Guadalajara who had always processed his papers ahead of time had given him the coyote this time. Juan Aguilar sent a telegram to Guadalajara, and was answered that the lawyer had closed up office and moved away. Aguilar sent another telegram asking where. And got the answer that no one knew. Maybe Mexico City. Juan Aguilar called Roberto, and they went off together to a private distance, and Juan counted his money. He had two hundred pesos left. Sixteen dollars. And one year ago he had come back across the border with more than twenty-two thousand pesos. Eighteen hundred dollars. Oh, how the money went. And to get new papers would take a lot of money, and to get advanced beyond these fifty thousand men would take even more mordida money. He asked Roberto if he had any money, and Roberto said yes, of course. He showed Aguilar that he had fifteen pesos left. One dollar and twenty-some cents. Juan rubbed the boy's head and pinched his cheek.

"Come! We are going to start thinking like thieves, wolves of the night, and find a way to shave these sheep." He patted his

.45 pistol, which he carried under his pants by his groin. They walked on and for two days could find no sheep. All fifty thousand men seemed to be wolves, as hungry and desperate as they. Then, on the third day, Roberto saw a man selling ice, and he got an idea and went to the dump and found some huge cans. He went to the sea—a thing that truly fascinated him—and scrubbed the cans all afternoon with sand and water. Late that afternoon he told Aguilar his idea. The other young men laughed and gave him innumerable reasons why it would not work. Pedro called him a fool, an Indian-without-reason. Juan Aguilar nodded, then nodded again, and went to buy the flavored syrup as Roberto went back to the dumps to get boxes for a table and dozens of small cans for serving. That night Roberto and Aguilar worked, getting things ready, and then in the morning Roberto went for the ice. By midmorning they had sold so many snow cones that the block of ice was almost gone. And hell, the day was just beginning, and already they had made their investment back, thirty pesos, plus a profit of well over two hundred pesos.

Roberto went for more ice. It took him almost an hour to return with it. That was too long. They lost customers. And hell, carrying a block of ice in one-hundred-and-ten-degree temperature was no easy task. He hired two of the boys who had laughed at him. He paid them on delivery. And that first day they made nine hundred pesos' profit and the next day they made twelve hundred and the third day the police came and asked for their business permit. They had none and were fined a hundred pesos after Aguilar assured them that they had made only two hundred pesos.

Now Roberto and Aguilar were alive once more. They had money. Over two thousand pesos. They ate. They drank. They were healthy men with eyes to see and a self to place once more.

Then as they walked through the crowd, Aguilar suddenly pointed. "Look!" he said. "See those two men in city suits! One is my attorney! The son-of-a-bitch who stole my money. And those workmen are setting up a booth and umbrella for him." He took a big breath. "This is our lucky day. I told you, luck, she is all woman. When she comes, she comes again and again, like a whore in heat, but when she goes ... my God—I've been there too. See the two flags they put up. Ahha, these coyotes, are the worst kind of wolves. They trick the people with those two flags, making them think that they represent both countries."

"Should we report them to the police?"

"No," said Aguilar, and he smiled a smile that made Roberto tremble. Then Juan Aguilar lit up a cigarette and took out a small bottle of tequila. "No, we will watch them like buzzards to the death."

"But he cheated us, you said. We should report him."

"No . . . kill him."

"Now?"

"Young one . . . you talk too much. Let me plan this and enjoy the planning. You see, you can't get much from a dead man. Little cash. Nothing more. But with planning, you can get sweet revenge and much much more. Watch. And learn."

Roberto nodded and didn't say anything more.

"Good. You're learning."

And so they squatted down at a distance and watched. Hour after hour. Circling buzzards watching wolves at prey. Then Juan Aguilar said, "I got it. Stay here while I go talk to them, but talk to no one. Not one word. Understand? Not one word."

"Will there be danger? I can fight."

Juan laughed. "Of course not. I'll talk to them as sweet as honey."

And two hours later Juan Aguilar had five hundred more pesos in his pocket and he and Roberto were out telling men that they had just given their papers to these attorneys, and surely they would be across the border in eight days. These lawyers had given it to them in writing! The American way! And men ran and fought to get in line by the tens of hundreds and pay their three hundred pesos so they could also be across in eight days. The next day Juan Aguilar went and got the rest of the deal. One thousand more pesos plus some forged immigration papers. He gave two hundred pesos to Roberto. Roberto now had nearly eight hundred pesos. More money than he'd ever seen. And he was happy.

Juan Aguilar pocketed their forged papers, and he smiled. He had nearly two thousand himself. He patted Roberto on the head and said that this was nothing. And that afternoon Juan bought Roberto some socks and underclothes. The first Roberto had ever owned, and then they also bought swimming suits. Roberto had never even seen such a thing. And they went to the sea to bathe.

At the sea there were a few local girls. Young and plump, brown and pretty. Aguilar walked out in the water and began splashing himself and glancing around for all to see him. He was well-muscled, big-boned, light-complexioned, and very good-looking. Roberto tried to follow his example but felt so very timid in his bright green swim pants. Then Juan Aguilar walked out farther and dove beautifully into a fair-size wave. Roberto tried to do the same but didn't go deep enough, and the water knocked him about and into the sand, and he lost his feet and couldn't get up. He ate sand, spat water, and was terrified by the time he finally got up. He ran to the shore. Aguilar laughed and laughed. Some girls on shore joined his laughter. Roberto blushed and went for his clothes. That night they went to town where the local people lived. They went to a restaurant, such a restaurant that Roberto's eyes jumped from his head at the luxury of tablecloth, silverware, and napkins, and Juan laughed and showed Roberto how to use the silverware, and then, after the meal, how to use a toothpick, and Roberto copied his every move. Aguilar truly liked this innocent boy. Maybe he would keep him. Maybe he would return him home safely. He had never taken time to have a son, and he liked his boy.

Afterward he took Roberto to a cantina with women, and Roberto had his first whore, and the next morning he felt bad and went to church and lit three candles and prayed a long time, but by afternoon with a few beers and money in his pocket it was all much better inside his soul, and he went back to the cantina with the women.

One girl, young and dark and lovely, came up to him and told him he was so wide-shouldered. So strong. He bought her a drink. She sipped and gripped his pants, and his organ burst forth, and she said he was so thick and heavy and huge. Truly incredible! One half time larger than men twice his height. She kissed him and said my God, to please, for the love of mercy to meet her at the beach after midnight. His mind whirled. She laughed and said that they would swim in the nude and then make love on the beach just like in the American movies. His mind leaped! This was so fantastic to have a girl. Such a beautiful girl wanting him by the sea. He swallowed. Not noticing that many men were watching. All he could see was a girl who wished to go swimming with him at midnight. He ran and told Juan. Juan laughed and told him to take care, and he, Juan, continued playing poker. He was five hundred pesos—forty dollars—ahead, and he now smoked cigars once again. He gave a cigar to Roberto. Roberto lit it and then began coughing, and everyone laughed. He went out. He'd wait at the beach for the girl. Hell, it was almost sunset, and it would not be too long before midnight.

He whistled his way toward the beach. He went to the long bridge which went over a finger of sea between Guaymas and Empalme, and there he froze. Carved in midair. By the bridge were people, and one girl was nude.

My God, and his eyes leaped until finally he saw that she was not really nude. She wore a little thing over her breasts, and another little thing on her butt, and he wondered if she was a whore or if she was so poor and shameless that she didn't bother to buy clothes. He wondered. She looked so slender, so skinny, and yet she was with a man who was well-fed and dressed expensively. Then, inconceivably he saw them walk toward a car with no top. The car was parked this side of the bridge. It looked shiny and new. These people had money. They had a car. They could not be hungry. And he watched her hips, her legs, her golden hair, her movements, and he believed her to be the strangest thing he had ever seen: an ill-fed, rich, beautiful woman.

Someone slapped Roberto on the back. He leaped and saw a man, dark like himself, laughing at him.

"Boy! Put your eyes back in your head! That is only a gringa. Not a person from the moon!"

But still Roberto could not pull his eyes back into his head. Now she turned, getting into the small low car, and her ombligo, her belly-button, oh so smooth, trim, and lovely, and now, as she bent to get in, her rounded behind, the mango cheeks of her ass, and he gasped and grew so excited that his knees went wobbly and his mind went dizzy. He swallowed. He breathed. He watched them roar away. And then, after a while, he walked on. And he waited by the shore of the Sea of Cortez for his own girl. He waited until midnight, until daybreak, but his girl from the cantina never showed up, and with the sun coming, and feeling so lonely, so stupid, so naïve, he remembered home—his family, and his mother coming up the river and bellowing her love; and then, hearing a cock crow in the distance, he recalled the bueyes, the blind horse, and his eyes began to water.

He knelt and began to pray to God for forgiveness. He had forgotten all about them. How awful. He had money. He had to send them some this very day. He took out his money. He counted it. He had more than seven hundred pesos. He would ask Aguilar if he could send them six hundred. He got up to go, feeling much better.

During World War II there were few men at home, and men were needed for farm labor. So the United States imported Mexicans. They were just south of the border, and it seemed very practical. So they legally contracted Mexicans to do a certain job on a certain ranch for a guaranteed wage, and these legal laborers came to be known as braceros, *arms, and between 1941 and 1944 fifty-five thousand were imported.*

Then after the war, having a taste of this good cheap labor, the farmers and ranchers of the southwest U.S. sent lobbyists to Washington to say that they needed this cheap labor. There were no Americans willing to do this back-breaking stoop labor. And so a few million Mexican-Americans and Okies and Arkies and Filipinos, who had done this farm labor before the war, were forgotten and the importation of braceros *was extended for a few more years, and it became big business. Huge! One hundred thousand were imported that first year. And more and more every year, so by 1954 more than four hundred thousand were being imported yearly, and God only knows how many wetbacks, illegal* braceros, *came across the border* a la brava.

For now it was the dream of every young man in Mexico to come north and make his fortune, and in Mexico many farms were forgotten, as the strong young men came north. Legal or illegal did not matter. Hell, the American dollar was the god of the earth.

CHAPTER FOUR

Roberto stretched in the early-morning sunlight. He went to the sea and washed his face with seawater. He breathed and he felt good. He would send money home. He smiled and went back toward town. At the bridge he stopped. The ocean was going. It was lower, and it was dragging away, and there were fish in it, and then suddenly ... there came a big roundish wobbly thing of such fantastic colors of green and blue and purple, glowing like a light, and he stood ... in wonder. It was so beautiful. Quickly he ran off the bridge and began taking of his clothes. He would dive in and get it and sell it for one thousand American dollars. Not pesos. Dollars!

A man yelled, "Don't, you fool!" He was fishing from the bridge. "Don't!"

"It's mine! If I get it first! It's mine!"

The man laughed. "No. I'm not disputing ownership. I'm just trying to tell you that it is worthless. It is a jellyfish, and they go out in the tide by the dozens. They are truly worthless." Roberto looked from him to the jellyfish. "Truly, they are no good to eat or anything. And if you touch one, it will burn you and cause great blisters and infection." He smiled at Roberto and saw that he was dark and wide-faced. He was an Indian, stubborn, and wouldn't believe him unless he showed kindness so he added, "Come here. I have an extra pole. We'll fish together."

Roberto saw his kind smile and put on his pants, checked his money, and went to the man, and they fished all morning and it was true, as the sea went away he saw many beautiful jellyfish, and then other kinds of fish, too, and all was so fantastic. So lovely. They caught several fish as the sea went away and the man explained about the sea, and Roberto was so happy that he forgot about home and about the girl who had caused him to wait all night and he didn't start back for town until midday. As he neared town, a pickup drove up beside him.

"Hey, boy!" called an old Mexican man from inside the truck. "Do you want work?"

"Sure," said Roberto. "That's what I came for."

The man smiled. He wore a straw hat and had a big moustache. "Good! I'm glad to finally hear someone talk like that. Do you have any friends who want work?"

"Sure. There are seven of us, and we all came to work."

The man truly smiled. "Very good! Where are your friends?"

Roberto told the man.

"Good, get in. We'll go get them."

Roberto had never been in a pickup. He didn't know how to open the door. The man opened it for him, and he got in and they were off, and Roberto felt very grand ... up high in a private vehicle and watching all the other men afoot. He smiled. The pickup owner saw and asked where he was from.

"Michoacán," said Roberto proudly. "High in the mountains."

The man nodded and explained his situation. He needed men. Lots of men. He and many other farmers were losing their crops because of lack of men. Roberto shrugged. He couldn't figure it. There were men all over this place with nothing to do. He said nothing, and they drove over to the railroad. It was terribly hot. He found Aguilar and Pedro in the shade of their railroad car. Pedro was telling some stranger to get the hell out of their area and go find his own damn shade. The stranger retreated. Roberto came up and told them about the offer of work. Pedro yelled at him.

"You fool! If it is so good a job, why can't he get more than enough men? Hell! There are thousands all over the place. You fool! You're supposed to be in line so we can get to *los Estados Unidos*. Just because you got lucky with that ice-syrup, you think that you're special. Eh?"

Roberto looked at this man, Pedro, and after a moment said, "Okay, if you're so smart, you tell me, we have no real papers, so what's the purpose of staying in line?"

Pedro exploded. "That makes no difference! You do as we say! We're the experienced men! Do you understand? We!" And he pointed at his own chest and poked himself hard. "We! Not you!" He was terribly angry.

Roberto looked at him, but didn't answer. He told Aguilar about the man in the truck. That he had cotton and he needed men. Right now. So he would drive them out to his place, charge them nothing for the service, and pay them top price for each kilo of cotton. Juan Aguilar nodded.

"And you believe that!" shouted Pedro, spitting on the floor. "*¡Muchacho pendejo!*"

Roberto jerked upright. Visibly.

"Pedro," said Aguilar very slowly. "No use insulting each other." Then to Roberto, "Come. Let's go and see. We'll feel this man out."

Roberto turned to go. Slowly. Quietly. Since the word "*pendejo*," stupid, he had needed to close up, shutting his eyes. Revenge ... it was not the proper time yet. But, oh, God, how this Pedro was drawing the line thin.

"You go! I stay! I'm not losing one second's chance of getting across the border." Pedro lay back down on the floor of the boxcar.

Juan Aguilar nodded and agreed that maybe Pedro was right. They should keep their minds on their immediate business of getting across the border, but still ... an ace in the hole was good. He went out with Roberto into the white sunlight and got all the information necessary, and then told the man that maybe tomorrow they would be out to his place. The old man threw up his hands.

"For the love of God! I'm paying top price. I cannot afford to pay any more or I'll go broke!"

"*Señor* ... it's not the price. The price is more than fair. It's just that we've got to talk things over tonight as a group and figure what is best."

"Sure. Sure. I've heard that before!" He started the motor. "You'll all stay here, preferring to starve with the dream of gringo money! Sure. I know! And I'll lose my crop this year again. Sure. Sure. These son-of-a-bitch bastard *americanos* have ruined you men! Made you crazy!

"Look! Look! You two are well-nourished! But look over there!" They looked. There were thirty or forty men under two palm trees. They looked drained. Thirsty and tired. Eyes closed and moving as little as possible. Some didn't even bother knocking the flies off their face anymore. "They are dying of sun and empty stomachs! But will they get out of this anthill and come and work? No! They will not! They'd prefer to die here! Waiting! With the hope of getting across to the American side!

"Insane! Insane! These dirty gringos have driven them *loco*!" And he drove off in a big cloud of dust, honking and pushing his way through the mob of sick and tired men.

Nine thousand were contracted that day. Four thousand new ones came in that day. And so the mob of waiting men remained at forty to fifty thousand, and the coyotes kept moving about, knocking off the weaker ones. The more innocent. The ones who were still worth knocking off.

Days passed, and Roberto couldn't sleep well. He and Aguilar were making so much money that he was always afraid of being robbed. He just knew that every face he saw knew that he was filthy rich. And there were tens of thousands of faces.

He and Juan Aguilar had kept broadcasting for the crooked attorneys and then also developed other methods of playing the coyote and shearing off these lost sheep, and hell, there were so many innocent sheep that now Roberto felt naked not to have five or eight hundred pesos in his pocket at all times. Finally he sent home some money by money order like Juan Aguilar showed him. Five hundred pesos—forty dollars—to his mother. But in care of his sister. And he now felt better, truly great, and so he walked tall. Much taller than his five-foot-seven, one-hundred-and-fifty-pound frame. He went to a store and bought needle and thread. He went to the dump to hide. There, well out of sight, he sewed his front pocket shut. Hell, he still had seven hundred pesos that he didn't need. All he needed was thirty or forty to live on for a whole week, and ... he was scared, so he hid at the dump and sewed his pocket shut and then walked back among the mob of men. Still scared but feeling a little better.

The days grew hotter. He couldn't sleep and soon began to lose weight. He felt dirty and sick. Men began fainting by the hundreds. Six died in one afternoon. One man leaped on a fallen one and ripped off his pocket with his knife and ran. Roberto raced after him and tackled the thief, and they went rolling about in the confusion of legs of waiting men. The thief kicked free, leaping up with knife in hand, and his eyes were mean and red and his face was scarred. He circled about Roberto, and men gathered, forgetting the fallen one as he lay choking to death with the dust of dragging feet. It was a mob, and they were watching the action. Roberto backed up and tripped. The scarred man came at him as quick as a snake. Roberto threw sand in his face and leaped to the side, barely saving his life. The man laughed and came again at Roberto, knife long and glistening white in the sun. Then came a shout. It was Juan Aguilar. He wished to stop the fight.

Pedro was with Aguilar, and he laughed and said, "Let the boy fight. Hell, we've seen no action in days. Here!" And he drew his knife and tossed it to Roberto. Roberto caught it. "Let's see what you know. Eh? *¡Muchacho!* Smart-ass!"

"But I've never used a knife to fight," answered Roberto. "I know nothing."

Hearing this, all the men around began to laugh, and the many-scarred man joined their laughter and said, "Don't worry, little one, I'll teach you how. You cut like THIS!" And he slashed at Roberto and cut his arm. The men burst out laughing.

Juan Aguilar yelled, "Roberto! You fool! If he gets you again, I'll kill you myself! You are my boy! Use knife and rock and kill that ugly bastard!"

"Oh!" yelled another. "You're for the Indian boy! Hell, I'll bet he dies. That one he fights is from Chihuahua, my state!"

"Shit!" said Aguilar. "My boy is from the mountains of Michoacán next to Jalisco. My state!"

"Jalisco," said a red-haired Mexican. "Hell, I then bet on him! He's my countryman. But I'm not Indian. I'm from Los Altos de Jalisco. Come on, *muchacho*! Cut him good!"

And so the money passed around as Roberto took up a sand rock and the other did also, and they circled. Eyes of men focused on the intent to kill. Eyes of eyes ... they circled like fighting roosters. Then the many-scarred one faked with the knife, and threw the rock, and hit Roberto on the head and rushed in, figuring he had Roberto, and he slashed! But Roberto was so high on adrenalin that he never really felt the rock and just staggered, crushing the sandstone into sand and throwing it in the scarred one's eyes.

"Kill him!" yelled Aguilar. Roberto now had the advantage. The other could not see. "Kill him now while he's blind."

"But ... ?" asked Roberto as he turned to Juan Aguilar. "He can't see."

Men laughed. Pedro began roaring and slapping Aguilar on the back.

"Damn it! That's why!" yelled Aguilar. "Watch out!" Roberto turned, leaping away but he was too late. He didn't escape the blade this time. He got it across the ribs, and blood began to flow. The thief laughed and tossed his knife to his other hand and came at Roberto. Roberto backed up, holding his side, then raised his hand and saw the blood.

His blood!

And in that moment, with red blood and white sun and men all around, something happened inside Roberto. Something that he had never experienced before in all his life. He began to tremble, lose control, and he thought he was afraid. Terrified. Completely. But then the trembling ceased, and an icy smooth feeling began moving down his spine to his groin, and he screamed. Savagely! All his self was gone. Gone beyond his own control, and a stranger leaped out of his being ... to kill!

And so, slashing and screaming, he took the thief by surprise and cut his knife hand, drawing blood, and he saw and smiled. Oh, such a smile, and the scarred thief saw, believed, and circled to the right, away from Roberto's knife.

Pedro yelled, "Eh! This is getting good!"

And so the knife fight of right and wrong ended, and a profound game of death began, and it was a good one. One of those awful standoffs where two well-matched men cut at each other until they are weak with the loss of blood. Like cock fights, they circle and attack in a fury of slashing and screaming, kicking and faking, spitting and throwing, and then break ... and circle with eyes of death on each other's very souls.

Man, the deadliest of beasts since time began.

And Roberto, without even knowing it, was now smiling as he circled, and the scarred man—experienced with knife fights and such smiles—grew weary. For this boy was now *a la prueba.* And death, a good death, was now the proof of life, and the many-scarred man made the sign of the cross over his own person and advanced. This was it. All one in the same: life and death all in the same self spot.

Roberto saw and smiled, made the sign of the cross also, and the finest of fighting began, and men watched. Big-eyed, hearts pounding, and so very happy. Time stopped. Now. Here. And knives slashed. Circling now, faking then, then stopping, holding, and staring eye-to-eye. For whole minutes with no man moving a muscle as they waited, bleeding and growing weak for the other's death. Some of these standoff circling knife fights have been known to last for hours. Until each man is down in a pool of blood and unable to get up, but still they try one last stab. For the one who never quits is then called *gallo de estaca* and, in this state of self, it truly doesn't matter if he dies. For this is *a la prueba*, and that is where Roberto now was. Body and soul.

Completely! Now, weak and bleeding, he circled and was finally beginning to force the scarred thief back. Eye-to-eye, knife-to-knife, while the mob of men watched in ecstasy. The divine comedy of man. A need to kill off the body and transcend into pure soul. They, the mob, smiled with pounding hearts and talked and approved with great admiration. These boys, these men, were *gallos de estaca*, cocks of the stake, and this was tremendous—as good as any bullfight!

Roberto staggered. The other looked faint. Juan Aguilar yelled, "Enough! This is my boy! And I need him alive!"

Pedro and the mob yelled, no! That it was all *a la prueba*. No turning back from sacred death.

Aguilar stepped out and bellowed to stop! Now! Immediately! Or be prepared to deal with him.

Hearing this, and having learned much about self-protection in the last half-hour, Roberto now acted like he quit at Juan's command. He turned, knife down, and the scarred thief lunged like a snake. Roberto, expecting this, dodged, threw sand in his face, and kicked. The thief stumbled. He couldn't see. He slashed about blindly. Roberto waited, then stepped in and kicked him in the balls. The man fell with a cry. Dropping his knife and gripping his groin.

"Kill him!" yelled Pedro. "Kill him! Kill him!"

Roberto whirled, bloody and weak, and screamed, "Kill? Kill? You!" And he lashed at Pedro. Pedro leaped. Roberto went after him. Juan Aguilar grabbed Roberto and forced the knife from him. Men were screeching and saying that this was good! This boy, Roberto, would fight anyone, anywhere, anytime. He was *muy macho! ¡muy gallo! ¡muy hombre!* and all *a la prueba* as a man should be!

"Enough," said Aguilar. "The fight is over." And he took Roberto under his armpit and carried him away. Roberto was so weak his legs wobbled. They took Roberto to town to buy first-aid for him at a drugstore. A doctor would not be needed. Aguilar knew how to care for wounds. And the thief was left in the dust of moving men to cough and choke and eventually die like the victim, the fallen one, whom he had robbed not even an hour ago ... over there. In the dirt and sun.

Several hours later Roberto was not better. He was worse. He was sweating and running a fever, and the cutting to his ribs had gone in more than Aguilar had thought. Juan took him to a doctor. It was late at night. The doctor was not in. Aguilar gripped the young girl by the neck and shoved a hundred pesos into her hand and told her to get that doctor now! Fast! Yelling, she went to the back. The office was also a house. Very clean and nice. In minutes the doctor appeared. He asked Aguilar about his money before he looked at Roberto. Aguilar showed him rolls of money. The doctor apologized and said that, my God, there were so many dying like flies that, oh ... it was awful. The Americans, who had caused it, should call it a disaster area and send their Red Cross. All these people. And no money. Roberto, he said, looked well-nourished. He'd pull through. He mostly needed salt, food, and rest. He was drained.

And so in 1959 American field workers labored harder and harder for less and less until they were down to sixty cents per hour. Running. Racing. Working like frightened animals. Desperately afraid to lose their jobs. For there, coming in the night like hungry dogs, were braceros *and wetbacks. By tens of thousands. Dying to get work in the land of plenty at any damn price.*

And so in 1963 the bracero *program was stopped by the U.S. The Mexican-Americans, Okies, and Arkies were out of work, and the U.S. had to protect their own. And a drive to deport Mexicans, like the huge "Operation Wetback" of the 1950's, began, and police were quoted as saying that they herded Mexicans like pigs. That they were illiterate, degenerate, filthy people, and that they, the law, had to protect their real citizenry. An officer in the San Joaquin Valley was asked why he beat them and he said, "You got to let out blood. They're not like you and me; they basically like to get beat. Hell, if you don't let some of their blood run, you can't trust them. I know. I've been dealing with them all my life."*

And so one of the largest but least known migrations of men was stopped . . . but not really. For Mexicans had always been coming and going across the border for centuries and so it now simply went underground and got much worse.

CHAPTER FIVE

Rumors of the knife fight spread around, and men began to take note of Roberto and Aguilar and realize that they were the same ones who had been broadcasting for the attorneys.

Juan Aguilar became aware of this fact and knew they had to get out of Empalme. These coyote attorneys would sneak out one of these nights, and then they, Roberto and he, would be left holding the bag.

"Come," said Aguilar to Roberto. "Now is our time for sweet revenge." And Aguilar smiled. "These coyotes figured us for fools. So we'll double-cross them before they double-cross us."

They went to the attorneys' umbrella with the Mexican flag on one side and the American flag on the other side ... all so very official and proper to the eyes of these desperate people ... and Juan Aguilar began yelling, demanding his papers.

"I paid! And it's been eight days! I paid, and I say you are coyotes!"

The two attorneys and their assistants, all dressed in suits, tried calming him down. There were hundreds of men watching. Some had already given their money, and others were in line ready to give theirs. Men began rushing up. Aguilar's ex-attorney reached under the table. Juan Aguilar drew out his .45, shoving it in the man's ear.

The attorney froze. Carved in motion.

"Up," said Aguilar. "Easy, and give me that gun." The lawyer wouldn't move. Juan hit him in the temple with his .45. The man spilled, and the other men in suits stepped away. Terrified. "Roberto," said Juan, "go around. Get the gun and get us back our money." And he turned to the mob. "All I want back is my own money! My three hundred pesos! Fair is fair. You people better all get your own money back too." "They"—and he pointed with his

.45—"have your *dinero*!" He turned to Roberto. In a low voice. "Quickly! Grab some money, act like you count it, and throw the rest! Fast!"

Seeing the flying money, the mob closed in. Hundreds of raging mad faces. One assistant screamed for mercy.

"They did it!" He pointed to the attorneys. "Not me. For the love of God! Believe me! I thought this was a legal thing!"

Aguilar grabbed another handful of money, threw it one way, and rushed the other way, and Roberto followed him. Men screamed! Bellowed! And Roberto, well-rested from the knife fight, fought hard to go against the sea of men and barely got away with his life.

He gripped his still-cut side. He breathed and watched with a twisted face of fear. Men were being trampled to death as they fought to get to their money, and the attorneys . . . the attorneys . . . the attorneys? . . . Oh, well . . . they were being ripped and torn. Destroyed beyond human recognition.

From a safe distance Juan and Roberto now watched. Silently. A mob so angry and hysterical that it bit at itself like a wounded rat. A disemboweled coyote rushing about in a circle devouring its own intestines. Fear snapping at pain. Pain enlarging and giving more fear. Around and around. And Roberto swallowed. It was a nightmare. He made the sign of the cross, and his eyes began to water and, he didn't know why, but he wanted his mother. He, outside of danger, was now more afraid than when he had been in the knife-fight danger. He could not watch. He turned and saw Aguilar's face . . . ecstasy. Why, Aguilar was actually licking his lips and preparing to light a cigar. Roberto's stomach moved. He had to hold himself so he wouldn't puke. Eyes closed. The last few crying screams of the coyotes died away in death.

"Revenge," said Aguilar, "how sweet she feels." He patted Roberto on the shoulder. "Come. The fun, it's over."

Roberto heard the words and opened his eyes. Staring. And couldn't believe what he saw. Now, grown men with callused hands, knives in their belts, were falling down and weeping. Crying like children. Cursing like Satan. And others were drawing their knives and fighting to get money from one another.

Juan Aguilar grabbed Roberto. Hard. And turned him about and they went off. They had money. They had made money on this very incident, and they had to get out of Empalme. Men would be coming after them . . . to kill. They walked the two or three kilometers to the bus stop. No bus would be leaving for a couple of hours. They went back to the boxcars. They couldn't find their *camaradas*, their group of friends. They lay down to nap. Suddenly Roberto awoke. He reached for his money pocket, which was sewn shut. It was gone, and there was a man with a knife in hand bent over Aguilar. Roberto yelled! The man took fright and slashed at Roberto. Roberto rolled away. Juan awoke, gun in hand, and the blasting fire of the .45 automatic echoed throughout the boxcar as the man screamed and lunged forward, falling dead over Roberto.

Roberto kicked hysterically.

Juan Aguilar pulled the body away and gripped Roberto. "Luck! She is now starting to go against us," said Aguilar. "Come. *¡Pronto!* Get your money. We are going." They jumped out of the boxcar; men were all around. They ran into Pedro and the others of their *camaradas*. "I killed a man," Juan said. "We are going. You know, the old back-to-our-homeland trick. Okay?"

"Okay," said Pedro. "Let's go. I'm sick of it here."

"No," said another *norteño*. "I stay. I'm going to try something new tomorrow. Hell, today they only legalized two thousand according to the bullhorns. Last week they were legalizing nearly ten thousand every day. I'm getting across before it's too late."

"As you wish," said Aguilar. "And if anyone asks about this shooting, say nothing. Or, if forced, say that we went back to our homeland. The mountains of Michoacán. And that will be that. No law would dare hunt a man in our mountains."

Roberto and the group left, going back south. They caught the bus that night and went to Ciudad Obregón. They got off. They waited until daylight. The country was flat and humid. They had decided to hide out in a work camp and get a few days' work. They found where the cotton picking was and walked out of town five miles along the Yaqui River and found work. They were sold sacks, twelve feet long and which were reinforced where they dragged, and they straddled these sacks and began picking. It was Roberto's first attempt at cotton, and he was doing very poorly. Juan Aguilar began coughing. He had to stop. He went back to the barn where they had beds by the hundreds. He lay down to think. He knew that many men had already been turned down by the Americans because of his type of cough, and so he had not put in their new forged papers for legalization. He would not take the chance of himself, personally, being rejected and the men knowing about it. He would rather have them all think that they had not been selected, and then they would all be forced to go *a la brava*.

By the end of the week Roberto was a good cotton picker and knew the tricks. He would start early, an hour before sunup, and he and Juan and their group would have their bags half-full before the sun came up. And, by doing this, their cotton would be heavy with morning wetness, and at the weigh-in—where they got paid so much per kilo—their bags would be much heavier and they'd make good money and be done with their work before the heat of day, while others, going to the fields at the foremen's call, worked late into the day's heat, and many passed out.

One old man died right next to Roberto. He, Roberto, had been picking, straddling his bag, when suddenly he saw this old one begin to breathe strangely. He was breathing and talking to himself, asking for water and yet not stopping to get water. Instead, faster and faster he picked, and talked more and more, and then fell down, gasping. Roberto went to him. His face was ice cold. Ice cold even in this heat, and he was oozing with sweat. Roberto tried to pick him up, but he growled, and hissed, and pushed Roberto away, and began jerking in convulsions. Other men came and they called the foreman. The foreman took him in his little tractor, and after work Roberto learned that the man had swallowed his tongue and choked to death.

That night Roberto took his salt tablets, which they were all ordered to take, and went over to Juan Aguilar who had a poker game going. It was a big game. The men had just been paid this afternoon, and everyone was drinking beer and playing cards and loosening up after a hard week of picking.

Roberto left. He had a girl friend. She was mute. She lived at a local *rancho*. She was not pretty. In fact, she was ugly, but she was young and hungry, and he told her he liked her and bought her a dress, and she told him she loved him, and they began making love every night. They'd get together in the fields between the rows of cotton in the coolest part of the night, and Roberto would lay his sarape on the soft earth, and he would mount her. And she knew a lot, much more than he, and she began silently teaching him different ways. One, two, three times a night, night after night, he would mount her, and she would moan and gasp and scratch and say she loved him by patting her heart, gripping her heart, and handing it to him with an outstretched hand and such eyes of sincerity that he would say, my God, this had to be love! And he would mount her again, and this night he took her seven times, until she died that small death so many times that she screamed ... NO MORE! She was going insane, coming, going, dying, and the woman in her person was busted forever. Open, open, to all a man and woman could be. Now. Here. Yes. Together forever.

Then, moments later, the earth stopped spinning, and they awoke, and he remembered. He was supposed to be at the poker game to help Juan Aguilar get out. He told the mute girl good night and began to get up, but she didn't want him to leave. She moaned and made sign language, and with her eyes begged him to stay. He looked at her and he tried to explain, he had to go. He would be back. She hugged his legs and began crying. He knelt down, kissed her and hugged her, and the moon shone down on them between the tall rows of cotton. Finally, not knowing what to do, he gave her some money. She saw the money and leaped at him with her nails set. She clawed him. He knocked her down. She fell crying. He stood there ... money all around. Night breeze stirring quietly. He breathed, he swallowed, feeling terrible, but didn't know what to do, so he walked away. Hearing her sounds of muteness far into the night.

And so the joke of closing the border was now done. Completed. And safely put in the law books like so many things of the nation are put in the law books and then shelved.

For example, in 1963 the U.S. Congress stopped the bracero *program, gave one extra year's grace to some cases, and by 1965 all was stopped. Definitely. Or so the legal world thought.*

But coyotes in Mexico and labor contractors in the U.S. were not letting a hundred-million-dollar business disappear. Hell, no! In 1955 braceros *in California alone earned $65 million, and in 1956 they earned $85 million, and in 1961 they earned $91 million, and no one knows how much more was being made every year by wetbacks. So this was no small game. It was big business. And so big politics were put to work, and laws were moved, and the stopping of the* bracero *program—which was a big victory to the César Chávez Union and U.S. American citizens who worked in the fields—was a sick gesture. For Mexicans were now being nationalized into American citizens by tens of thousands, and the ones who weren't, were being smuggled across* a la brava, *and the war for cheap labor continued, expanded, and went underground to high-risk, quick-profit, and the tactics became gangsterlike, and Mexicans were being found dead along the U.S. highways by the dozens.*

And, thus, this least known of human migrations continued through the late 60's and 70's and into modern times—growing larger and larger and more desperate each year.

CHAPTER SIX

"Give me your money!" yelled Juan Aguilar.

"I gave you most of it already," said Roberto.

"Boy, don't give me explanations! Give me *dinero*!" Juan Aguilar was drunk, and he had lost all his money plus most of Roberto's, and he was raging. They were not playing poker anymore. They were placing bets on cock fights. And the men in camp were happy. All week Juan Aguilar had been taking them in poker, and now he was losing everything on these cock fights. He kept betting on a man who had cocks from his home land, the mountains of Jalisco, and he kept losing, but he had such state *orgullo*, pride, that he would not stop betting on these cocks. "Roberto!" He drew his knife. "Cut that pocket of yours open and give me your money! Or I'll cut you open myself!"

"You best go along with his wishes," said Pedro. "You are his boy, and you would have nothing if it weren't for him."

Roberto was scared and respectful of Aguilar, so he nodded and accepted the knife from Juan and slit his front pocket open and gave the money to him.

"Okay!" yelled Juan. "I cover all bets! I take that cock from my mountains. He is game! Look at his great colors! At his breeding! English ancestry and Mexican improvement. Strengthened by the mountain air of my beloved Jalisco."

The bets were made. The tequila was passed around. The cocks were teased at each other. Their razor-sharp spurs were uncovered, and they were then tossed at each other. The cock fight began in a leaping fury of knives and feathers. One cock fell. The other stood up proudly. And they had won. Juan and Roberto had won. Their mountain rooster had cut the other to pieces, but then ... their rooster walked away, and Juan Aguilar, in a frenzy of bellowing emotions, screamed to his cockman to retrieve his cock and show its killer bravery.

"*¡A la prueba! ¡A la prueba! ¡A la prueba!*"

All the men were screaming *a la prueba*, and both cockmen picked up their cocks and teased them toward each other, and the dying one seemed more interested, more game to continue fighting, even though he was dying.

Juan yelled, "Put them down! And we'll see their style of death!"

So the cockmen put them on the ground to see which one was the bravest in the face of death, which one kept style until his last breath, and Juan Aguilar bellowed for his cock to get back there, show style, and finish the other one off. Because if his cock walked away, even though he was the better, he lost! Because true killer bravery was what won. And if the dying one showed more sign of wanting to continue to fight, then he won.

Juan Aguilar bellowed.

His cock, the better fighter, was walking away, uninterested in fighting this hurt and dying rooster, and the dying cock was getting up, staggering, and still wanting to fight. So he, the dying one, was the winner!

Men burst out laughing.

Roberto didn't laugh. That better-fighting rooster was acting like he, himself, Roberto, had acted in the knife fight. Why fight a dying man? Eh? Why? But all the men were laughing.

And Juan Aguilar leaped into the arena, ripping off his shirt, and screamed in a frenzy, "I'M BROKE! I've lost everything! But I say, I came into this world naked and hungry! So all I wear and feel inside is PROFIT! So I'm still ahead in life! I breathe! I spit! I FEEL!" And he grabbed his cock and balls and pulled them upward. "And have profit here! Where it counts for a man!" And he leaped up and down, bellowing his fortune of life, that no man could beat him; kill him, yes, but not beat him. "I'm a man! And man cannot be defeated! Destroyed, yes! But not defeated!" And he drew his .45 and shot his rooster who had won but walked away, and men froze. Now he was shoving his .45 at them.

"*¡Manos arriba!* Hands up!" He told them all to lie down on the ground and throw their money to him. They did so. He told Roberto and the other *norteño* to collect the money. Not all the money. Just half. And throw the other half up in the air over the crowd. Roberto did as told. The crowd began fighting to get back some of their money, and they—Roberto and Juan and their *camaradas*—took off into the night.

They ran along the Yaqui River. They got to the outskirts of

Ciudad Obregón. They stopped a truck. They paid the man a few pesos, and he took them to Empalme. They got off. The men—the tens of thousands of men—were not around. They were only hundreds. They walked out to the American warehouse with the offices. The barbed-wired field where the men waited for processing was almost empty. The booths, the carnival of temporary structure, were mostly deserted. Then they saw the Mexican and American Red Cross. There were trucks and tents, and they had taken over a large building. Men were dying by the dozens. Despair and exhaustion in this terrible heat were killing men like flies. Both federal governments, Mexican and American, were trying to feed the men who had not been legalized; then, they were sent back to their homes. Men were crying, preferring death if they couldn't get work in the U.S. of A.

Juan Aguilar asked around. He found out that the Americans were legalizing only two or three hundred a day. No more thousands a day. Something about a *pocho* union. That a *pocho*, a goddamn Mexican born in the United States, named César Chávez, and Congress were quitting the Bracero Program. Juan Aguilar said, "Come!" They all walked off to a private distance. "What do you say, eh? Let us go *a la brava*!"

"Why not?" said Pedro. "Like that old man in the boxcar always kept saying ... I hope, I hope! They give me nothing, so I can go *a la chingada* once and for all!" He laughed. "Shit, we got nothing to lose. And a man with nothing to lose is indestructible. So let's go and take from the gringos who robbed our lands."

"Right!" said Juan Aguilar. "Let's go! And I defy the devil himself to intervene. *¡A la brava!*"

"*¡A la brava!*" they all yelled. Roberto said nothing. These men were becoming so strange to him. So desperate. So loco, with no fear. He, personally, was very much afraid. So he held ... quietly, trying not to show his fear. They went to town, had a big breakfast, then boarded the bus to go to Mexicali. North. Several hundred-some odd miles. They rode all day, and the hot and humid weather grew even hotter. Then, soon, not very humid. Just hot as hell. They were traveling across such barren deserts of sand and rock that Roberto felt he was not on this earth. Never had he seen anything like this. His mountains back home were heavy with pine and oak, and the lower lands were rich with tropical forests and banana trees. He kept quiet and began to think of home. For weeks everything had been going so fast that he never thought of home, but now, with all his hometown friends asleep as this dog bus raced on, he thought of home and recalled his mother following them on the other side of the moonlit river and her crying out that he would never return. He would get killed. And he thought, my God, how many have I already seen die? Three? Four? No, five, six, oh, so many. And how many others have I heard of but not seen? Dozens. Maybe hundreds. And in his mind he saw his mother coming along the river. Dark and squat and old. She was only in her early thirties, but she looked fifty. She had given birth to eleven children, but four had died at birth.

The bus roared on, and his mother kept coming along the moonlit river until she fell.

He too fell down. Exhausted. He was terrified. He swallowed and remained still. They, a *camarilla* of twenty-some men, were at the border. It was midnight, and they were by the American canal about seven miles west of Mexicali. A U.S. border-patrol car had just driven by, and they were belly-down on the bank. They waited. Hearts pounding against the earth, and then, on the word of Aguilar, they jumped up and began their slow lope along the canal. There were twenty-some men, and most of these Roberto did not know.

A few miles farther into California they came to a road. Highway 98. They left the canal and went across the flat fields of sandy dirt, climbing over fences of barbed wire. They saw lights coming. One man panicked and yelled as he ripped his leg on the barbed wire. Another man hit him.

All was silent.

They waited. Hearts against the earth. The lights passed by. They got up and began running. The man with the cut leg began dragging behind. No one waited for him. They crossed the highway and came to another fence. One wire. There were cattle in the field. One man touched the wire. He screamed. This wire was electric. Suddenly lights came on from over there, and a bullhorn yelled in English, then in Spanish, to stop! Men scattered, running every which way. Juan gripped Roberto and they went back toward Mexico. A few others followed them. The patrol ran after the ones who raced toward the north. Juan Aguilar turned, going east, and ran with all his might, and Roberto was right beside him. Later they, a camarilla of about fifteen men, turned north once more, and they ran until they fell down gasping.

Juan coughed and coughed, and then got up and said, "Boy,

now your power of youth starts paying its way. Give me a hand, and let's go!"

Roberto, tired and sweaty, jumped up and gripped Juan by the belt and began running.

"Faster!" said Juan Aguilar. "Pull faster and never stop until my legs fold or I drop."

Roberto gripped and pulled, and they went on. Mile after mile. There were only ten others with them now, and they were all blowing hard like dogs. Suddenly Roberto gasped and choked and fell down spitting and heaving.

"What is it?" asked Juan between his own heaves for air.

"I swallowed! I swallowed!" And he pointed to this great mass of insects which they had stirred up. "I swallowed a mouth full of 'em."

"Oh." And Juan took out their plastic milk bottle. It was filled with water. "Drink! Wash and spit out these damn American bugs. Quickly! They're probably sprayed with poison." Roberto drank and coughed. "Here, one more swallow and . . . okay. Okay! No more. Let's go!"

They were off once more at a run, and like that they ran and walked most of the night. Through bugs and insects and over electric fences and across fields of produce. Then up ahead through an area of granite and brush, and worst of all, little slopes of deep barren sand. They went on. Escaping into the land of plenty. They came to a freeway. Such a road that Roberto stopped, forgot he was hiding, and just stood upright and looked in wonder. Such a fantastic sight. And all man made. Juan grabbed him, and they crossed and went on and on, and then Juan said, "Okay, see those lights over there? That mountain of lights? That's the plant where they make plaster. So we go this way . . . " he pointed northwest. "I know a place where we can get more water." He turned to Roberto. "How much water we got left?"

"Not much."

"Well, come on. We must go far before daybreak."

There were just ten of them in total now. More had fallen. And so they, the able, now headed for a small light in the distance, which Aguilar said he knew was a farmhouse with water, and only a few miles away. For hours and hours they traveled. Up the rich Imperial Valley at the southeast end of California. And the light in the distance never seemed to get any closer.

Finally one man, a stranger, said, "Look . . . I don't think you know where we're going. I think that light might be forty miles away."

"Then don't follow. Go where you damn please," said Aguilar, and he went on toward the light in the distance.

Daylight found them no closer to the distant light. They were in a field of produce, and an airplane was coming. It was coming low and loud, so they hit the ground, chest to the good earth between the rows of green, and there they lay in the misty dawn of the first light of day. Hearts pounding and nostrils raging as the plane came down in a sweep and sprayed a blue-green cloud of chemicals all about them.

Juan Aguilar began coughing. Quickly he covered his mouth and nose with his shirt sleeve, and poked Roberto to do the same, and the plane swept upward in a huge roar of power and then circled and came by two more times, and each time it swept up and the pilot couldn't see them, they would get up and run. Leaping over rows of green, and then hitting the good earth, trying to rest as the plane came down again with its deadly spray of man-made chemicals. They breathed. Deeply. Then raced on, escaping farther into the land of plenty as the plane clouded the dawn with spray.

By sunrise they were coming out of the fields of produce and going into dry desert. They came across an irrigation pump. It had a big tank on posts some ten feet high, and in a pile on the ground were huge empty bags; and water, or what seemed to be water, was dripping down one side of the tank. The stranger who had earlier talked back to Aguilar now felt this dripping with his fingertips and then smelled it and looked at the pile of empty bags and read their labels and said, "No, don't drink. It's bad."

"You can read English?" asked Aguilar.

"A little," said the stranger. His name was Luis.

"Oh," said Aguilar, and nodded. "Well, then, I'll just rinse my mouth a little."

"Don't," said Luis. He was tall and thin, and his face was all covered with pock marks. He had a big moustache and large open eyes.

"What are you saying to me!" said Aguilar. "No one tells me what to do." He began gathering the dripping liquid in his hand.

"I wouldn't fool with it," said Luis. "It may be poison."

"It may not be. Hell! I'm thirsty! I'll just rinse out. It can do me no harm if I don't drink."

Roberto went to join Aguilar, who was catching the dripping water, sipping it, slapping it about his face, and refreshing himself. The stranger gripped Roberto.

"No, don't. Believe me."

Roberto stopped, and he and Luis watched as the other men freshened themselves, and then they all went on. They went out of the cultivated land and into the barren desert of sand and scattered brush. Soon the heat began to sing and dance with glistening bright nothingness.

The flat sand would reflect heat waves of dancing whiteness. The insects would sing in eery outer-space screeches. The sun rose higher and higher, and soon the insects screeching and the heat waves dancing all began numbing the eyes and ears, until all was not here. But over there. Up ahead. And here, all around, was nothing. *Nada. Nada. Nada. Nada.* And Roberto instinctively began to pray memorized prayers as he walked on, numb. All alone. Separated from all men, all life, he felt his human awareness evaporating into the huge infinite nothingness of all sealess deserts since before recorded time. He continued to mumble prayers as they walked on. It was only mid-morning, and men were beginning to stagger. They walked over to a pile of rocks. They kicked some rattlesnakes out of the shade and lay down like dogs. Panting and hurting and trying to gain moisture from deep within their throats. The men who had drunk from the tank had a little whiteness about their lips. Some began to babble *nada* words. The others all rested. Not saying one word. Roberto, being strong and young, was able to go right off to sleep and truly gain rest for both body and mind, and he dreamed. He was killing and robbing and gathering money, but his father was drunk and begging a drink from a man in a fancy shirt.

He awoke. His tongue felt dry and coarse as sandpaper. He glanced about. He saw Pedro. And he felt good that Pedro was still along, and Roberto's heart uplifted with the good feeling of revenge. He stood up. Aguilar saw and smiled.

"Well, one of us is still strong. Come. Let's go a little farther." Aguilar was trying to act strong, but he looked sick. "Find a place with better shade."

"No," said one man. "I stay here. My head. My stomach. Oh, God."

"I told you not to drink," said Luis, getting up.

"Telling us of the past does not help. Why don't you go back there to the cultivated fields and bring us help! Oh, for the love of God, are we not all brothers?"

All the men who had drunk were yellowish-looking, but only two were truly complaining and getting sick in the head.

"No help from me," said Juan Aguilar. "I drank, but I don't cry. Stay and die if you're so cowardly."

"My friend?" said one sick man. "We're all of *la Raza.* Please, don't leave us."

"All my friends died," said Aguilar, and he began getting up, but he groaned with pain.

Luis shook his head. "No, I don't think any of us are going to make it, especially not you people who drank."

"Bullshit!" yelled Aguilar. He was sick, but he still had gut concentration. You could see it in his eyes. "Me and my boy are going on." He got up. "Roberto, give me a hand."

Roberto obeyed.

Luis glanced around. "Well, at least we got to try."

Some men yelled not to leave them. Others began scrambling to get up and give it a try. Aguilar leaned on Roberto, and they began. Men cried out in fear of being left.

Luis stopped and said, "Don't be fools. Stay here in this shade, and I promise you, if I make it out, I'll send you people help."

Luis turned, going after Roberto and Aguilar and Pedro, and little by little, the cries of the ones left behind began to blend into the great numbing silence of the eery screeching bugs and insects, and then were gone. Not here. But over there. Ahead. Everywhere. And in the next few miles two others fell, but still they, the strong, walked on. Into the dancing, singing, eery bright nothingness of *nada nada* desert.

Near the Salton Sea on Highway 78 there is a restaurant at Ocotillo Wells with a historical landmarker, and the landmarker says that six skeletons were found there. They were Mexicans. No doubt trying to make it across the desert border to get work in the land of plenty.

Also, in a two-month period in the late 1960's, seventeen dead were found in Southern California by the border patrol and local law enforcements. And one old border patrolman said, "That's nothing. Imagine how many are never found."

CHAPTER SEVEN

By high noon they were in the desert mountains south of Palm Springs and all was glistening white, and a terrible wind was beginning, but they moved on. Staggering against the wind. In the low places below sea level, the wind blasted their faces with sand and blinded them, and on the high land the wind jerked them about like weightless toys and rammed the sun and wind into their very bones.

They headed toward some rocks and scrubby trees. They would rest out the day there and then go on at night. There were only six men now, and this morning crossing the border they had started out with more than twenty.

As they approached the shade, a motor suddenly started up, and a vehicle came rushing at them, grinding high in four-wheel drive and shooting sand in all directions. Aguilar yelled, "*¡La migra!*" He burst out running, and they all ran except the Mexican stranger, Luis. He stood still. "*Amigos,*" called Luis. "Save your strength. We're caught."

But the men were running, falling, trying to escape, and Roberto was the fastest. He was off like a rabbit. The patrol wagon took out after him, passing all the others and spinning sand and rock in their faces as they screamed on after Roberto. Finally, after a terrible two-hundred-yard chase over sand and rock and cactus, Roberto fell. They leaped out, standing over him. Two officers. Dressed in uniform. Wearing dark glasses.

"Boy," one immigration officer said in Spanish, "why run? Eh? *El sol . . .* it's too hot."

Roberto said nothing. He had sand in his face and mouth, and he was bleeding, spitting, and coughing terribly.

The other immigration man yelled, "Okay! All of you! Come over here. No more running. You're caught!" A few men began obeying. "Come on! There are six of you. We've been watching you coming along.

"*¡Pronto!* Come over here. We got cool water for you. Plenty of *agua fresca*. Hey! Only five. Where is that tall fella with the big hat? Come on, plenty of *agua* here, but no one gets any until you're all here."

Luis said, "The tall one went that way. Send his young friend to get him. He and these others drank *agua mala* from a tank. They're all sick, but won't admit it."

"Hey, boy!" called the older immigration officer. "Go get your friend before he drops dead."

Roberto was scared. These men in uniform had guns and belts and dark glasses and a car that could leap over rock and sand. He got up and obeyed. He found Aguilar behind some rocks. He was gasping and mumbling that he'd lost his favorite hat. He was sweating like a waterfall. Roberto shouldered him, and they went back to the vehicle. They were given good cool water. But not too much. Then salt tablets and more water. They were then put in the shade to pant and moan like a pack of done-out bloodhounds. Then, later, they were asked questions, and Luis told the officers of the ones who had been left behind. Sick and dying. The two immigration officers, Lou and Jack, radioed in for help, and Jack, the younger one, was told to go and investigate the ones left behind. Jack got in the four-wheel-drive International station wagon and drove off. Lou sat down and lit a cigar. He began telling them all a story of how lucky they were. He spoke good Spanish, and he told them that down in Texas, ten years back, he and his partner had found three wetbacks dead in the desert. They were so dead and sun-dried that they were like jerky. Like mummies. Hell, their flesh and bones had dried out so much that the wind was blowing their bodies about like dry leaves.

"*Muchachos*, I kid you not. I found one body blown up against a cactus bush. All that remained was his leather belt, part of his shoes, and a few shreds of clothes.

"For the love of God, you don't know how lucky you are that we caught you. Why, we rightly saved your lives." Lou then asked them where they were from, and told a story about each place where they were from. He, Lou Martin, had been all over Mexico. He loved Mexico. He planned on retiring by Lake Chapala near Guadalajara. He talked and talked, smoked and smoked, and spat cigar juice and asked questions, got answers, and laughed, red-faced and jolly, as he did his job in a friendly manner.

Aguilar felt better now, and so he went and got water. He and

Pedro drank together, talked, then suddenly Aguilar drew his gun and shoved it in Lou Martin's face. Lou froze. Carved in mid-air. Cigar two inches from his mouth. Eyes cross-eyed as they looked down the barrel.

"Your gun," said Aguilar. "Or I'll part your head."

Lou took out his gun, a .38 special revolver, and handed it to Juan Aguilar. Juan took the gun, shoved it in his pants, and said, "Roberto! Fill up our jug with water. We're going. You can come or stay," he said to the others, "I don't care."

Luis, the Mexican stranger with the pocked face, stood up. "*Amigo,*" he said, "please, give this *migra* his gun back before we all get in serious trouble."

"What?" said Aguilar.

"You heard me," said Luis. "Use your head. We can't make it. They radioed for help, and all they'll do is track us down. So give him back his gun. At present, we are not criminals. We are just *alambres*. Wetbacks. Honorable workmen. Nothing more. But if we keep his gun ... oh, *amigo mío*! we are in trouble."

"He's right," said Lou Martin. "And besides, you don't have a chance."

"*¡Cállate!*" yelled Aguilar, and went to hit the old patrolman.

"No!" yelled Luis and he jumped at Aguilar, grabbing his gun hand. "We got to use our heads."

"Let go of me!" Aguilar fought.

"No!" said Luis.

And now it was a fight. The patrolman got up. Pedro pushed him down and picked up a rock to hit him. Roberto saw Pedro going to hit the old man—Pedro, who'd belittled his father—and he screamed, leaped, and grabbed Pedro, and now it was truly a battle. Roberto and Pedro; Aguilar and Luis. Finally the stranger disarmed Aguilar, who was sickly. But there, rolling on the ground and biting, were Pedro and Roberto.

Pedro screamed, trying to crush Roberto's head with the rock.

But Roberto bit him in the face, tearing flesh and blood. Pedro yelped, screamed, trying to get away, but Roberto was still biting and raging like a wild animal. Luis gave the two guns to the patrolman. The officer thanked him and stood up and fired into the air. But the fight wouldn't stop. Roberto was a madman. Finally they pulled Roberto off Pedro, and Pedro's nose was missing and his face was an awful bloody mess as he continued squirming in agonizing pain.

" ... ever insult my father," Roberto was saying, "I'll eat you alive! You son-of-a-bitch!"

Luis began laughing. It was all so bloody terrible and completely insane. "Here we are," he laughed, "dying in the sun, and this boy brings family feuds from old Mexico. You must be from Jalisco or Michoacán. Where else are people so full of ridiculous pride?"

"Okay," said Lou. He had his gun in hand. "Back to the shade. My God, that boy has teeth."

They all waited for the other patrol car. Two hours later a panel four-wheel-drive Ford came up. They loaded the men up. They drove into the desert. They found Jack, the younger patrolman. Jack had one live wetback, one dead wetback, and two were missing from the last ten. But how many were missing from the original twenty-some, only the desert wind knew. And it, the wind, was now blowing dark and blinding. The patrolmen had to use compasses to find their way back across the desert and to the paved road.

César Chávez and his American farm workers celebrated a victory. The border was legally closed and now the U.S. agribusiness would not be able to fight poor against poor and keep the wages down. But this celebration was short-lived. Because in one year three hundred thousand braceros *were legally switched about and made into American citizens before anyone ever knew. And smugglers charged Mexicans two hundred dollars apiece and loaded fifteen in a camper, or six in the trunk of a car, or tied two underneath the frame of a pickup, and smuggled them north, where, on delivery, a labor contractor paid another sum.*

And so, the war of cheap labor continued all through the 1970's and 80's and into more recent times.

CHAPTER EIGHT

The stranger's full name was Luis Espinoza, and he was very different from Pedro and Juan Aguilar. He was from the northern part of Mexico, the State of Sinaloa, and he didn't carry a gun or knife. He knew how to drive a tractor, change a tire, speak English to the boss, and he was wanted up north in the San Joaquin Valley, the mecca of the wetbacks, by many farmers. They wanted him up there now. Immediately. To work this season, and if he wished, any one of these farmers would legalize him as a citizen.

Roberto and Juan Aguilar were with him now. They were just across the border in Mexicali. The immigration office in El Centro was so overloaded with illegals that they weren't punishing or flying illegals down deep into Mexico so that it would be difficult for them to get back across. No, the Border Patrol Office was too overloaded. So they put Roberto's *camaradas* right across the line from Calexico, California.

Now Roberto and his group were waiting for a pickup to drive them west on the Mexican side of the border. Past Signal Mountain, through the desert of La Laguna Salada, and over to the mountains of La Rumorosa. There they would once more sneak across the border, up the mountain to Jacumba, and be picked up by a Hertz rental truck and then be smuggled north to Bakersfield in the San Joaquin valley. Luis Espinoza had made all the arrangements, and they were all going together. Along with twenty-two other men. Pedro was not going with them. He was still in the hospital. His nose and face had become badly infected. A human bite was worse than a dog bite. Roberto truly had strong jaws.

The pickup came. They and ten more got in back. They headed out of town to the west. Another pickup joined them, and they passed through streets filled with people. Mexicali was swarming with no-faced people. Half of the fifty thousand from Empalme, who had not been contracted, had come to Mexicali to try to sneak across *a la brava*. Another fifty or sixty thousand had swarmed in from the local area when they learned the rumors associated with American citizenships. Now Mexicali was an anthill of more than three hundred thousand. Men were everywhere, and yet the local Mexican farmers could get no workmen because they were all dreaming of going to the land of plenty. And the local Mexican farmers were raging. Their crops were going to rot. They could find no men willing to work for the old pesos. Thirty, forty, or even sixty pesos a day made no difference. All these men dreamed only of dollars. Gringo money! Worth twelve times Mexican money.

The pickup slammed on its brakes. A man had jumped out of the mob, directly in front of the vehicle. He was begging the driver to take him along. That all he had been able to get was fifty dollars, but for the love of God, to please take him!

The driver refused.

The man, draped over the hood of the vehicle, screamed a threat to inform on them if they didn't take him. That now there was a standard reward for informers.

The driver and his partner talked it over and said for him to get in. He got in the back. He went to sit by Aguilar. Juan shoved him away, calling him *un cabrón rajado*! A bastard stoolpigeon. He moved away from Aguilar and sat very quietly.

Luis Espinoza lit a cigarette and said, "*Amigo,* you were not truly going to report us, were you?"

The man, thin and scared, said, "No. Of course not." He tried to smile. "I just wanted to get up north. You know how it is." He smiled a gold-toothed smile to Roberto, who was sitting beside him. "Eh? Aren't you the one who was in that great knife fight in Empalme?"

Roberto began to answer. Aguilar cut him off. "What the hell difference is it to you! You goddamn stoolpigeon!"

The man saw Aguilar, saw him well, and froze in silence. The rest of the truck ride went very quietly. They passed out of town, out of the green ranches, and into the desert. Pale brown and barren and flat, and up ahead were the glistening white salt flats, and beyond were the tall rock mountains of La Rumorosa ... towering up from the desert six and seven and, in some places, ten thousand feet.

That night at the Rumorosa, the would-be-informer begged for his life as the others were led into the mountains by one of the drivers.

Roberto said nothing, heard nothing, and thought nothing as

he followed along in the night behind Luis and Aguilar. So much killing and robbing had happened in the last six weeks that, hell, a little more didn't seem to matter. They, twenty-five men, followed the driver along the mountains for three hours. It was a half-moonlit night and no wind was blowing, and there was a little snow in the low hidden places and Roberto was very cold. The coldest he'd ever been in all his life, and yet, when he saw the snow, he forgot his coldness and marveled. Never before in all his life had he seen such a thing. He touched it. He tasted it. He followed Luis and Aguilar. He felt good that Luis Espinoza was with them. For this stranger, Luis, seemed very intelligent and didn't carry a gun and never seemed to be in the company of trouble.

Later, they were across the border. They came to a road. They were told to wait. The driver left and came back in a little while and then led them to a big Hertz truck hidden in some trees. It had an enclosed bed. They got in. The big bed was all metal and completely enclosed. The big rear doors were shut and bolted, and they were off. Soon the metal room began getting hot and stuffy. Men began coughing. One man vomited, and then many began pissing, shitting, and vomiting. Aguilar began pounding on the front and yelling for the driver to stop and let them get some air. Luis sat down and did nothing. Roberto followed Luis Espinoza's example, and the Hertz truck went on in the night. Screeching tires on the curves, and moving swiftly in the straights. Men were now beginning to pass out.

Juan Aguilar continued to pound. Several men joined him, but soon their fists were bloody and raw. Luis sat still. Half-asleep. And Roberto followed Espinoza's example.

Later the truck stopped and the metal doors were opened and the men piled out in a mad rush. They were told the situation. They had to get north as fast as possible. They were given ten minutes to breathe and clean out the shit and piss, and then they were put back inside, and they went on into the night. They traveled for hours. Men began passing out again. Others began vomiting and pissing. Juan Aguilar began pounding on the front again.

The truck stopped. The doors weren't opened. Aguilar began coughing and bellowing that they had been abandoned. Luis said to shut up, that maybe the *migra* was nearby, that maybe they had just pulled over for gasoline, or something like that. Aguilar quieted down. They waited. And waited. And waited. And then even Luis Espinoza became upset, and he began looking about at the frame of the metal box for a way to break out. Men were coughing and choking, and some were beginning to pray.

Roberto knelt down. He began to pray. He began to think of home. Of his mother and sisters and brothers and father, and he prayed. Praying and coughing and feeling faint. He saw his mother. The moonlit river. Weaker and weaker and weaker. Most of the men were down now. Only he and a few others were still conscious. His eyes were watering and his head was throbbing and his nose was beginning to bleed, and, oh, God, he hung on ... mumbling faster and faster. And, then, a noise. A noise at the bolt of the big metal doors, and the doors opened, and there were two young people. Strange long hair and funny clothes, and they were wide-eyed at all the dead bodies, but then ... Roberto bellowed from out of the dead and shoved bodies as he burst for the outside. The fresh air struck him like a stone wall and his mind whirled and his chest cracked in pain as he fell out of the truck, spilling onto the asphalt. Death and life were one—one and the same- -and he fell through eternity.

Darkness.

A pain rushed from his mind and chest, through his entire body, which went numb ... blending off into *nada, nada, nada.*

Two hundred years ago the philosopher Schopenhauer said that man would eventually become tired of making this world easier and easier and that people would then turn about and revolt against easiness. For we need resistance to push against. We need obstacles in order to strengthen, anger, and grow. "Life without tragedy would be unworthy of a man."

And so during the 1960's in the U.S. of A. things began to happen. The well-off youth began to feel the need of attaining impossible dreams.

In 1963 John F. Kennedy was assassinated and the whole world wept, and in Mexico people were as moved as if Christ had just been crucified. Mexicans? Identifying with a gringo?

In 1968 Martin Luther King was assassinated. Youngest Nobel Prize winner. Ever. A Black.

In 1968 Robert Kennedy (days before his assassination) received Holy Communion with César Chávez after César's twenty-some-day fast. Fasting? In the twentieth century?

And so Dick Tracy was moved off the front page and Charlie Brown and Snoopy moved in and a new generation began their revolt. Why? For the SHEER HELL OF IT! For life, viva la vida, *was meant to be LIVED with* gusto y grito*!*

CHAPTER NINE

The two youths were trying to get Roberto into their Volkswagen van. Roberto, between coughs, was trying to tell them to get Aguilar and Luis. Finally the boy with long blond hair understood and jumped in the Hertz truck and had Roberto point them out. Luis was able to crawl out on his own. Aguilar had to be carried out bodily. Others were coming to and wanted a ride. The boy with long hair and no shirt or shoes told his girl to get in their VW and make ready to drive. Then, in very poor Spanish, he explained that he could take only a few. He would take five in total. The ones most fit. This was guerrilla-war tactics. He'd learned it in the U.S. Army in atomic war training. He told the others to hide and he'd see about sending a friend, Paco Miller, with another white van truck.

Roberto and his group lay down in the VW and breathed quietly as the girl and boy with long hair got back on the freeway and drove on. The girl wore shirt and pants and boots, and the boy had wild hair and no shirt and no shoes and he spoke a little Spanish. He said his name was Little John, Juan Chiquito, and he and his girl Mary lived on a ranch in San Berdo. Short for San Bernardino, California. And that he would take them home and introduce them to his family and then they would figure out what to do.

At the ranch, Roberto and his *camaradas* washed off with a hose and tried to figure out how Little John's family worked. There were only three children. Mostly his family consisted of good-looking young women with long hair, but they were so poor that their clothes were old and dirty, and they wore no shoes—this was the land of plenty?

Roberto said nothing. Luis could speak English, and he was talking with Juan Chiquito, who was laughing, and jumping, and saying no no no and then yes yes yes. And Mary and all the girls were big-eyed and listening, and then one of the girls, a very young one named Adrene Jones, came over to Roberto and sat on his lap and kissed him.

Roberto froze. Heart pounding and terrified. He expected to see guns. She kissed him again. Juan Chiquito burst out laughing and leaped up, coming over to Roberto. Roberto did not move. Fully ready to receive death but, to his surprise, Little John said, "*Mi casa es tu casa.* Do anything you please. We're free as birds of God."

Now the girl truly began kissing, and Roberto, confused and terrified, still waited for guns. But no *retrocargas* were drawn. Then the girl took him by the hand and began pulling him away, and everyone was laughing. Roberto said nothing and followed her. She took him to a small back room with no glass in the window. They had newspaper nailed over the window, Mexican-style, and Roberto didn't know what to think. This was supposed to be the land of wealth.

She began undressing.

He swallowed, huge-eyed, and looked at her ... truly seeing her for the first time, and his heart was moved with pity. There she was, undressing, and smiling, and he, Roberto, could now see that her teeth had wires and silver on them. The poor girl. Her teeth were falling out, and now, there she was nude, and she was so skinny. Oh, God, this poor little girl could not chew her food, and she was dying of hunger. And now, there she was, doing something to her eyes. She was bending over and sticking her eye with her finger and ... oh, *Dios mío*! she was taking out her eyes and putting them into a little metal tub, and ... he swallowed. Terrified. Then she came toward him. Naked, arms open, and with no teeth, and no eyes, and he glanced around for escape, saw a door, opened it, and there was a kitchen with food. He rushed to the food, completely forgetting her.

Later, after having eaten and drunk the good cold milk, he felt better and more at ease, and he understood the poor girl's desire. She wanted to absorb his health. And so Roberto went with her to the small dark room, and she took him. Again and again, and he never looked to see if she was diseased, for she was so hungry and ... surprisingly strong for one so ill-fed.

That night Little John studied maps and got together with another guy and they made plans about how to smuggle these wetbacks north to Sacramento, California.

Shit, it was kicks!

Finally, after much arguing and fun as they tried to think like cops, they decided to do it in the daylight. Cops would expect smugglers at night. Then Little John got an idea and went to a pay telephone and called the Border Patrol and asked them, in a very good tone of voice, where their main points of inspection were. He said that he was a newspaper reporter for the *Los Angeles Times* and needed to interview officers in the field. He got the information and came back and they refigured which route to take. They decided to leave San Berdo by way of Freeway 15 and turn off at Hesperia on Highway 395, eventually making their way to Bakersfield. There, in Bakersfield, they'd call the Border Patrol again. Or maybe the Highway Patrol, and figure out plans from there.

They had a feast of hot dogs and Coca-Cola, and Roberto's eyes grew big as they translated hot dogs, *perros calientes*, but he said nothing and ate half a dozen of these dog meats with mustard and horseradish, and his eyes watered. My God, these gringos ate hotter food than Mexicans. Then, with full stomachs and much laughter, the two guys and five girls got in their VW and began smuggling five wetbacks up toward Sacramento. Radios blasting loud and VWs speeding out in the morning the young Americans felt like outlaws, happy and wild.

Outlaws! The hunted, the wanted, the greatest feeling within, except for maybe the emotion of the hunter himself. The searcher. The killer. The two-eyed focus of being, of man's reach into the future from out of all his prehistoric darkness ... to survive, to create, to go against the boring-norm of society.

Then came the news—a Hertz rental truck with an air-tight bed had been found in Colton, California. Four illegal immigrants from Mexico had been found dead, suffocated in the enclosed truck, and five others in critical condition had been found hiding under a bridge by the freeway.

Little John laughed a nervous laugh and continued speeding across the high desert up Highway 395. California, U.S.A.

César Chávez is nothing new. His efforts are old. As old as the territorial wants of man. As old as the borders between nations, races, cultures, and religions. And he is not the first or last ten-foot-tall figure. Ernesto Galarza, who wrote the Merchants of Labor, *was ten feet tall when he tried to organize a union in the Imperial Valley in the 1930's. A time in which it was truly impossible to do such a thing. Carey McWilliams stood tall when he wrote* North from Mexico *in the 1940's and used such plain language as "Los Diablos Tejanos, Gringos and Greasers, Blood on the Pavement, Politics of Prejudice," and used a quotation from King Fisher, a fine Texas Ranger, to demonstrate the core of the border situation. Someone asked Fisher how many men he had killed. He said, "Thirty-seven. Not counting Mexicans."*

You see, Mexicans were not even worth counting, and thus it has continued in many ways to this very day.

CHAPTER TEN

Juan Aguilar wanted Little John to take them into Sacramento and drop them off in the streets so the farmers could come and get them and they could negotiate for work. He knew that during harvest time even the Border Patrol looked the other way, for the *rancheros* were strong and the Border Patrol did what the growers wished, and the best thing was to go into Sacramento.

Luis Espinoza shook his head and said, "No, that's no longer true. The Chávez Union is as strong as the *rancheros* now, and the Border Patrol doesn't look the other way anymore. They'll pick us up and deport us if they find us. So I suggest," continued Luis, "that Juanito take us to a work camp I know south of Sacramento. There, in camp, we'll be safe from *la migra.*"

"No!" said Aguilar. He was angry. He had to keep face. This Luis was contradicting him too often. "If we go to a camp, they'll have us by the balls! They'll give us whatever they want. I say we take our chances in Sacramento. We are illegal, so we're free. And there we can get work by contract. Not by the hour. And by *contrato* a good man in one day can make thirty dollars. *¡Dinero americano!*"

"*Mira, amigo,*" said Luis quietly. "What you say is true, but this is not like a few years back. Times are changing. Chávez is getting us *alambres* driven out and fast. We've got to go easy, *amigo.*"

"That damn *pocho*, Chávez, I'd like to *chingarlo*!"

"That's not necessary. This camp I know is safe. I, personally, know the owner, Mr. Davis, and I think I can get us work by *contrato.*"

"Truly?" asked Aguilar. "By *contrato*?"

"Yes. I think so."

"Well, then ... " said Juan Aguilar, and he glanced around,

then spoke strongly. "Maybe we should consider this camp."

Luis smiled. "Yes. I think we should."

So Luis spoke to Little John, who was driving, and asked him if he could please take them to a camp in Acampo, this side of Sacramento. Little John said, "Yeah, man!" But then he asked, "Hey? Why are you guys talking bad about César Chávez? I thought he was trying to help unionize all you poor farm workers."

"*¡A su madre!*" yelled Aguilar. "*¡A su madre! ¡Es un cabrón pocho!*"

"*Pocho*?" asked Johnny. "What's that?"

"*Pocho*," said Luis, "is a Mexican born here in *los Estados Unidos*."

"Oh ... and you guys born in Mexico don't like them?"

"Well ... "

"*¡Son cabrones!* They are half-breeds who wish to cut our *tanates*!"

Roberto smiled with the word "*tanates*," and Adrene Jones, sitting next to him, drew close and rubbed her head against his shoulder. They were being lovers at the far end of the VW.

"No," said Luis. "Aguilar is being too unreasonable. They don't wish to cut our *tanates*. They simply wish to protect their own way of life. You see, we from Mexico come up here and work a few months and make ... oh, maybe one thousand dollars, and then get caught by *la migra* on purpose and are then flown back to Mexico free of cost, and that thousand dollars is big money back in a small village in Mexico. But here, for these *pochos*, a few thousand dollars for a year's work is very bad. Everything costs so much. So Chávez is trying to get us all put out so he can bargain for higher wages."

"Cut our *tanates*! That damn *pocho*! He is lazy! That's all that's wrong with him. He is lazy and *muy coyote* and wants everyone to give him so much per month so he can get rich. He is *un cabrón*! And if I ever lay eyes on him, that will be that. Last year he had a *huelga* where I was picking, and I had to sneak out before they found out I had no papers. They are no good, I tell you! They don't allow a man to be free and work. I know! So don't tell me any bull!" He yelled so loudly that everyone went quiet. Juan Aguilar wasn't sick anymore, and he was big, well-built, and very impressive.

The VW van drove on, and the weather was hot. They all drank Olie beer and ate hot dog meat in tortillas with mustard—Little John's favorite type of eating—and then Little John asked, "How about you, Roberto? What do you think about Chávez and his union?"

Roberto sipped his Pepsi and shrugged. "All I know is that I came a long way and my family is hungry. So, well, I've got to get all I can."

Little John nodded. "Good answer. Basically, every man for himself." And he nodded some more and drove on in silence. They were past Bakersfield, California, now, approaching Fresno.

Late that afternoon they got to the camp. The camp was twenty miles south of Acampo in a huge orchard. They, five *hombres a la brava*, gave their thanks to Little John and asked him to please come by the following weekend when they had money so they could treat him to a night in the barrio. Juan Chiquito laughed and said sure. Mexican *mariachis* and *enchiladas*!

And Adrene Jones hugged Roberto and said that if Little John didn't come, she'd come anyway. She loved Roberto. He was so cute. She kissed him, and all the men laughed, then she got in the VW with Little John and they were off, going across the windswept field and disappearing into the orchard. With its trees in long straight lines, and the earth clean and smooth. Roberto watched, and breathed, knowing instinctively she would never return. She'd shown him a picture of her parents' home. She was from North Hollywood and was rich. He was only a game to her.

Luis patted him on the back, and they turned, going toward the tin buildings, the *barracas*. And these buildings, old ex-military barracks, were lined up one right next to the other in two rows, and each row had five buildings, and these rows were seventy-five yards apart; between these rows were two larger tin buildings that looked like barns, and these tin barns were each about two hundred feet long and separated by forty yards. One was the kitchen and the other was the baths.

A bus came roaring up. It stopped. Men got out. Big hats and dirty work clothes. Someone came out of a small well-lit building and yelled at them on a small bullhorn. In English. Then in Spanish. They were told that the kitchen would open in half an hour and remain open until eight o'clock, but no man, not one, was allowed in there without showering and changing clothes. His first! That was the law. The sanitation law, and it was good for them. A shower would help their bodies relax. Then all the new men were told to come to the office.

Luis turned to his *camaradas*, telling them to come along, that he would do the talking. He knew the *patrón* personally. Juan Aguilar smirked but followed. They went into the small building. Luis asked the secretary for Señor Davis. The secretary asked Luis in Spanish if he knew him. Luis said yes, of course. She nodded and went into the back room and in a few moments out came a big red-headed American. The big man saw Luis and smiled. "Luis! Where the hell have you been? Come into my office."

Luis went through the swinging gates, passed the secretary, and into Señor Davis' office. The four remaining men couldn't believe it ... and in moments Luis came out smiling again, and said they all had jobs by *contrato* and would get a ten-dollar advance right now.

Juan Aguilar grumbled. Roberto stood up in admiration.

The secretary had them fill out forms, sign their X's if they couldn't write, and then gave them each a check for ten dollars and told them to get the things they'd need at their little store. Roberto didn't understand. He had clothes. He had everything he needed. Why did he need anything else? But he felt embarrassed to ask, so he followed Luis and Aguilar and said nothing. They found the store. It was dark now, and the store was a truck that had open doors on the sides and lights showing its goods like a real store, and Roberto smiled and said, "These gringos. These incredible gringos!"

He watched Juan pick out a khaki shirt, a pair of Levi's, a big red towel, a bar of soap, and so he did the same, but then the seller said, "No!" And took the pants away from Roberto. "Here. Those aren't your size."

He told Roberto in Spanish, and Roberto asked, "Size?"

"Yes. Clothes go by size."

"At home we always get the biggest and then just tighten our rope."

"Well, not here. Here you get your size. I'd say twenty-eight waist, thirty length for your pants and ... let's see your shoulders. Thirty-eight or forty in the shoulders. Here, take a large towel." Roberto pointed. He'd seen Luis get one of those. "Oh, that's a toothbrush. Do you want one?" Roberto stopped and figured. "Do you know what they're for?"

Roberto nodded. "Yes. Of course." The man gave him a red one. Roberto took it in his hand and turned it about. He'd never seen such a thing. But Luis had got one, so he would get one, and whatever Luis did with his, he would do with his own.

"How about toothpaste?" asked the seller.

"Toothpaste?"

"Yes. To soap your teeth with your toothbrush."

Roberto figured ... he looked at his towel and bar of soap. He said, "I have soap."

"Yes. But you need ... oh, hell, try it like that for a few days."

And so they got their things and then went to the shower building. Inside, the long building was divided in two. On one side were shower spigots along the walls. About forty of them. On the other side were huge wash-basins. Some of the basins had scrub boards on the floor beside them. They undressed. It had been a week or two since Roberto had bathed. He smiled. He watched the others and then walked up to a spigot and turned the knob hard. He yelped. It was all hot water. Luis laughed and patted Roberto's head and showed him that one knob was for cold water and another was for hot. Roberto asked where the hot water came from? Did they have a boiling spring like back home? Juan, at another spigot, snapped, no, they had heaters. Shut up. No more questions. He was tired ... truly. And so they showered in silence and then went to their assigned tin building. Number seven. Each building had a concrete floor and three rows of beds. Each row had fifty beds. They took an empty bed. An orange crate was at the head of each bed. It served as a dresser. They put their wet towels over the orange crate. They put their belongings inside the box. Each bed was the same. A box of iron with springs, an old mattress, and one blanket and no sheets. Roberto jumped up and down on his bed. He'd never slept on a bed before.

"Stop that racket!" said Juan. He was mad. "*¡Cabrón!* My head hurts."

Roberto stopped, and then they went to the kitchen. The kitchen worked like a cafeteria. Everyone picked up a tray and got what he wanted and then went over to a table with old tin chairs. They had to eat in fifteen minutes and move out. There were other men waiting to eat. Roberto wanted to know if he could get more food. He'd never been offered all he could eat in his life. Luis told him sure, go ahead. Juan said he'd see them back in their barracks, and he left. Roberto smiled, got in line to eat again, and Luis drank his coffee and watched. Roberto's eyes were huge. There was fried chicken. There was rice cooked in chicken. There was chicken soup. There were loaves and loaves of white bread. There were beans and chile. There were apples and peaches and bunches of grapes. There was so much! He had more fried chicken, more beans and chile, more bread, and two apples. Then ... he also noticed that they had cartons with a little cow's head. He had not seen these last time. He asked if these were cow's milk. The Mexican behind the counter said yes and to take all he wanted. Roberto's eyes lit up ... these gringos, these fantastic gringos, and he took two cartons and smiled happily as he went back to the table to eat some more.

Afterward he and Luis went back to their tin building, number seven, and Roberto was told by Juan to go wash their clothes, and he, Juan, would stay and protect their belongings. Roberto asked where and how, and would it cost money. Juan said to follow Luis, and, no, it wouldn't cost money. Roberto obeyed, and he and Luis went back to the shower building, and he learned what the scrub boards under the huge basins were for. Then he saw him use his toothbrush on his teeth so Roberto took his out of the pocket of his new khaki shirt, brushed it across his bar of soap, then added water, and brushed his teeth. It tasted terrible. He spat. He threw the toothbrush away.

"These stupid gringos!"

Luis burst out laughing. "You need toothpaste. Pick up your brush." Roberto got his brush, and Luis gave him paste and showed him how to do it.

"Good!" said Roberto. "That tastes *muy bueno*!" And he smiled and put his toothbrush back in its plastic container and put the container in his new khaki shirt and looked in the mirror, and he was proud. New shirt, new toothbrush. He smiled. "These gringos! These gringos!" he said with real admiration and warm honest pride.

Luis finished shaving—Roberto wasn't shaving yet—and they went back to their barracks. Juan Aguilar was asleep. Snoring loudly. Roberto saw how the others had hung up their wash on a wire rope by the beds. So neatly. So orderly. So he did the same and went to bed but didn't like it. Every time he turned, the iron springs made such noise that he awoke.

"These stupid gringos!" he said, and took his mattress and blanket off the iron bed and slept on the cement floor. There ... that was much firmer. Much better. And he quickly went to sleep. Dreaming. Dreaming of a *jacal* with an open crack and a formation of stars, the *arado*, high above in the heavens.

The ex-Army barracks were enclosed by barbed wire; and the rancher's son said, "You think these bracero *camps are bad? You should have seen the wetbacks before the program. They came by the thousands and lived under bushes like dogs. And some ranchers, the white-trash type, would call in the immigration and get them picked up so they wouldn't have to pay them.*

"Now, those years of the 1940's and 1950's were bad, but they've got it made now. All's legal, and the sanitation department checks regularly on their food and bedding, and their wages are federally-controlled.

"Myself, I think Chávez and Kennedy and McGovern and all these do-gooders have hurt the Mexican. They're making a big deal where it isn't, and using lies and exaggeration to further their own personal careers."

"What do you think?" he asked the interviewer.

The interviewer was still looking at the camp enclosed with wire and lights like a prison. The rancher's son saw.

"Oh, the wire? Don't pay any attention to it. Everything is sanitary and legal." And he smiled proudly. "Federally-controlled!"

CHAPTER ELEVEN

All was dark when the huge alarm went off. Roberto leaped, fully dressed in his new clothes, glancing about. He was terrified. Luis Espinoza laughed and told him it was nothing. It was just time to go and eat so they could get to work. Aguilar didn't laugh. He cursed at the alarm, cringing.

"What is it?" asked Roberto.

"I don't know," said Juan. "Before, my cough was my only trouble but now ... my bones even hurt. Especially my legs."

"Should we tell the office?"

"No, you fool! They'd take me off work." He yawned. He stretched. He looked very tired. "I'll be all right as soon as I move around a little. The run in the desert, and that climb in the mountains, took a lot out of me. Here ... help me."

Roberto put his shoulder under his armpit and walked him around and around until Juan felt loose and able, then they all three went to the showers, relieved themselves, and Roberto read a sign that said, "*Lave sus manos.* Wash your hands." They went out. It was still dark.

Roberto said, "It said on that sign that we are to wash our hands." "*Muchacho,*" Aguilar said, "I'm tired, so don't be showing off your ability to read to me!"

Roberto nodded, figuring that Juan Aguilar was just too worn out. And besides, last night they had washed all over, so that should be enough washing for a month.

Inside, the kitchen was very active. There were hundreds and hundreds of Mexican men. Big hats, dark faces, many moustaches, and heavy work clothes. They were eating quickly, then going to a table and putting food in a brown bag and going out fast as hell. Roberto picked up a tray and got in line behind Luis. Aguilar was in back. Luis told Roberto not to eat too much or he'd get sick in the field. Roberto, looking at all the food, said he'd never got sick from eating.

Luis said, "Okay. Learn the hard way."

Roberto smiled. There was so much food to choose from. Bacon. Fried eggs. Scrambled eggs. Toast. Butter. Peanut butter. Jelly. Cartons of milk and orange juice. And, on the lunch table, plates of bologna and cheese and hot dogs. So much. Roberto took some from each. Peanut butter he had never seen, but he would try it. They went to a table. Juan Aguilar sat down and dropped his head into his hands.

"What is it?" asked Roberto.

"I don't know. God, my head. My bones."

"I have the same thing," said Luis. "The very same. You know ... I think it was that plane that sprayed us when we came across the border."

Juan nodded. "Maybe. But if that is true, then why doesn't this boy feel sick? Look at him eat. Not an ache in his body, and he was there with us."

"True. But he is very young. Never been exposed to chemicals before. And we old *norteños* have much spray in our bodies from past years."

"Maybe. But I don't think so. I think it was the heat in the desert, and we're just old and tired. Hell, I'm thirty-six. But with a few more days of good food and steady work I'll be okay." He looked at Roberto. He was eating his eggs with the peanut butter. "No. You fool. That stuff is for making your sandwiches. You use that and jelly and make a sweet sandwich. And you use the bologna and cheese to make another sandwich."

Roberto made a peanut-butter and jelly sandwich and tasted it. "*¡Bueno! ¡Bueno!*" And he smiled. He was so very, very happy. "Oh, this is good! These gringos! They can even make something that looks like baby *caca* taste so good!"

Juan smiled and rubbed Roberto's head. "Eat, boy. Eat. For believe me, from now on, you are going to work like five *pochos*!"

Roberto went and got more peanut butter and jelly and made himself five sandwiches and put them in a brown bag with two bananas and a pretty white paper towel, called a napkin, and they went out. It was still dark. There were a dozen buses by the entrance of the tall wire, and men were being loaded. Quickly. Fast as hell. Each bus went to a different ranch. The whole area of Sacramento was in harvest, and everyone needed men. Luis knew their assignment, and he found the right bus and called them. The three of them would be going to a produce ranch today. They boarded the bus and in moments they were going. Out of the orchard, on the highway, and into an area of produce. Quickly they were dropped off and the work began, and by sunrise Roberto had a good sweat going and he was thirsty. Luis told him not to drink. It would only make him more thirsty in the heat of the day. Roberto obeyed and kept working hard, and by eleven in the morning it was so hot that many people were beginning to stop their labor. Roberto marveled.

People could just stop working?

My God! In Ciudad Obregón in much hotter fields than these, one could not do such a thing as quitting without the foreman yelling and threatening.

Roberto and his *camaradas* worked on. They were picking tomatoes. Thin-peeling tomatoes. Over there in another field the thick-peeling tomatoes were being picked by a machine. Those thick ones the machine could do, but these thin ones with more juice and more flavor the machine could not do. By noon there were only a few people still working. Most people had stopped and were resting in the hundred-degree shade and waiting for the buses. The buses came at two in the afternoon. A wind was beginning, a hot dusty wind that cut the face and all the way back to camp Aguilar coughed and jerked in convulsions. When they got to camp everyone climbed out of the bus slowly, tired and dirty and drained. The bullhorn yelled in English and then in Spanish. Everyone was told the kitchen would open in an hour and for everyone to first shower and change clothes. For no man would be allowed in the kitchen until he was clean. This was the law. Besides, a shower would refresh them and help relax their bodies.

"*¡Chíngate!*" yelled Aguilar into the wind of dust and heat. "I already showered yesterday! You goddamn bastard!" But he didn't yell loudly enough. The wind was against him. So he turned, grumbling, and went off with the other men toward their different barracks. Inside, Aguilar dropped on his bed and began coughing. Roberto asked if he could do something.

"What can you do?" snapped Aguilar. "Shoot me! Like a horse with a broken leg?" He doubled over in a jerking cough and then breathed. Deeply. "No ... *gracias* boy, there is nothing you can do. But I'll give you this advice, make all the money you can now that you are young, for we, the field workers, don't last too many years." And he lay down and waved Roberto away. Roberto and Luis went to the showers. They showered and when they came back, Aguilar was gone. They asked around. One of the men had seen him go off in a new car with some other workmen. Three brothers. They'd most probably gone to the cantina up the road. Roberto and Luis went to eat. There was fried chicken, rice, beans, Kool-Aid, and platters of cakes and cookies. Roberto ate hungrily and took handfuls of cookies with him. They went back to their barracks to do their wash. Outside the sun was going down but the day was still hot. In the barracks it was hotter than outside. Aguilar was still not back. They went to the baths and did their wash, and Roberto carried his toothbrush in his shirt so all could see, but he forgot to brush his teeth.

Later they went out behind the barracks by the tall wire so the building would protect them from the wind and dust and they played cards and told stories with the other workmen. One man brought out a guitar. He leaned back on the wire mesh and began to sing ranch songs, *rancheritas* and *corridos*, from his State of Zacatecas in old Mexico. Other men smiled, smoked, and joined the singing. They were waiting for the sun to go down and the barracks to cool so they could go in and go to sleep. The alarm would be going off in not too many hours.

Later, Aguilar and the three brothers drove into camp in a brand-new Ford car. They slammed on the brakes. They were all drunk, happy, and loud, and Aguilar wasn't coughing anymore. One brother, the older-looking one, was laughing and singing, kissing his fingertips and saying he had seen so many girls.

"So many girls *y cada una estaba hermosa*! Oh, yes! And each and every girl was beautiful!"

"And the big tractor that kissed you? Ah? Was that one beautiful also?" asked another brother, who was young and baby-faced.

"Oh, yes! Especially her. *¡Hermosa!*"

All the men laughed, and the other brother, the huge fat one that was a cook and everyone called Gordo, said that the woman they called the "tractor" was as wide across the ass as an ax handle. Bigger of ass than he was of shoulders, and also she was cross-eyed!

"Oh, yes! Cross-eyed and beautiful!" laughed the older brother. "And can she drink! She cost Gordo five dollars' worth of beer, and he never got *nada*!"

Aguilar came over and slapped Roberto on the back and bellowed, "*¡Mañana!* We get 'em by the *tanates* again. Shit, are we making money. Today I bet we made more than thirty American dollars. Apiece! How about that? Eh, *muchacho*? We make more here in one day than back home in ... "

Luis got up. "*¡Amigo!* Come with me. Please, I want to show you something." Quickly Luis took Aguilar away from all the other men. "Look ... no one must know that we are from Mexico. No one must know that we are illegals. What's wrong with you? Ah, *amigo*? You want to get us deported?"

Aguilar swayed back and forth. "Of course not! I just forgot. Tell me ... who will report us? Eh, one of those brothers? I'll kill him! Now! Before he talks!"

"No, *amigo*, killing isn't necessary," said Luis. "I don't think anyone will *rajarse* this time, but ... no more talking!" Aguilar's eyes narrowed, trying to figure if this man was telling him what to do. Luis saw his eyes and smiled. Tactfully. "Okay?" he asked. "No more talking? *¿Amigo?*"

Aguilar stopped staring, and his eyes opened up happily and he said, "Of course. No more talking. You are right."

"Good," said Luis. "So let's now go and get some rest. Okay?"

"Okay. And *mañana* we get 'em again!"

Roberto followed and they went inside the barracks. The tin buildings were a little cooler now. Roberto undressed for bed. Aguilar did not. He just dropped on his bed and passed out. Snoring loudly. Roberto looked around ... beds and beds and beds, and he took his blanket and went to sleep outside. Outside the night was beautiful ... stars and sky and breeze in the trees, and he slept, dreaming, and all was fine until a guard with a dog awoke him. He awoke large- eyed and frightened. The dog growled, and he was asked a few questions and then told to go back inside to his own bed. He obeyed. Quickly. And the whole barracks echoed with snoring. Roberto had a hard time getting back to sleep.

All was dark and the alarm went off. Men began cussing, yelling and getting dressed. Fast as hell. They went outside in the dark to the baths, relieved themselves, and went to the kitchen. All was ready for them. They ate, got their lunches, and boarded the ten or fifteen different buses. All was still dark. They, Luis and Aguilar and Roberto, waited inside their bus until it was completely full of dark men with large hats, and then they were off. Out of the miles of orchard and on the highway, traveling fast, and then into the fields of produce as far as the eye could see if it had been light. But ... it wasn't light. It was dark, and they turned off the highway, and suddenly ... cars turned on their lights and came roaring from the darkness and began following the bus. One man grew nervous and yelled, "What is it? *¿La migra?*"

"Keep still," said another.

"But look! There must be five cars." The cars were all around them, and horns were blowing. "Who are they?"

"It's probably Chávez and his damn union," said another.

"What's wrong with Chávez? Eh? I say you shut up!"

"Oh? Is that what you say?"

Cars were all around. Aguilar drew close to Roberto and whispered, "*Cállate.* Not one word. Understand? Whatever happens ... not one word."

"But who are they?" asked Roberto.

"It doesn't matter. We came to work. We didn't come to get involved."

"But their lights. God! They just appeared out of nowhere."

"Aguilar is right," said Luis, and he put his hand on Roberto. "Just do as you're told, and not one word. Understand?" Roberto looked at Luis, saw his huge asking eyes, and nodded. Car lights were behind their bus and in front of their bus, and people were yelling on bullhorns in Spanish. "Not one word. Hear them. They're Chávez' men ... and they'll be on us all day. So keep calm. We came to work. We must not get involved."

The bus turned on another dirt road. Up ahead were lights and machinery and a few trees enclosed by a tall wire fence. The bus turned in there and stopped. The bus driver leaped out excitedly. A foreman, who was already in the field in his pickup, yelled at him to keep calm. He'd already radioed for the sheriff. The driver eased off. The five or six cars with bright lights stopped on the side of the dirt road some forty yards away, and men with lights and bullhorns got out of their cars and began yelling, "*¡Huelga!*" Then the bullhorn said, "There is a *huelga* here. Please, *amigos* of the field. Understand, there is a strike here! For wages, and justice, and the dignity of us, the field workers! The *campesinos*!

"Help us! Help us! Please, come and help us! For united we will win, and justice for the *campesino* will be done!"

And then all their voices united with the bullhorn in one word, one call, and it echoed: "*¡HUEL-LLGAAA! ¡HUEL-LLGAAA! ¡HUEL-LLGAAA!* STRIKE! STRIKE! STRIKE!"

Roberto and Luis and Aguilar sat in their bus and listened to these shouting, yelling, pleading voices as the sun—the light of the world—began breaking in the distance and its rosy yellow light came shooting out across the flat rich valley and the strikers lifted their voice of protest in a harmonious chant, and Roberto's heart began to pound. Pound hugely with the cries of these thirty or forty people, and ... it was a sight to behold.

So fantastic! Out of nowhere!

Roberto felt a chill, a strangeness, going up and down his spine and ... he didn't know whether to get angry or jump up and join these voices of human cry.

Outside they sang, and inside men waited ... silently still in the bus; and the sun, the light from darkness, began growing more and more as it came shooting through the valley, and the song echoed that they together would overcome, for deep in their hearts they did believe that all men, when united, were indestructible and pure in heart.

Solidaridad Pa' Siempre	*Solidarity Forever*
En las viñas de la ira	*When the union's inspiration*
Luchan por su libertad	*Through the workers' blood shall run*
Todos los trabajadores	*There shall be no power greater*
Quieren ya vivir en paz	*Anywhere beneath the sun*
Y por eso compañeros,	*For what force on earth is weaker*
Nos tenemos que juntar	*Than the feeble strength of one*
Con solidaridad!	*But the union makes us strong*
Solidaridad pa' siempre	*Solidarity forever*
Solidaridad pa' siempre	*Solidarity forever*
Solidaridad pa' siempre	*Solidarity forever*
Que viva nuestra unión	*For the union makes us strong*
Vamos, vamos, campesinos	*They have taken untold millions*
Los derechos a pelear	*That they never toiled to earn*
Con el corazón en alto	*But without our brain and muscle*
Y con fe en la unidad	*Not a single wheel can turn*
Que la fuerza de los pobres	*We can break the growers' power*
Como las olas en el mar	*Gain our freedom while we learn*
La injusticia va inundar	*That the union makes us strong*
Solidaridad pa' siempre	*Solidarity forever*
Solidaridad pa' siempre	*Solidarity forever*
Solidaridad pa' siempre	*Solidarity forever*
Que viva nuestra unión	*For the union makes us strong*

Chávez's young attorney made out a police report and went to the judge and the judge scratched his head, paused, began, paused again, and then ... evaded the whole issue. The police report would have to be taken to the district attorney's office. At that office a well-dressed district attorney told the young Chávez attorney that he would have to send an investigator out to the strike area to make out an official report.

"But this is an official report. I want action done now! A boy is in the hospital, and I've got ten witnesses. I want to file this complaint today."

The deputy D.A. stood up. "Listen, boy ... come back in a week or so and I'll let you know what's developed. Good-bye."

The young attorney left, and the boy in the hospital lost his foot and two more such incidents happened that same week and ten days later the complaint could still not be filed but ... the young attorney and all the other witnesses were given a subpoena to appear in court by the rancher.

For trespassing!

CHAPTER TWELVE

Roberto watched, and the *huelga* was on. The sun was up. The sheriffs' cars were parked between the strikers and the workmen. The workmen were getting out of the bus and being ushered into the fields. The strikers were in line along the public dirt road and yelling in chant. There were four sheriffs, and their two cars were parked on the farmer's property. One sheriff, the one with stripes, was leaning on his car. Arms folded. He watched silently. With his back to the farmer's property as he faced the *huelguistas*, the strikers, who were calling, yelling, pleading, and begging for the workers not to go to the fields, but to quit and join them. Now. Quickly. To come to them, their brothers, their fellow field workers, their brother *campesinos*. And not be afraid.

The foreman, thirty-some yards behind the sheriffs, was telling the workmen to get out of the bus and go into the fields. That everything was okay. Not to pay attention to those troublemakers. Roberto and his two friends obeyed and followed the other workmen out of the bus, by the big tractor machinery, and into the fields. They began to work.

The *huelguistas* screamed!

The sheriff, the one with stripes, put on his sunglasses as the sunlight brightened, and there he stood. By his car. Uniform and gun. Arms folded. And the others copied his style, and they all watched silently. The sun climbed higher, and the heat of the day began, and the *huelga* continued.

Now Roberto and his group of field hands, *campesinos*, were working in mid-field, and the *huelguistas* were far away. Way over there on the public dirt road, and their calls were not too loud or bothersome. Roberto now worked fast and picked many tomatoes. He wiped the sweat from his brow. He looked across the field and saw the line of *huelguistas*. They were dressed much like himself, and they were waving flags and calling. He watched.

"Boy! Get back to work!" It was one of the foremen. A *pocho* Mexican foreman. There were now many foremen on this job, and they were all moving about and telling the workmen that everything was okay. Not to worry. They were doing the right thing. That those, on the road, were just lazy, no-good troublemakers. "I said, get back to work! ¡*Pronto!*"

"Hey," said another foreman to this first foreman. "Don't yell at our men. Take it easy." Then this second foreman smiled at Roberto. "He didn't mean to yell at you, kid. Go back to work." He smiled again. Roberto thought his smile-of-concern seemed very unnatural, but he said nothing and went back to work. Picking fast. Carrying fast. Dumping fast. And once again picking. Soon they were by the edge of the field again, and there were the *huelguistas* on the public road. Very close. They were waving red flags with a black bird in the center and calling and pleading, and it was all so very loud that Roberto could not do his work. He stopped and looked at the *huelguistas.* Many other workmen had stopped also. Even Aguilar and Luis were not working so good now. The *huelguistas* stopped yelling and began talking. They explained that this particular ranch was on strike. On *huelga.* For them to go and work elsewhere. That this ranch had a particularly bad reputation for treating *campesinos,* field workers, very unjustly. That they paid bad wages and lied about the number of boxes one picked. That they robbed one. To please come with them. That united they could overcome ... for the hearts of men were ...

Suddenly a car came racing at the strikers. Roberto, in the field, watched. The car was new and golden, and it was coming up the road, raising dust, and going straight at the line of *huelguistas.* The *huelguistas* watched, mouths open. And the car came. One striker ordered everyone to keep his place. The *huelguistas* stood their ground. The car kept coming fast. Not showing any intent of turning, and now the long golden El Dorado was only a few feet away from the group of strikers, and one *huelguista,* a young Mexican boy of fourteen, screamed and dodged away, and then all the strikers scattered. The car came to a skidding stop. Dust clouding all around, and a big man leaped out of the car. Bellowing! He was tall, raw-boned, and dark and very un-Mexican. His arms were hairy, his head was balding, and his face was shaved but shadowed with beard. He continued. Cigar in mouth.

"What the hell's going on here!"

The sheriff with stripes came over to him. Slowly. Respectfully. And began explaining.

A *huelguista*, young and tall and very much the all-American type, came over. "I'm an attorney!" he shouted. "And I want this man arrested!" He was yelling at the sheriff. He was very excited.

The sheriff and the big man with the cigar looked at the young man, and, together, they said nothing. The clean-shaven man ran his finger through his longish blond hair, looked at the four sheriffs, and trying to keep cool, said more quietly, "I'm an attorney, and I want this man arrested."

"Who's he?" asked the big man, and pointed his cigar at the young attorney.

"I don't know," said the striped officer. "One of Chávez' attorneys, I guess. But getting back to my point, we're here to keep the peace, and please, Mr. Anderson, I don't want you doing things—"

"Boy!" said Mr. Anderson. The attorney had come closer to them. "What's your name?"

"Michaels. Jim Michaels."

"Well, Jim Michaels ... get back over there." He pointed with his long cigar. "This is private property."

Jim Michaels backed up three paces to the public road. He yelled, "Sheriff! I want that man arrested on attempted hit and run!"

"Hit and run?" laughed Anderson. "Hell, who's running?"

Jim Michaels shuffled his feet in the dirt. He was twenty-five and so uptight that he could hardly think. Last year he had graduated second in his law class from Stanford Law School and he knew the law, and this damn sheriff wasn't doing his job. "Arrest him for the ... Sheriff, hell, you saw him. Do your duty!"

"Look, boy ... " said the sheriff, and drew out the word "boy." "I'm doing my duty. I'm keeping the peace. And I suggest you go talk to Mr. Chávez and find out what your duty is. Understand?"

The young attorney kicked the dirt. He was boiling. He went back to his group of thirty or forty *huelguistas* and they began talking on the bullhorn to the workers in the field. Roberto and the others all stopped their labor and listened. Even Aguilar and Luis. The car and the scattering of the strikers had caught their attention. They now listened. Giving their undivided attention. The sheriffs all drove off. The big man, Mr. Anderson, turned on his car radio real loud. Blasting rock music. The man on the bullhorn had to speak louder. The foremen began coming up to the workers and telling them individually that everything was okay. That legally these lazy troublemakers were in the wrong. That the sheriff had gone to get a warrant for their arrest.

Two pickups came up, in front and in back, of the long golden

El Dorado and put on their radios also. More blasting modern music. The workmen began going back to work.

The bullhorn screamed.

It was a Mexican girl on top of the old van, and she was a sight to see. She wore black pants and black boots and had one hand on her hip, another on the bullhorn, and she was screaming, cursing, and laughing. Roberto smiled. There she was, tall and slender, and she was *a toda madre*, a real live mother, and many men stopped their work. This woman, this girl, was not asking them nicely to stop their work and come and join them. No! She was yelling at them, saying they were cowards, not men, if they allowed a *patrón* to rob them of their dignity. Then, having their attention, she moved her hips and called to the heavens for them to be men, true Chicanos, Mexican-Americans, and not crumble to this gringo boss! That they too had their rights! That sure, right now, they were young and all the fields were in harvest and they were making good money. But let the work die down a little, and they'd be fired! Or get a little old, reach the age of forty or just thirty-five, and they wouldn't be given jobs!

"And you know what I say is true!" she continued as the radios blasted rock music in front of her, trying to drown her out. "My own father, not yet forty, cannot work because of a back injury he got on a ranch. And does he get compensations, no! He doesn't! Because farm workers had no disability compensation until a few years ago, while all other workers have been getting it for years! And years!

"And unemployment. Do we get that? No! While all other workers have been getting unemployment insurance for years! Please, be men! And see the future and think of your children. Your children! And improve their world! Their chance for education and a better world! Join us! For, UNITED WE CAN OVERCOME ... " A roaring echo began coming from the distance. Roberto stopped watching the girl on top of the old van and looked; two gigantic tractors were coming. They were pulling plows, huge steel discs, and raising a great cloud of dust. The girl stopped, she saw, and her face twisted with fear, but then she held ... swallowed and continued talking as fast as she could. "Think of your children! Do this for them! Join us! And united we shall overcome!" The two tractors, driven by two Mexicans, came on. Anderson and his foremen got in their vehicles, radios blasting loud, and drove off to a comfortable distance. "Oh! Deep in my heart, I do believe that we shall overcome someday ... We'll walk hand in hand, someday we shall ... We are not afraid ... "

The first tractor, huge and all iron, passed by in front of her and threw up a fantastic wall of dust with its huge steel disc. The girl began coughing and choking. A *huelguista*, a young Chicano with an Ivy League shirt and longish hair, leaped up on the van with her and tried to help her down. She pushed him aside. She screamed, "JOIN US! NOW! DON'T YOU SEE WHAT THEY DO?" She was choking and crying, and now Roberto, for the first time, wished to quit and go to her. To them. Over there. He threw down his tomatoes. He began to go. A foreman yelled. The girl saw. She screeched with delight. The first tractor had gone by, and she could see. "Come! That's right! Please! Give me your name! Give me your name!"

Roberto began to speak. Aguilar grabbed him.

"Don't!" said Aguilar.

Roberto looked at Aguilar.

"Leave him alone!" yelled the girl. "If he wants to quit, it's not your concern!"

Aguilar was saying, "Don't be a fool! We're illegal. You'll be deported."

Roberto's eyes blinked and he held back ... remembering all his months of labor to get here.

"Leave him alone!" Then, in a very feminine voice, "Please, good-looking. Tell me your name."

"Roberto," he said, shaking his arm loose from Aguilar. And eye-to-eye he stared at Aguilar, but then went back to work as the second tractor came in front of her.

"Roberto?" she called out. "Did you say Roberto?" The second wall of dust raised up in front of her. She coughed, she choked, she called, "Roberto? Robert! Bob! Oh, that is my father's name, and he is brave and strong and would not let them ... "

She was drowned out. The two tractors were now going back and forth in front of her and the *huelguistas* and all was a wall of dust and the roar of the tractors and the blasting radios from the owner's El Dorado and his foremen's pickups was all too much. But still the *huelguistas* held their ground on the public dirt road in the cloud of dust and kept chanting their protest as the tractors raced before them dangerously close. Finally a few strikers backed up across the road and got inside their cars and rolled up their windows. The girl was choking and coughing, but she held her post on the old van and continued using the bullhorn. The two tractors picked up their pace. Going by, cutting near the edge of their property line with their great sharp discs, turning about and coming back. Then the van was bumped. It rocked. The girl fell.

Huelguistas rushed to her aid. Someone screamed.

Screamed a sound of pain. Not protest. And Anderson rushed forward. His face truly looked concerned. He stopped the tractors. The dust was terrible. No one could see anything. Anderson stood there. Tall. Boss-solid. And waited for the dust to settle.

Roberto, in the field behind Anderson, was not working. No one was working. All eyes held in wait.

Finally one could see. The girl was down, and there were a group of *huelguistas* around her, and someone was crying in terrible pain. Anderson walked up and saw ... the person in pain was a young boy. The one that had panicked when Anderson had raced up in his El Dorado. His leg was all bloody. It looked like his foot was cut off. The girl who had been up on the van was bent over him. She saw Anderson. Savagely she turned and leaped at him.

"You murderer! You pig!"

It took the attorney, Michaels, and two others to get her off the big man. Still she screamed at him. She had clawed his face and he was bleeding, but she wanted more. Michaels told two *huelguistas* to hold her. He went back to Anderson.

"Mister," he said very evenly. "We're going to sue you. Believe me, we're going to sue you, and you're going to pay with every damn cent you've got!" Anderson said nothing and touched up his face with a handkerchief. "Look at that boy! Not even fourteen, and your tractor cut off his foot!"

"The boy was trespassing," said one of Anderson's foremen. "I was over there, and I saw the whole thing. One of them"—he pointed to the *huelguistas*—"got in the van and backed up into the tractor and knocked the girl off."

"Liar!" yelled the young Chicano with the Ivy League shirt. "I was going forward, and your tractor ran into me!"

"Bullshit!" said the foreman. "You backed up and knocked the girl off, and then this kid, trying to be a hero because he was a chickenshit a little while ago, rushes out to help her and goes into the disc!"

"Liar! The tractor came at us!"

"No sirreeeee!" The foreman shook his head with much vigor. "That tractor was within our property line. You all were trespassing, and that's a fact!"

"You goddamn liar!"

"Listen, punk!"

"All right," said Anderson, "enough! We can each tell our story when the sheriff comes." He turned to Michaels. "Michaels, I'm radioing into my office for the sheriff. Do you want me to get an ambulance out here?"

Michaels looked at the young boy. "No. We'll take him. It will be faster." He turned to his fellow *huelguistas*. *"Amigos, por favor*, help this boy to my car. And you, Teresita," he said to the young girl with black pants and boots, "get in with him." And he shook his head, kicked the dirt, mumbled to himself, and got in his car, a small foreign-made station wagon, and drove off. Down the road he stopped. He yelled for somebody else to drive. He had to stay. He had to make sure the sheriff got the right story. The Chicano with the Ivy League shirt ran up, got in the little wagon, and drove off.

Michaels came back to the scene of the incident. "Everyone step back," he said. "Don't destroy this evidence. Please, get back. Don't mess up these tractor prints." Anderson was with his tractor drivers. They were starting up the tractors. "Anderson! Don't you dare! Those tractors stay where they are!"

He rushed at Anderson, yelling and ordering. Roberto and all the men in the field watched. The foremen weren't telling them to get to work anymore. The foremen were all watching, too. Michaels was raging. Anderson, twice as wide as Michaels, smiled, cigar in mouth. Michaels yelled at the tractor drivers and told them that these vehicles were evidence, and if they moved them, they would be breaking the law. One driver stopped his tractor, turned off the motor, and got down.

"Keep your tractor," he said to Anderson. "I quit!"

The *huelguistas* yelled, "*¡Bravo! ¡Bravo!* Tell it to him again!"

The tractor driver smiled hugely and yelled, "I QUIT!" And he walked over to the strikers. The strikers cheered him and rushed forward to meet him, embrace him, and give him many compliments.

The other tractor driver, a *pocho* Mexican also, was hesitant. He sat on his tractor. He looked from boss to young man to boss. Anderson took the initiative and walked up. He mounted the abandoned tractor. He started it up and drove off. The other driver followed him. Halfway down the field he, Anderson, stopped, called one of his foremen, and told him to take the tractor into the yard. The foreman obeyed quickly, and the other driver followed. Anderson lit up a new cigar, smoked, watched the two tractors go down the way, and then turned, coming back down the field. Tall. Alone. Boss. Solid. And all the foremen saw him, became his men once more, and began telling the workmen to get back to work. Quickly. Quickly. Aguilar went back to work. Roberto didn't.

Luis patted Roberto on the shoulder and said, "Tonight, we'll talk. Not right now. Come. Let's get back to work."

Roberto nodded ... and he went back to work, but he couldn't figure things out. Hell, where was Aguilar's bravery? Where was Luis' smartness? What were they doing letting an old balding boss and a bunch of fat-ass foremen treat their people like this?

He jerked at the tomatoes. Hard! He was mad. A foreman yelled at him. He whirled. Ready to fight. The foreman, a big fat *pocho* Mexican, stepped back. Surprised. Roberto looked at him, eye-to-eye. Unto death. Ready to go *a la prueba.* Then he felt someone pulling him around. It was Aguilar. Aguilar was telling him to get back to work. Aguilar was apologizing to the foreman. Aguilar shoved Roberto to the tomatoes. Roberto, after a minute, began picking. And across the field on the public road the strikers were with their flags once more, and they were chanting: "*¡Huelga! ¡Huelga! ¡Huelga!*" And the sun climbed higher and the day grew hotter.

Later, sirens were heard in the distance. Anderson got out of his air-conditioned car, lit a cigar, and walked over to meet the coming sheriff. Michaels followed him. And the *huelga* continued. *¡Huelga! ¡Huelga! ¡Huelga!*

An old favorite story of the Mexican Revolution of 1910 is about an ex-schoolteacher in Villa's army who was trying to talk a bunch of campesinos *into taking a fortress. He told them that it was for liberty, dignity, equality, and the creation of a new constitution.*

They all scratched their heads. They thought he was crazy. He saw and said, "Hell, come on! In that hacienda I hear tell there's gold! And tequila! And if we take it, we will split it up among ourselves, and the lands, they will be ours, and then our children's future will be ... "

He wasn't even able to finish his words. The men now understood, and they attacked immediately and took the fortress.

And like this, some men joined Chávez. Not really knowing why. Just knowing he was one of them and he was not afraid ... no, he was brave.

CHAPTER THIRTEEN

They worked only half a day, then Roberto and the other workmen were put on the bus and taken in when the sheriff arrived and began questioning. And, back at camp, there was another *huelga.* There were five men with flags, red flags with the symbolic black bird, walking back and forth at the entrance of the camp's enclosing wire. Roberto got out of the bus, saw them over there by the gates, and he heard one man say, "Damn them! We only got half a day's work because of those bastard *huelguistas*!" Roberto looked at this man. He was oldish. He wore an old-style Mexican hat and looked very tired. "Is not a man free to work in peace? I'm leaving. I tell you. I'm leaving!" He kept walking. He was not really talking to anyone. "But how can I leave? I got family here."

Inside the barracks Roberto and Luis and Aguilar got together. They sat down on their bunks. They grouped in privacy. Aguilar wanted to leave now. Immediately! Luis was calmer.

"I suggest we go to the office and explain our situation to the camp owner. He's my friend. Maybe he can send us to work tomorrow to a ranch where there is no *huelga.*"

"Ha!" snapped Aguilar, making an ugly face. "Are you a dreamer? I say, this *huelga* has all these owners by the *tanates*! And they don't care about us. Particularly not us, the ... " He stopped. He glanced around. No one was close by. " ... the illegals. We," he poked his chest vigorously, "got to look out for ourselves! The owner, the foreman, or any one of these legal ones here will turn us in the first chance they get." He glanced around the barracks. More men were coming in. Lots of men, and they looked disgusted. It was only about one in the afternoon. They too had only had half a day's work. "What happened?" called Aguilar.

"Chávez," said one, and lay down on his bunk and said nothing more.

"You see," said Aguilar. "It's the same at all these ranches. We got to go far away. Maybe back south to Bakersfield or over to Salinas."

Luis nodded. "Yes. I think you're right." He nodded some more. He took off his big straw hat and showed a white line on his forehead. Below the line his pock-marked face was dark with sun and dirt. Above the line all was white and clean, and his pockmarks were more noticeable. He lit a cigarette. American. "But I still wish to go to my friend, the owner of this camp, get our wages, and explain to him why I, personally, must leave. He has always been good to me. I must be straight with him. I do not wish to run out and leave a bad reputation behind me. I am a workman." And on the word, "workman," he stood up. "Shall I get your wages for you, or are you coming?"

Aguilar stood up. "We'll come. But then we'll go. Okay?"

"Okay," said Luis.

They turned to Roberto. He hadn't stood up. He sat there looking from one to the other. They waited. He said, "But no mention has been made of the *huelga*?" He looked from one to the other. They didn't say anything. "Well, what have we to say about that boy whose foot was cut off? And the girl who was almost run over? Eh? They are our people. They say they are our friends and they're trying to help us."

Luis shook his head and drew close to Roberto. "Look," he said softly. "You must not forget our own situation. We are ... "

Aguilar laughed. "Our friends? Trying to help us. Bull! All my friends died when I was born!" He breathed, and he was big-boned, big-faced, good-looking, and strong. "What the hell's the matter with you, *muchacho*? Have you forgotten your family and the hunger in your village? Eh? Did a girl with tight pants turn your head to stupidity?" Roberto stood up. "Good. Get angry. Anger cleans the soul and kindles the blood, then the brain can truly know what one feels." He patted Roberto. "Come, let's go to the office. We've come too far and paid too much a price to have our heads turned. We've got to work. Make money. Now! While the harvest is strong!"

Roberto held ... and then nodded yes. They went out of the barracks to the office. At the office they were told the owner was out. They waited. The phone rang many times. The secretary seemed on edge. They waited. Finally he came in. His face was long. He saw Luis. He tried to smile.

"Yes. Can I help you, Luis?"

"Yes," said Luis. "I need to talk to you. It's important."

"Well, ah ... " He turned to his secretary. "Any calls?" She nodded. She handed him a bunch of small papers. He glanced through them. "Come into my office," he said to Luis as he went through the memos. Luis followed him. Roberto and Aguilar waited. In moments Luis and the owner came back out. The owner smiled. He shook his head. He ran his fingers through his thinning red hair and swayed back and forth on the balls of his feet. "Damn! I don't know what to tell you." He turned to Roberto and Aguilar. "You illegals have got it better than anyone I know. Hell, I envy you." Roberto looked at him. This man spoke very good Spanish, and Roberto understood his words and couldn't believe what he heard. The owner laughed. "You don't believe me, eh? Well, I'll tell you what, if I was in your shoes I'd work here and there, not pay taxes, save my money, live cheap, and in a few years open a little business in Mexico. Down by Mazatlán, where my wife and I spent our honeymoon." He smiled. Remembering fondly. "It's good down there. The law is crooked, but hell, one knows where one stands. Here in the United States ... " He breathed. "Half these ranchers are running scared ... nobody knows what's going to happen. And in the meantime it's going to be rough. We can't pay more for labor here and have them pay less in Texas. We're in a competitive business. We'd price ourselves out of the market." He stared down at the ground. Hands in his back pockets. Swaying back and forth. "Believe me, you illegals have it made. You're free. You can pick up and leave anytime you like.

"Sure," he said to Luis, "I understand. If I was in your shoes I'd take off too. Come back in an hour. Your checks will be ready. Good luck, my friend. I got to get on the phone now." His face hardened and he took his hands out of his back pockets, and one hand was clenched in a fist. He stood up tall. "I've got to ride this thing through. Bye."

He turned and they said good-bye to him, but he didn't hear them. He was off. Walking fast and straight. He was a labor contractor, one of the few good ones to both laborer and farmer, and César Chávez was directly opposed to him. They had never met, but they were enemies.

That night in camp they found out that the three Mexican brothers who owned the new Ford were leaving also. Many men were leaving. Luis made a deal with them for thirty dollars. And the brothers agreed to take them south toward Fresno and find a ranch without a *huelga.* The brothers also wished to find a ranch without a *huelga* so they could work in peace. At midnight they left. Quietly. They didn't want to run into any of Chávez' people and be turned in to the *migra.* They drove out of the camp. They went out of the orchards, past the fields, and through the town. They stopped at a liquor store. The brothers wished to buy beer. Aguilar agreed. Luis was opposed to it but said nothing. It was their car, and they could have charged them much more. He had to keep smiling, be friendly, and agree with their silly ways. These brothers were legals. They had green cards. They had immigrated, and in five years they could take a test and gain the right to vote and be full American citizens. They bought two six-packs of Lucky, one six-pack of 7-Up, one family-size bag of Fritos, and they were off. They took back roads. The three brothers laughed, told jokes, poked fun at each other, and drank beer, throwing the empty cans out their car window. Aguilar joined them. He drank beer but ... he didn't joke. These brothers ridiculed each other, poked vicious fun about women and sex and bravery, and Aguilar didn't like it. He had gone out with them a few times and he'd come to know that they had no self-respect. All their talk of knives and guns, *tanates* and women was silly, naïve, and very dangerous. So Aguilar now drank beer with them but made no jokes. He smoked his cigar. Sitting up straight.

Luis, on the other hand, didn't drink beer. He drank 7-Up, his favorite American drink, and joked a little with them. But not too much.

Roberto drank first a beer, then a 7-Up, as he watched, noticed, and kept easy. This type of Mexican was different from all he knew. They used words of insult like *¡chinga tu madre! ¡Pendejo! ¡Cabrón baboso!* that back home, deep in Mexico, such words would have meant a fight to the death. Immediately. Brother or no brother. But here, between these Mexican brothers, these words meant nothing. Roberto asked the eldest brother, Pepe, where they were from. He asked the question politely and with good formality.

"T.J.," said Pepe. All three brothers were sitting up front. Pepe was in the middle. "And you?"

"Michoacán."

"Oh," laughed Pepe. "In the mountains. So then you are a goat man, eh?"

"A goat man?" asked Roberto very courteously.

"Of course. You do goats up the ass!" Roberto froze. Completely taken aback. The big brother laughed and drank his beer, and his younger brothers joined him. Laughing and laughing until they choked on their beer.

"Hey! You ever been to T.J.?" asked the youngest brother. He was driving, and one could tell that he truly loved to drive their new Ford. He looked at Roberto in the mirror. Roberto sat in the middle, between Luis and Aguilar. Luis and Aguilar were saying nothing. "Eh? You know T.J.?"

"No," said Roberto. "I don't."

"Oh, you haven't lived! Tijuana is the greatest city in the whole world! It's wide open!"

"Yeah," said Pepe. "Whores are everywhere. Hell, you can buy a fifteen-year-old virgin straight out of the Catholic convent if you want." Roberto tensed, feeling his skin crawl. This was truly against God. This was awful. The eldest brother, Pepe, turned around. White smiling teeth and big can of Lucky beer. "You don't believe me? Well, shit, that's nothing! Tijuana is so bad that dirty old men can buy little girls. No more than children, and do whatever they please with them." Roberto drew up tight. Pepe saw and laughed. "If this makes you upset, you should hear the real-life stories I know. Oh, your skin would crawl!"

"I do not wish to hear it," said Roberto.

"Eh? You hear that?" Pepe turned to his fat brother, Gordo, who didn't talk much. "We got an innocent one with us. All he knows is goats with quivering assholes!" he screamed with laughter. "After the harvest, we'll have to take him to T.J., then he'll see the Mexican at the gringo's feet. Shit! You people way down deep in Mexico got it easy. You weren't brought up knowing the meaning of the gringo's dollar. I, when I was five years old, was out in the streets of T.J. shining shoes and kissing ass until two in the morning. Night after night. Didn't even have a damn coat. I'd be shivering outside a bar, catching the drunk Americans as they came out. I'd offer to shine their shoes. I'd offer to go get 'em a taxi. I'd ... oh, God! It hurts to remember. They'd laugh at me and say, 'keed! You got a sister? Eh? Or a virgin mother?'

"I'm not lying. That is the truth. They'd laugh at me, throw me some pennies like to a dog, and insult my mother and ... " He leaped halfway over the front seat. He gripped Roberto by the neck. Roberto was taken by surprise. He froze stiff in fright. " ... and you know what I would do? Eh? you know!" Roberto shook his head. "I'd laugh and play back to them and say, 'Yes, Mister *Americano*, for you I got a virgin mother ... ' " He let go of Roberto. He dropped down in the front seat. His eyes were watering. "And I said it all to them in English. Good English. But not too good. I knew they liked for me to not speak too good.

"Hell, 'Come-fuck-my-sister' were the first American words I was taught. A taximan taught them to me. Hell, by ten I was one of the biggest pimps on main street. All the sailors and marines knew me. 'Hey, Pepe!' they'd call across the street to me. 'You got any new sisters?' 'Oh, sure,' I'd answer. 'Three new ones. Fresh from the convent!' And they'd laugh and call me over and I'd race to them. Like a well-trained dog . . . ."

He stopped. He said nothing more. The silence grew heavy. The fat brother, Gordo, put on the radio and pushed the buttons, looking for a Mexican station. He found one. It was Mexican ranch music and very clear. The car was a big new Ford and the three brothers owned it together and were very proud of it. It gave them big prestige. After the harvest season they'd go back to their slum area of Tijuana and drive their new Ford around, and all their slum friends would watch in envy as they'd cruise around. They'd park a lot instead of driving around because of the cost of gas. They'd sit there . . . parked. And they'd honk at the passing girls and turn up their radio. Blasting loud.

Up ahead they stopped at a roadside bar. They were out of beer. They wanted to buy more. Quickly. Before two o'clock. Luis suggested they go and find a liquor store. Beer costs too much at a roadside cantina, and besides . . . these trucks, these pickups parked all around were not Mexican-looking vehicles. They looked like Okie equipment. They had gun racks in the back windows of the cab, and some had decorative chrome horses or bullhorns on the hood.

"No," said Luis. "Let's not go in. I smell trouble."

"Trouble?" said Pepe. "Shit! I'm not scared of trouble. I'm a man *a toda madre*! *¡Un gallo de estaca!* And I'd love for someone to try and mess with me tonight. All week I've been taking it, and taking it, and I'm ready to burst! Eh, *Gordo*?" He turned to his big fat brother. The big fat brother, who usually got a job in the camp kitchens and never worked out in the fields, nodded. Said nothing, smiled, and nodded. Pepe laughed. "Stop the car! We're going in. What the hell! Is this not a free country? Are we not all equal? Eh? I fart and shit on all that bullshit. Open the doors. Let a man get out! You three stay here if you want. My two brothers and I will go in and get the beer."

Gordo got out. The car springs moved way up. *Gordo* was that huge. And he was black- brown and mean-looking in the face; he was a mountain of flesh. He was six-foot-five and weighed at least two-seventy-five. Maybe three hundred. And he now got out, smiled, said nothing, and rubbed his nose as he glanced around. His big nose twitched. He rubbed it some more. All the brothers were out now. Aguilar began getting out. Luis gripped his arm.

"*Amigo* ... let's wait here, eh? I think it's best."

Aguilar looked at his arm where Luis was holding him. Luis let go. For even though Aguilar was not in the best physical shape, he was big-boned, handsome, and a very impressive figure of just under six feet. Luis was the same height, but thin, small-boned, and almost delicate.

"Look," said Aguilar. "I know you're right. I smell the trouble too. That's why I go. To keep them safe so we can drive on."

Luis' large brown eyes softened. "Okay, *amigo*. But take care. I'll stay here with Roberto. All right?"

Aguilar nodded and turned to the brothers. The older brother and the younger brother were laughing and joking with insulting words at each other. *Gordo*, the mountain of flesh, was saying nothing and smiling quietly to himself.

"Come on," said Aguilar. "Let us hurry and get the beer and go on."

Pepe laughed. "I knew you weren't a coward like those others. Come! Let us go and see these Okie gringos."

Roberto began to protest that he was not a coward, but Luis gripped him hard. The others were now walking across the gravel parking lot. There were flattened beer cans everywhere. They passed by all the pickups and trucks. They headed for the entrance with a beer ad flashing off and on. They opened the door. Western music came pouring out. Loud western, Okie, hillbilly music. They went in. The door closed. All the sounds stopped. Roberto's heart was pounding. Moments passed. They still didn't come out.

"Let's go," said Roberto. "I'm afraid for Aguilar."

"No," said Luis. "They'll be out."

A crash was heard. Roberto bolted for the door. Luis tried getting him, but couldn't, so he got out also. They ran toward the entrance with the flashing beer sign. Luis grabbed a shovel out of a truck as he ran. Roberto opened the door. The place looked small from the outside, but inside it was long and open and it had two pool tables, and there were American cowboys all over the place. They had cue sticks in hand and were bluffing down the three brothers, telling them to stay put, and one man was fighting Aguilar. He was not much taller than Juan Aguilar but a lot heavier. He was potbellied, wore a cowboy hat and a big western buckle, and he had a cue stick in his hand, and he was bellowing. That he was a foreman! A superintendent! And that Aguilar, who was up against the wall with nothing in hand, was a goddamn greaser! A coward-ass Mex! A son-of-a-bitch Chávez' man! Aguilar didn't have his gun and he was glancing around for something to defend himself with. The cowboy swung the stick at his face. Aguilar ducked. The cowboy laughed. The brothers were cowed and offering no help. They looked like frightened little children. Especially compared to the mountain of flesh.

Roberto ran up in a rush, leaping on the cowboy's back before anyone even knew he was in the room. The cowboy went spilling into the wall. Roberto kept on his back like a monkey and was hitting, biting, scratching, and the cowboy dropped his cue and screeched. "Get it off me! Oh, Lord God! My eyes! My ears!"

There was a rush of men. But Aguilar now had the cue stick. He caught the first one with a terrific roundhouse to the head. The man dropped. Others came. Another fell. Gordo bellowed. Cowboys turned and saw, and they scattered. The mountain came down, catching two. His brothers shot in like snapping little dogs and hit at the two as the mountain held them. The two dropped. The mountain bellowed in ecstasy and turned to get some more cowboys. The brothers followed close behind. Ready to hit what he caught. But the mountain didn't catch anything. One cowboy had rammed a cue stick into his belly, and the mountain was turning white and rolling forward in a slow clumsy fall. Eyes turned over. All their whites showing. The brothers stood in panic. Yelping at their large brother like scared little dogs. Their brother responded. He didn't fall. He doubled over, all hurt, and rushed at his attacker with the cue stick and rammed him into the wall. And fell. The brothers saw other cowboys coming, and they bolted. Dodging and racing like rabbits.

Aguilar and Roberto were no longer fighting. They were up against a wall, backs protected, and Aguilar had a cue stick, and no one would approach them. They stood solid. Boss. And good. For the proof of them, *a la prueba*, lay there on the floor. Two unconscious cowboys, and one crying that a wildcat had clawed and bit him half to death.

"Lordy! Lordy! One of my eyeballs is hanging out. Oh, Christ-Jesus, help me!"

Two men were trying to help him. Three others had got chairs and were getting ready to make a go at Roberto and Aguilar when Aguilar roared. Swinging his cue! Busting a chair. Leaping and roaring.

"*¡Apártense, pulgas! Porque aquí viene el peine!*" And he was swinging like a man prepared to die. A man who didn't give a good goddamn. "Open up, fleas!" He roared, and men moved aside. "For here comes the comb!" And he kept swinging roundhouses. "You're goddamn right! I'm a CHAVISTA! A VILLISTA! A ZAPATISTA! And you're all INSECTS to me! You SONS-OF-BITCHES!"

The lights went out. Luis had turned out the lights, and now he was yelling to come outside. *¡Pronto! ¡Pronto!* And he'd take care of everything.

Men yelled. Cue sticks crushed. Chairs flew. Names and insults echoed. And men began running out the door, and there was Luis with the shovel, and he tried to distinguish which was which before he knocked their shins out from under them. And each swing to the shins brought out a roar of pain. A scream of terror. And when Pepe came, Luis recognized him but let him have it anyhow, and Pepe, the big brother, screamed like a baby, and after they were in the car and driving fast, he was still crying.

"Well," said Luis. He was now doing the driving, and the three brothers sat in back trying to console their big brother. "Mistakes like that happen in a bar fight. Maybe next time you'll be more careful."

Pepe raged and wanted to jump over the seat at Luis, but he bumped his shin and just fell back yelping, crying, and that was that. He was truly hurt. The shovel had cut him to the bone and sliced off his flesh all down his shin to his foot. His foot was swollen at the top of the arch. He would not be able to wear shoes or walk for days. Maybe weeks. Luis said nothing more and drove on. Everyone was very quiet and yet ... happy. Or as Aguilar so well put it, all day their race had stood in shame of the gringo's shadow, and this fight, this bellowing of words in the style of his mountain-home language, had made him feel good and clean, and next time a gringo said anything against Chávez, he would say he was a Chavista and splatter the bastard. Rightly or wrongly, he didn't give a good goddamn. His cough was bad. He was dying anyway. So, shit! He'd die proud. *¡Un gallo de estaca!* A CHAVISTA TO THE DEATH!

A few of the cowboys made out a police report, and the police were now looking for a newish car with some muscle men, professionals, whom Chávez had hired . . . and by morning the local papers had the thing pieced together. These professional musclemen had been hired to cut off foremen's feet in retaliation for the accident of the boy at the strike area. Three White Americans had injured shins, and one foreman had most of his foot chopped off.

And so this violence was put on the records and broadcast by radio, TV, newspapers, from police station to police station, while the current of real events continued rushing forward . . . untouched. Unknown.

CHAPTER FOURTEEN

At Madera, California, they stopped to see a Mexican family the brothers knew. Pepe was truly hurt. It was decided to leave him and the car there. They would go on with this man's son and their pickup. There was work in Firebaugh. The cantaloupe were in, and there was a shortage of men, and the pay was very good. They drove west to Firebaugh. They heard about their fight on the radio. The Mexican station made it very clear to them. The police were looking for a new car and a huge man. They got into Firebaugh about four in the morning. They drove around trying to find someone awake. They couldn't find anyone. They parked in an open lot and tried to get some sleep. The weather was good this time of the night. It was cool, the coolest time of the whole night. At five-thirty a little light began breaking in the east. They drove around. They saw a light in the kitchen of a work camp. They went in. It was a huge kitchen with enormous pots. There was only one cook. He was making coffee. They asked for coffee. He said, sure. They asked about the melons. He told them the melons had not started. There was no work in town. The cantaloupes began here in six weeks. Now the melon work was farther south. In Huron. Or anywhere around Bakersfield. They thanked him for the coffee, got back in their car, cursed the family who had given them the wrong information, and drove off.

Now as they drove through town they could see that this town was indeed deserted. Wind-blown. Resembling a ghost town. And yet, in six weeks, with the melons, this same town would be bursting with men. Booming! Like a gold-rush town. All the bars full. All the sidewalks covered with men. All the markets open most of the night. They now drove out of the ghost town and headed east to catch big Freeway 99 and shoot south. They would try Huron first; then, if they didn't have any luck, they'd go on to Bakersfield and out toward Pumpkin Center, Greenfield, and Weed Patch.

After many more bad leads and a lot of arguments about the gas, they found work in the melons south of Bakersfield, at the foot of the great mountains between Bakersfield and Los Angeles. There, in Kern County, one of the richest farmlands in the world, they found plenty of work, and they worked at the melons, one of the physically hardest of all farm labor. Starting with the first light of day, they would straddle a row, bend down, and pick with heavy sacks on their backs. There were six men on each side of each truck, and every man would have his own row and he would walk along bent over, move the leaves, select only the large, three-quarter-size, ripe melons, pick them, toss them over his shoulder into his sack, fill the sack, and trot quickly to the truck, race up the two-by-twelve ramp which dragged along behind the truck, dump his sixty or eighty pounds of melons, race down the other board, jump over the rows of melons, get to his own row, straddle it, bend over, and start selecting, picking, and tossing them over his shoulder, filling his sack. Quickly. The faster the better, for soon the sun would be too hot, and they were getting paid so much per truck.

Each *cuadrilla*, group, had twelve men, and each *cuadrilla* was paid so much per truck, and so they hurried. They ran bent over in the fields, they trotted quickly to the ever-creeping-along-beside-them truck and trailer, and then raced up the two-by-twelve board. Short quick steps, trying to keep balance, holding the sack of melons from swaying, yelling at the driver, who's always trying to creep ahead faster than the men can pick, slow down, dammit! or we'll quit loading you! The driver would act like he didn't hear, but still he'd slow down for a little while.

Then it was ten in the morning and the sun was hot and the men didn't run anymore. They began to walk, to lug up the ramp, flip-flop down the ramp, wipe the dripping sweat out of their eyes, line up at the five-gallon water tank tied to the side of the truck, take the empty can of Coors with a wire tied to it like a handle, fill it half up with ice-cold water, rinse, spit, drink, pass it to the next man, and return to the field. Refreshed. And so they would briskly walk out two or three or six rows, straddle, bend over, and begin selecting. Now it was truly hot. It was eleven, and all the melons were beginning to look bad. Too green. Too small. Too burned by the sun. And, for these bad ones, one didn't get paid. They'd get thrown out at the packing shed. Only the good ones were taken from the truck, boxed, and shipped, and one got paid by the number of boxes shipped per truck.

Then it was noon, and Roberto was still racing. He straddled, he bent over, he walked along selecting fast. Picking with his left hand, passing to his right hand, and tossing over his right shoulder into the sack. He picked and tossed and tossed and tossed. He yelled at Luis and Aguilar and Ramón.

"The melons! They're heavy over here!"

"Good," said Luis, and moved over to him. "They're thin here."

"I got plenty," said Ramon.

"Don't pick the green ones!" said Aguilar.

Ramón and Luis were all right, but Aguilar was tired and he was working near the ever-creeping truck. He was drained. The sun was blazing. It was at least a hundred and eight degrees in the shade, but they were not in the shade. They were out in mid-field, ten to thirty degrees hotter than the shade. The melons themselves that were not shaded by leaves were burning into wrinkled-up little balls. Roberto came at a trot over the rows with a full sack of melons. Aguilar saw him. He smiled. That boy could truly work. They'd already filled six trucks and trailers. As much as the best *cuadrillas*, and this boy was still running. There he went back bent under his load of melons. So many melons that they were up over the top of his sack. Three, four, resting on his back. Two others in his left arm in front. A good eighty or ninety pounds, and he hit the two-by-twelve at a run. Short quick steps, working to keep balance. He dumped, he turned, and came running down the other ramp as the truck moved forward. Aguilar called him.

"Boy, not so fast. Don't do work for the others. Save your strength for the whole harvest season. You know we all twelve split the number of boxes at the end of the day." Roberto smiled. Dripping with sweat. Soaking through all his clothes with dark wetness. Eight salt tablets a day he took. "Yes. But there is so much melon." He raised up his new American straw hat. A big golfer's type hat. "We're going to get rich! Six trucks and trailers today so far. Twelve loads. Maybe we can make fifteen or sixteen by two o'clock. Yesterday we made twelve." He wiped his face with his long-sleeved shirt. He blew his nose by putting a finger on one side and then on the other side. Dirt and sweat and snot blew out. He smiled hugely. Wiping his hands on his pants. "God, we'll maybe make thirty-five dollars apiece today." And he rushed over the rows, yelling at the six men on this side of the truck. Six men took six rows on each side of the always-creeping truck. "Hurry! Pick only good ones! Fill up these trucks! And by God! I'll do more than my share!" Some men laughed and yelled back at him. They liked him. He was truly a good, strong, enduring workman. Others said nothing. They just grumbled. They didn't like him. He was too good. He made them look bad, and yesterday, because of him, two men had been fired by the *cuadrilla* boss. Each *cuadrilla* had a headman who was elected by the men to keep count of the trucks, keep check on the men, and make sure of the division of their pay. This *cuadrilla* boss liked Roberto, liked the way he worked and talked and pushed the men in a good-happy manner, and yesterday he had reported to the foreman that he had two slow men in his *cuadrilla* and he wanted them replaced. The foreman, proud of this fast-working *cuadrilla* which made him look good to the field boss, took the two men and put them on a slow *cuadrilla* of old men and winos. These bad *cuadrillas* filled only two or three trucks and trailers in a whole day. And they made only twelve or fifteen dollars per man a day.

At twelve-thirty the lunch truck came. The men stopped work, the headman went and got their boxes of lunch. They all gathered around the truck they were loading and lay down in its shade, panting and sweating like dogs on a chase, and began to eat. Each man was given a brown paper bag with six tacos. Three of bean and three of dried-out beef stew. They bitched about Gordo's cooking. They laughed. They ate. Mouths open. The tacos were warm because of the sun. They drank water to wash them down. Coke and beer were available but cost extra. Twenty-five cents a can. Either one. Same price. And, in the wino *cuadrillas*, some wino would have a cold gallon jug of cheap mountain red and sell a can full for seventy-five cents. A fantastic profit.

With lunch over, the good *cuadrillas* would go back to work. Quickly. Renewed. Refreshed. And strong. While the bad *cuadrillas* would buy more beer, more wine, more Coke, and collapse.

Like that they worked hard all week, and many men were fired off the good *cuadrillas* and put on the bad ones, and in the bad ones two men collapsed that week. Fell down with their sacks on their backs, and that was that. They were winos, they were old men, they were no good for the melon work, and they were taken off the job. But in Roberto's *cuadrilla* no one fell. They were the best, and they worked on and never looked back. The pay was good and the season was short and they had to get all they could. Now! Quickly! Pick the melon, fill the trucks. The trucks were filled and the boxes were shipped east by rail, and the cantaloupe business was in full swing. Their grower-shipper-owner was moving fifteen thousand boxes per day and making good money. Depending on the day's market. Some days he'd make as much as two dollars per box. His cost was at a steady four dollars and fifty cents per box, and the daily market was keeping at six and six-fifty per box. That made him $22,500 to $30,000 per day. Everyone was making money. It was one of the best years in the last five years for cantaloupes.

Roberto earned $235.50 that first week for a seven-day week and was given $216.50, and out of this he spent only thirty-five dollars for his living: $24.50 for his board and room and ten dollars more for 7-Up, beer, and a few personal things. Aguilar took another fifty dollars from him. That was their deal. One-fourth of his earnings. He had $121.50 left. He kept the $21.50 and had the rest sent home to his sister through the office. He figured he had now sent home a total of one hundred and sixty American dollars, so he now wrote the letter to his sister and told her to give some money to their father so he could buy a milk cow. But for her not to give him the money until he promised not to drink the money. For her to read this letter aloud to him in front of the whole family.

"Father," he added to the letter, "this is my money. I've worked hard to earn it. If you do not do as I ask, I will not send you any more money. On the other hand, if you do as I ask, I will keep sending money and I will bring you home any gift you, personally, wish. A rifle? Or a many- shot shotgun if you wish? Or a radio that plays with batteries? Anything. There is much money to be made here. But understand, it is not easy like we think back home. Here, in one day, I work harder and sweat more than in a week at home. We are not in the mountains. We are in a valley. Flat and deep and hot, and richer than your highest dreams. The soil, you can smell its richness. And the rivers, they lose not one drop of water. They are enclosed in concrete.

"This land has water and soil and machinery and crops, such huge crops of the deepest richest green, that ten days on horse would not cross half of them. And each hectare is like gold. The soil's that rich.

"Father, take care of my money. It is ours. Our family's. And if I can keep finding work, we will soon be able to buy a ranch, and cattle, and be a people to whom the word 'Don' will be addressed."

Then he wrote some words of warmth to his mother ... to his mother and to the children and to his sister Esperanza, who would be in charge of the money, the correspondence, and all legal papers of their different purchases.

He breathed.

He lay down and dreamed of the future. He fell asleep. The alarm went off. He got up. Heavy. He was getting tired. This was not so good. But after eating he was strong once more and he worked all day, and the days passed, the weeks passed, and all was good for him, a strong young man. He worked seven days a week. He worked and ate and slept and had no time to notice how the faces were changing in his *cuadrilla.* The weaker were being put aside.

Then the melons were done. No more work. But they, the strong, were told to go north, and they were given a paper with an address. And these strong ones got rides on buses and cars, and they went a few miles north, and the work continued. More fields, more melon, more trucks and trailers, and another work camp much the same as the one they had left. Roberto worked, earning an average of two hundred dollars a week for a seven-day week. Aguilar began taking off one day a week. He said he needed a day of rest or he would not last the season. Roberto said, "Fine. But now you only get one-fourth of six days of my labor."

"What?" said Aguilar. He couldn't believe it. He leaped up off his bunk.

"Look," said Roberto. "Fair is fair." He swallowed. "Don't get angry. Please. We've been through much together. Let us be honorable with each other." Aguilar eased off. He lit a cigar. He was a half-head taller than Roberto. He was big-boned, and before the harvest, he had outweighed Roberto by thirty-some pounds. Now they were almost the same weight. He was tired, drained, bony in the face and caved-in at the stomach and chest. Roberto, on the other hand, had put on weight. Fifteen pounds, and all in the arms and chest and thighs, and his face and stomach were as lean as a running greyhound. "I know I owe you much. I know I would never have come without you. I know that you've brought me through hell, saved my life several times, and ... and ... " He choked up. " ... in many ways I've come to look upon you as my true father.

Aguilar's eyes blinked, then he smiled. "Yes ... I, I, I've come to look upon you as a son. You've never turned coward on me." He smoked. Cigar in mouth. Hands on his hips. "Most of the boys who come with me fall apart. But you ... I truly remember that day in the desert you stood up to go when all were wanting to lie down and die like dogs." He breathed. "I swear, I, myself, the great Aguilar, the *norteño* of ten years, was ready to give up too, but ... when I saw you stand up I ... I ... "

"You?" said Roberto, huge-eyed. "You were ready to quit?"

Aguilar nodded and looked at Roberto a long, long while and then smiled handsomely. "Yes," he said, "even I, with my style of gun and cigars, have limits. Like that night in the bar ... I was lost. You saved me when you leaped on that Okie." He nodded. He breathed. "But now, getting back to this about the money, tell me, how do you figure it?"

"Well," said Roberto, but he didn't feel so strong about it now. He looked at Aguilar. Aguilar smiled handsomely and said nothing. Roberto shied away.

"Well," said Aguilar. "Explain."

"Every day," began Roberto, "I pick more than you ... I thought I gave my fourth there in the field and ... "

"What! Are you loco? That fourth you do more of in the field is divided by the twelve men in our *cuadrilla*! That doesn't ... "

Roberto turned red before Aguilar. He, Roberto, had made a deal. He had heard the headman talking about Aguilar, saying he was getting slow. Roberto had told the headman that he would make up for what Aguilar didn't do. To please not move him to a lesser *cuadrilla*, and definitely not to mention to Aguilar about their deal. The headman had asked Roberto if they were relatives. Roberto had said no. The headman, a man about Aguilar's age who didn't smoke or drink and went to bed early each night, looked at Roberto closely.

"Tell me, why are you doing this for him?" Roberto swallowed. "You don't have to tell me if you don't want," said the headman. "But I'm curious. It's not often that you find men close like that. Not nowadays. Years back, yes. But now it's dog eat dog, and move on as fast as you can."

The man had waited. Roberto had said, "Well, you see, we come from the same town." He had said no more. And he had wondered why he hadn't told the headman the truth. Why did he feel so protective of Aguilar?

And now, as he, Roberto, looked up at Aguilar, he wondered the same. Why? This man had helped him, but hell, this man had also used him time and again. He began to tell Aguilar about his deal with the headman. Damn, he'd already paid Aguilar his fourth, and more. He'd tell him now and not give him anything from his check.

But Aguilar spoke first. "Well," he said, "it seems you have nothing to say. It seems you're just getting a little too big for your pants because the harvest is good and the times are easy. But, to show you I mean well, I'll tell you what, the days you work that I don't, you can keep for yourself. I won't take my fourth of those. How's that? Eh? Son?" And he extended his hand. "From now on we'll be *compadres*. To the end!"

Roberto's eyes blinked and his throat choked. Aguilar laughed and grabbed Roberto's hand. "Don't apologize. What the hell! Like you said, fair is fair, and we have been through much together and should be able to talk to each other head-on. Straight!" He smiled grandly. "*¡Compadre!* You are the manliest man I've met in years. You're *un macho a todo dar*!" Roberto blushed, and Aguilar pumped his hand. "No need to blush or thank me. I like you as a son. Come, *hijo*, let's go to the store. I'll buy you a beer. *¡A lo macho!*"

One very successful Mexican-American police captain, in the San Joaquín Valley, told a young Chicano bookwriter, "These people," meaning the unsuccessful Chicanos in the U.S., "are low- class people, and that's the whole problem in a nutshell. Hell, the Europeans who came here had to have money, ambition, and a little old-fashioned smarts to come across the ocean. These people who come across from Mexico are broke, illiterate; they're the lowest and most backward of all Mexicans. They just give me and you a bad image to all the Americans. And Chávez, hell, I know him since way back, and I say he was all right years back when he tried to work within the framework of our great society, but now it's all gone to his head. He's a puppet for foreign forces, a news-media gimmick, and ... you know, low-class."

"Oh," said the Chicano bookwriter, "but I'd understood that Chávez helped you get your present position."

"Well, he did," said the captain, "but that was before. When he was all right. Before he turned low-class."

"Oh," said the young Chicano, and it was by far one of his finest 'ohs.'

CHAPTER FIFTEEN

It was a long, hot summer day, and after work Roberto, Aguilar, and Luis went to town. The town's name was Huron, and it was only half a mile from their work camp. At the other work camps there had been no towns for ten miles or more. None of the brothers worked with them anymore. Pepe was back, but he was in a lesser *cuadrilla*, and his younger brother, Gordo, the mountain, was a clean-up man in the kitchen. This kitchen already had all the cooks it needed. So Roberto and Aguilar and Luis were now alone. They walked to Huron along the road and passed many men. Six weeks ago this town had been a ghost town, but now it was booming. There were five or six work camps in the area, and all the bars were full and all the grocery stores were open all night. There were *camaradas* everywhere, but they didn't look like the mass of men in Empalme. No, these men were laughing, talking, slapping each other on the back, and they looked happy and well-fed. Having a job changed a man's perspective about life.

And the town—these were not temporary structures. No, these were solid old buildings, and the main streets were blacktopped and the gutters and sidewalks were cemented, and there was a garbage system. The town didn't smell of dung and death and rot. It smelled of life and men and sweet cantaloupe. Why, the sweet smell of the melons was in the very atmosphere. The trucks that loaded in the fields had to pass through the main street of town to go to the packing sheds that were by the railroad tracks and melons fell from the trucks, getting squashed on the road.

Roberto and his *camaradas* went up the street and into the first bar with a Mexican name. Inside, the place was big, with a tall ceiling, and there were a lot of men but very few women. So these women moved around and kept smiling very friendly. Roberto, Luis and Aguilar went to the long tall bar. The barman, a skinny old Mexican, said he could not serve Roberto. He was too young. California had a state law of twenty-one. Aguilar angered. Roberto tried calming him down. Luis said the bar was no good anyway and suggested they buy beer at a market and go back toward camp and drink under some trees.

"What the hell, I'll even buy a radio. A transistor for the three of us," said Luis, and they went out.

At the huge modern market they bought beer, salami, chips, salsa and a transistor for $14.95 made in Japan. They went out of town and sat under some trees and watched the sun go down, as they drank and ate and listened to the radio. It was a good radio with a black vinyl case, and everything was fine. Later they went back to camp. A poker game was going on. Aguilar lit a cigar and joined the game. One man won a big hand, and so he quit and came over to Roberto and Luis, who were listening to the radio.

"Hey, I like that radio! I'll buy it from you."

"No," said Luis. "I just bought it."

"How much? Twenty dollars?"

Luis nodded. "More or less."

"Here, I'll give you twenty-five. Gringo cash!"

"Look," said Luis, "you can buy one tomorrow at the big supermarket for much less."

"But I want it now! I'm ahead in poker, and if I don't spend some money quick, I'll go back and lose it."

Luis began to protest. Roberto jumped up. "It's a deal!" he said to the man, and took the man's twenty-five dollars and gave him the radio. The man left. Luis sat there, hand outstretched as if he were still holding the radio. "Look," said Roberto. "I'll get you another one. Wait here one minute." And he took off running. He ran out of the barracks, up the road and all the way to the supermarket without ever slowing down. He bought a radio, black in color, and began to leave. But he stopped and looked at the other radios, the stopped. He bought another radio, a brown one, then ran all the way back to camp. "Here," he said to Luis. "Your radio, plus half of the profit we made on that first one." He drew close. "I bought this other one also. I'm going to sell it. Do you want to come in with me?"

Luis looked at him a long time. In the past he had always been against business. He was an honest workman, and business was only for crooks. But he now looked at this boy, Roberto, and he nodded and said, "Okay, but let's not sell it. Let's raffle it."

"Raffle?"

"Yes, like the chances back in Mexico. We'll sell fifty chances at fifty cents apiece, and—"

"Oh, I see ... I see ... " said Roberto, and his heart began to pound, and his eyes grew happy and far-seeing. "Wait. We'll sell these chances for a dollar apiece, and ... .How much money you've got? We'll go back to the store and get some beer and have two more people, after the winner, draw for a case of beer each, and then ... " He smiled, very catlike. "They'll share the beer with the others, I'm sure, and then no one will feel a loser, and we'll be able to have a raffle every night." Luis was looking at Roberto, and his eyes were huge with surprise. Roberto saw his surprise, so he said, "Aguilar ... taught me much. We'll include him. Okay?" Luis nodded, but said nothing. "Good. I'll go borrow twenty from him. We'll each put in twenty dollars every night and ... .Oh, it makes my stomach flutter at the possibilities!"

And so a business began, and by the last week of the melon season in Huron, Roberto was buying TV sets for two hundred dollars and raffling them off for five hundred chances at a dollar apiece.

Luis couldn't believe it.

Aguilar believed it easily. He was now working only five days a week. He was organizing poker and dice games and kidding Roberto about buying a car. A brand-new car, and raffling it off at the end of the harvest season. Roberto would only blush ... but then one day he found out through Gordo that they were losing their new Ford. They needed cash. Roberto's eyes got big, and he went and talked to Aguilar and Luis, and they came up with a deal. Roberto and his partners would give the brothers enough cash to pay off the whole car, get them out of their debt, and maybe give them a few dollars. They accepted, and Aguilar's joke became a reality and Roberto was out selling chances for three dollars each on a new Ford, and people now knew him, knew he paid off and didn't cheat, so many men wanted lots of chances. He made these men a deal. He'd sell them fifty chances for one hundred dollars, and he and Luis and Aguilar brought in $4,525.00 in one week and gave the brothers $2,650.00 to pay off the car and another three hundred for them personally, and Roberto and his partners had $1,575.00 profit. Cash money. American. Plus the eight or nine hundred dollars they had made on radios and TVs, and then ... the melons were done and the car was raffled and a man from another camp won it and that was that. The season in Huron was over, and they all had to move on.

They went to Firebaugh next, and it was the same there. The

town that had been a ghost town was now booming. But the raffles didn't go so well here. In the second week one man accused Roberto of cheating and drew a knife and rushed Roberto, but he was so drunk he fell over his own feet and stabbed himself, dying instantly. The boss of the camp stopped the raffles. The melons were in, and he, the boss, didn't want extra problems. He had enough. Chávez was in the area ... and he was striking the tomatoes, and several big ranches weren't using as many men, and no one knew what was going to happen next. Chávez moved so quickly. Here at dawn, over there at night, and the sheriff's department and the private detectives of the growers could barely keep up with him. His tactics were hit-and-run, very confusing, and seemed to come right out of the U.S. military manual on guerrilla-tactics.

Roberto was doing well. He'd now sent home a total of twelve hundred dollars and had put another seven hundred in traveler's checks. The checks he'd sewed in his pants. He was truly doing well, and his sister was writing him regularly and telling him that all was going well. That their father was not drinking the money, that he had bought the milk cow and now had bought some pigs, and one of the pigs was a huge female and she was already bred and would soon have a litter. Also, the supply room had food and she and their mother each wore a new dress. That all was fine. Their father was working. It was inspiring and soon they would start looking around for *un ranchito.*

Then she added that their mother was expecting once again and she sent her love and thanked him, her eldest and dearest son, for she was eating well and surely this coming child would live and not die at birth like the last two. Esperanza then closed the letter with much love and said she so wished to come to the United States.

Roberto breathed ... yes, maybe Esperanza should come. After all, she had been the one always wishing to leave their pueblo, and yes, she had inspired him to leave and come north. He breathed again, thinking about his sister, his mother, and about his father not drinking. Something was wrong. It all seemed too good to be true, or maybe it all was true, and he had just become too pessimistic and rotten inside to believe. Hell, it was all too confusing to figure, and so he went to sleep. Dreaming. Dreaming of a little *rancho* with goats and *bueyes* and calves and pigs and ... a big drunk man came stumbling in and fell down, breaking everything. Roberto awoke ... and for moments couldn't distinguish dream from reality.

Then, the melons were done in Firebaugh and they headed north. Back up toward Sacramento. They went to Acampo. To the camp that Luis' friend Mr. Davis owned. It was deserted. There were no men. Only one family, who were given free room for keeping watch over the camp. The family was Mexican, and Roberto and Luis and Aguilar had coffee with them and were told that Mr. Davis was gone. That a great tragedy had happened here last month.

The man of the house, Joe Sánchez, was doing the talking. His wife was over by the stove rolling a great mass of dough and gripping pieces of dough, rolling the gripped pieces into balls about one-third the size of her fist, and piling them up as her two daughters—girls about seventeen and eighteen—took each ball and flattened it, rolled it out with a rolling pin, and put it to bake into a delicious tortilla. Roberto, between sips of coffee, watched the two girls. They were so young and quiet and blushing and so lovely. He sipped, trying to listen to the man of the house and be proper. Courteous and formal. But it was very hard.

" ... God forgive me for gossiping, but ... you are friends of Señor Davis, and Señor Davis has always been good to me and my family, and last week his wife took the last of his money and ran off with a young Mexican boy. A no-good boy. A troublemaker from Zacatecas who only works when he feels like it. Not a man like you or me who works steady and hard and tries to do the whole harvest season and save for the winter." Luis stood up. He threw up his arms in disbelief. "I know, I know, that's exactly how I felt when I first found out. Why did it have to happen to Señor Davis, who has always been so good to the Mexican people? Why didn't it happen to some no-good gringo?"

The older girl was blushing, and Roberto was so upset he couldn't sip his coffee. He was blushing and trembling and yet trying so hard to be formal and proper and listen to this man's story. Both girls wore boots, pants, long-sleeved shirts, and big bandanas. They looked like they had just come in off the fields. The older girl was giving such quiet hidden eyes to Roberto that when she went to flip her next flour tortilla from hand to hand, she missed, and the tortilla went sailing. She jerked upright, gasped with surprise, and blushed all red, covering her mouth. Her younger sister burst out laughing. The mother slapped at the older girl's arm and scolded her for not paying attention to her work. The older girl apologized and bent down to get the tortilla, and her sister nudged her behind and she fell. The young sister laughed. The fallen girl leaped up ready to claw her laughing sister. Their mother stepped between them. The embarrassed sister ran off crying toward the back. The mother yelled after her, then turned, and pulled the laughing girl by the ear, and scolded her and then went back to work.

The men smiled, stopped watching, and went back to their business. Señor Davis' wife was gone, and Davis himself was now trying to find work. He had gone over toward Salinas. He had a brother near King City. He needed money very quickly or he'd lose everything.

"So," Joe Sánchez, the man of the house, concluded, "I suggest you go to King City. There is work there now. My two eldest sons are over there with Señor Davis right now." Then he stood up. "Come. Let us sit down to dinner. *Mi casa es su casa.* Please, the honor is mine."

So they stood up and went to the long table with long benches, and as they were getting ready to sit down, in came the older girl in a red-and-white dress, and she was beautiful. Long black hair and red lips and brown arms and legs. Roberto breathed. And the girl saw and blushed, and her younger sister laughed. The mother yelled at them, and they became quiet. The men sat down, and children came running in, and the women began serving, talking, and moving about so swiftly.

Roberto breathed again . . . smelling the tortillas, the beans, the *carne de puerco en chile verde*, the strong heavy Mexican coffee, and he felt such a warmth, such a good clean warmth throughout his person, that he smiled happily, and then the sister in the red-and-white dress came by and he smelled of her also and . . . oh, God! the sweetness of her freshly soaped body. He melted, feeling at home for the first time since he had left home . . . ten thousand years ago.

"Look," said the police captain, "in a nutshell, I'll tell you all. I come from the fields, but I now work with the growers, so I know both sides, and no one can pull the sheep over my eyes. Of course there are problems. Huge problems, injustices, and gross abusements—mostly because of neglect—in the fields.

"Hell, no one cares about migrating people: here today, there tomorrow. And there is no dignity in laboring under the sun in the dust and wind. Field workers have always been the lowest and will always be the lowest. I say César Chávez is a fool, impractical and ignorant, to try to improve the conditions for the Mexican in the fields. I say to hell with the Factories of the Field. Let them remain awful! Encourage the Mexican to get educated and get the hell out of the fields. That would be the humane position for Chávez to take, but no, he just wants to stir up trouble."

"But . . . " said the young Chicano, "who would then pick the tomatoes, the melons, the . . . "

He leaped, suddenly raging with anger. "Who gives a shit? Let the Okies do it! The Niggers! The Hippies during their summer vacation! I don't care! I made it; they can make it." And there he stood, a tall, big-bellied police captain of Mexican descent, positive about his position and not going to give an inch.

CHAPTER SIXTEEN

The youngest daughter was named Lydia, and she wore pants and was seventeen. The older daughter's name was Gloria Sánchez. She was eighteen, three months younger than Roberto. She wore dresses, and was very beautiful. Their family came from Chihuahua. Their father had been an immigrated green carder; then, five years later he had become an American citizen and brought his family over from Mexico. His two daughters had been born here in California and he no longer followed the harvest from Yuma to Sacramento to Salinas. He lived here, near Acampo, permanently so he could send his children to school. Gloria, the most educated of the family, had finished high school and last year had gotten a scholarship to attend a junior college. She had always loved to read books, go to school, and study history and geography, and in high school her Spanish teacher had come to talk to her parents and told them she would try to get her a scholarship. Gloria was a good student, and in the last few years, because of Chávez and Kennedy and many others, Mexican-Americans now had a much better opportunity to get scholarships. So Gloria's Spanish teacher finally got her a scholarship and now she only worked at picking fruit in the summers so she could buy her school clothes and not be too much of a burden on her parents.

After dinner Gloria and Roberto talked at the table while her mother and Lydia did the dishes. The men had gone outside. Roberto stayed behind on the pretense that he was still hungry. He now sat there, playing with his food, trying to eat another bite, but unable. The mother smiled. She guessed his situation. Gloria was telling Roberto about her scholarship and how the great César Chávez helped her and all Chicanos. Roberto said nothing. Gloria asked him what he thought of the great César Chávez. He shook his head and said he didn't know ... *nada, nada.* All he knew was what he had seen at a certain *huelga.* She became interested, and he told her the story of that strike as he had seen it.

"And you didn't walk across those picket lines and help! Eh?" She was terribly upset. "What kind of Mexican are you? A coward!"

"Gloria!" snapped her mother. "Hold your tongue! You have no right to raise your voice at this young man."

But Gloria would not be silenced. No, she continued accusing, demanding, and yelling. Roberto was red in the face. He finally stood up. Fast! Gloria's eyes grew large. There he stood ... heavy. Boss. Good. And the bird of fear flew through her, and she was afraid, and yet ... the woman in her could admire the powerful look of this young man.

"Thank you for dinner, *señora,*" said Roberto to their mother. He was speaking very formally, but he was not addressing Gloria. "I have not known such wonderful cooking since I left home ... ." He stepped back and picked up his straw hat. "And I thank you," he said to Lydia in a less formal tone of voice. Lydia was over there finishing the dishes. "And of course, thank you for your thoughts," he now said to Gloria as he turned to leave.

Gloria said nothing and Roberto was going out the door when the younger girl, Lydia, who was a senior in high school and not such a good student, said, "Please, tell me one thing before you go." Roberto stopped. She brushed back her hair with the back of her hand. Her hand was covered with white wet suds. "Tell me, did you make more money or less money when Chávez came?"

He blinked his eyes. He had not really noticed this girl all evening. She was still in boots and pants and long-sleeved shirt. She looked more like a boy than a girl and she was tall for a Mexican girl. She was five-foot-six and could pick fruit faster than most men. She had quick hands and quick feet, and at school she was on the track team. She loved sports and outside work. Books bored her.

"I lost money," said Roberto.

This young sister, Lydia, smiled, nodded, and went back to doing the dishes. "I thought so," she said. "Chávez isn't so good. A real worker doesn't need him."

"No!" yelled Gloria. "You are wrong! You and my ignorant brothers don't understand. We are being discriminated against and ... " She turned to Roberto. "Did you make good money all year long?"

"Yes," said Roberto. "I worked hard and made a lot of money."

"How much? Do you have any idea what the national average

is? Eh? Of course you don't, and this winter you will starve! You will not be able ... "

Roberto bowed courteously. "With your permission, *señora*," he said to the mother, "I'm going outside with the men. Thank you." And he went out without addressing the girls, and he heard Lydia, the younger sister, burst out laughing, telling Gloria that she was one very dumb woman. She knew so much from books and yet a good-looking boy turns her on and she insults him and sends him running. Gloria yelled at her. Lydia laughed. The mother spoke loudly. Then they all became very quiet.

Roberto took a deep breath ... approaching the men. They were under a tree by the tall wire fence. They were smoking and passing around a small bottle. He sat down on the good earth. The earth was warm to his Levi's. The heat of the day lingered long into the night. He sipped from the bottle. It was whiskey. He made a face and gave a sound of relief as it traveled down his throat. He exhaled and listened to their conversation. They were talking about Chávez and his union.

"Oh, no!" said Roberto to himself, and his face twisted, and so he took another swig. Then, wiping off the mouth of the bottle with the palm of his hand, he passed it on. Mexican style. And the next man drank, and they continued talking about Chávez and his union, and Roberto ... cursed the damn Chávez under his breath. And the long summer day closed.

The next day Luis and Roberto and Aguilar contacted a *pocho* with a car and they paid him to take them down to Stockton, over to Tracy, and then south on big new Interstate 5 toward Los Baños, where they turned west over the mountains, by the new dam, through the Pacheco Pass, and into the coastal valleys heading towards King City. A few miles out of King City they found Davis, and he put them to work with Joe Sánchez' two big sons, and Roberto and his *camarada* worked, earned money, and all was well until ...

There came Chávez again.

Chávez and the Teamsters were at war, and the Salinas Valley was their battleground, with newspapermen, TV crews, and thousands of well-meaning nothing-better-to-do young people swarming to the area.

Roberto raged! A fist to the heavens. "This goddamn *pocho*, Chávez!" he said. "He's everywhere all at once! Why the hell is this man like this? Why does he fight so hard?

"Why did Zapata fight so hard?" asked Luis. "Why have different men all through history fought so hard? Last year Chávez himself came to the camp where we were working and, I'll tell you, he didn't look like much. Just a regular farmworker. But when he spoke and he told us that the ranchers weren't our enemy, but we had to unite to get ahead, he made so much sense."

"Bullshit!" said Aguilar.

"No, let me talk this time. I say Chávez is a good man, the best, but we just happen to be on the other side, so, well—"

Just then the two Sánchez boys came rushing up. They were both very excited.

"Quick!" said Marcos, the oldest. "You people have got to get out of here! Chávez' attorney has been hit by a foreman and he's in the hospital. The Chávez people are mad. They're trying to get the goods on these ranchers. They have spies looking for illegals everywhere." Roberto tried to talk. "*No, amigo, ¡pronto! ¡Vámonos!* Chávez is really pissing mad! He's going to get these ranches by the *tanates*!"

They quickly left in the pickup with the brothers, and as they traveled north on Highway 101 they saw campfires at the different entrances of the many ranches with tall rows of mighty eucalyptus trees. Around the fires huddled men with big hats, work clothes, and large red and black flags. *¡Huelga!* And these serious men warmed their hands and held vigilance through the night. Until dawn. The war was on. Picking up and getting heavy. As heavy as the symbolic colors of the flag. Red for blood, black for death, and of course the bird for hope. It was the same way in Mexico ... these colors were universal.

In Soledad, where there was a prison just south of Salinas, they stopped for gas. Next door was a bar, and all around were pickups with gun racks in the back and ... the racks were not empty. Marcos wanted to buy beer.

Roberto looked at Aguilar, then at Luis. Roberto said, "Marcos, you are legal ... if we get in trouble, nothing will happen to you, but we, who are illegal, will be deported."

Marcos smiled, standing tall alongside the pickup, and began to laugh. "Tell the truth. You are just afraid of these gringos and their guns."

Roberto got angry and began to get up. Luis pulled him back down. "Keep still," he said to Roberto. "It's the truth. We are afraid."

Marcos laughed. "I thought so."

"Okay," continued Luis. "So you're right. Now, let's go on. Up ahead, I'll buy you a case of beer."

"Okay," said Marcos, and pushed away from the bed of the

pickup. Roberto, Luis and Aguilar were riding in the back. Marcos and his brother, Jesús, were riding in the cab. "Now you talk my language. We'll go on. But not because I, Marcos Sánchez, fear these *cabrones gringos*! And he made a fist. "*¡Yo los chingo! ¡A toda madre!*"

Roberto looked at him but said nothing. He was tired. Really tired.

Luis patted Roberto on the shoulder, pinched his cheek roughly, and said, "It's okay. Don't you know that to pay attention to fools is to make them important? You know," he laughed, "*hacerle caso a pendejos es engrandecerlos.*" And he pinched Roberto on the cheek again, trying to loosen him up. "We did all right."

Roberto nodded, saying nothing, but thinking about Luis' words.

"Yes," said Aguilar, "we did right, considering the circumstance. Otherwise he would be dead."

They traveled north and saw many campfires surrounded by men with flags. They decided to return to the camp in Acampo, going by way of San Jose, Fremont, Hayward, and over the mountains to Stockton.

At the camp, Mr. Sánchez invited them to stay until things blew over. Roberto and his *camaradas* stayed put. Hiding and getting nervous. One day Mr. Davis arrived from Salinas, and he didn't know what to do. His wife had returned. He stayed and got drunk with Luis, and that night he cried. He'd lost everything, and his wife was as much to blame as Chávez, and now she was back. He didn't want her, but what the hell, they had children.

Then, later that month, as Roberto and the other young people sat around outside, a blond woman drove into the deserted camp. She was about forty, forty-five, and she asked Roberto where her husband was. She spoke Spanish. Roberto answered her question. She smiled at Roberto, telling him he was very good-looking, then turned, walking away. Tight pink slacks, melon cheeks moving, tall, with very short hair.

Roberto swallowed. Recalling how Mr. Davis had cried that night.

Gloria and Lydia said nothing. Marcos and his brother, Jesús, laughed at Roberto and said he had been picked out. He was next. Roberto looked down at the ground. Gloria didn't. She said it wasn't funny. It was awful. Mr. Davis was such a wonderful man, and she, Mrs. Davis, was a tramp.

She stood up and looked at her brothers and Roberto. "And if any one of you gets involved with her, then you're no good also!"

Marcos, the eldest, told her to hold her tongue. No one was getting involved with the woman, but ... if someone did, it was still not Gloria's business.

"Gloria," he then added, "I swear, you talk too much."

Roberto nodded.

"See," said Marcos. "He doesn't say anything, because he has manners, but ... he nods his head."

"Oh, you men! Why don't you all return to Mexico and suffocate in your *machismo* and double standards!"

And she went off, and Lydia laughed and stayed with Roberto. Her two older brothers were now telling Roberto about baseball. They no longer talked about Chávez and the daily newspapers. That only seemed to make them all very angry and divided in opinion. So they were now telling Roberto about all the money in baseball. He'd never heard of such a thing. He'd thought it was a game for little kids. At first, he wouldn't believe it. It didn't seem right. Money for a game? Marcos was telling Roberto that there was money, and that he, Marcos, was twenty-two and wished he could go to a college just so he could play. Marcos was very good, but then, on the other hand, many boys with more opportunity than he were very good. He needed a contact. Or maybe he'd try his hand at boxing also this winter. He was fast and had quick hands, and he could do good in just about any sport. He had been the champion in their old barrio in Fresno.

"Have you ever boxed?" he asked Roberto.

"No."

"Would you like me to teach you? We're just about the same weight. One-hundred-sixty, and then, when you get good enough, you can spar with me, and this winter I can go to Fresno, Sacramento, or San Jose and make some money boxing."

"Well ... " said Roberto. He didn't really want to. He had seen Marcos get mad in camp last month, and he beat a guy up very badly. He got mad too easily and became a big bully. "I don't know how ... you two, you and your brother, do it first and I'll watch. Okay?"

"Okay," said Marcos, and he leaped up and began jabbing lefts at his brother, who was twenty and tall and skinny.

Roberto watched them and rubbed his head and breathed. He'd been hiding out for two weeks now, and he was getting nervous. They all were. Only Luis and Aguilar were working, operating a spray rig way out in the back country away from Chávez and all this union mess. Aguilar was coughing a lot. Roberto felt edgy. He couldn't stand clowning around and losing valuable time. And also, he'd not gotten word from home for over one month now, and last week, with the help of Gloria, he'd sent a special-delivery letter. Certified and everything. He was very anxious. He'd made twenty-eight hundred dollars this year—after paying Aguilar his fourth—and he'd sent home a total of twenty-five hundred American dollars, and the last five hundred he'd sent for a down payment on a piece of land with an old house. Esperanza had sent a wonderful letter telling him that the litter of pigs had been born and their father was truly working hard and had picked out the old ranch in the canyon going out of town. That the house was in ruins, but their father, an excellent carpenter, could fix it up. He, Roberto, had sent the money, and ... they'd never written to him again.

The brothers now stopped boxing. Marcos had hit Jesús too hard and cut open his lip. Jesús was mad and wanted to really hit his brother. Marcos was saying no. It was better to stop now. That was their father's rule. If one got mad, he had to quit. No matter what. Jesús calmed down. Marcos came over and punched Roberto. Not really hitting him, but more like pushing him off the bench. Roberto fell on the ground. He leaped up reflexively. Marcos hit him. Hard. Gloria had come back out, waving an envelope, telling them to stop. Marcos was laughing and saying he was just teaching Roberto the art of self-defense. It looked like he truly needed it.

Roberto crouched, moved in, and hit Marcos in the stomach and dropped him. Marcos leaped up. Astonished. He rushed at Roberto. Swinging wild and savage. Roberto ducked, dodged, came in from the side, and dropped him again. Marcos couldn't believe it. No one had ever done this to him. He was a killer, a fighter, a boxer. He leaped up, bounced around, jabbed and jabbed, and hit Roberto in the face. Roberto took a few jabs, and his nose began to bleed, and he then walked in and hit Marcos so hard on the arms and ribs that Marcos dropped his arms.

"My God!" he yelled. "I'll kill you!" He raged into Roberto, slugging and kicking, and Roberto tried to keep away and not hit him so he would calm down. But still Marcos screamed. "I'll kill you! I'll kill you!" And finally he landed a good roundhouse, and Roberto dropped. "There!" he yelled. "And if you get up, I'll kill you again."

Roberto looked up at him and didn't know if he should laugh or not. It was all so ridiculous. This hitting at each other for no profit. So he, Roberto, shook his head and stayed knocked down, and then he heard ... Gloria was yelling at him.

"Shut up!" Gloria was yelling. "I have a special-delivery letter for Roberto from home. It must be important."

And she bent down to Roberto. She was very much concerned. Roberto saw ... and he took the letter. He began to open it. His hands began to tremble.

"Please," he said to Gloria, "read it to me. It's bad. I feel it."

Gloria took the letter. She sat down on the back steps of the deserted barracks. She opened it. Her eyes went large. Lydia took Roberto's hand. She too was concerned.

"Roberto," Gloria began reading the letter, "our father has been killed." Roberto stood up. "He was shot to death in the cantina last night. I want to explain to you everything before anyone else gives you false rumors.

"First of all, we did not buy a ranch." Roberto's facial muscles quivered. "We only bought a cow and a pig, and, as you can guess, the rest went into our father's drinking and night life. And last week, he sold the cow and pig to buy a gun and be like the other *norteños*. That is where the main trouble began, him trying to be a *norteño*, and bullying the town. Please, understand and forgive him, and also forgive me ... all the money you sent is gone." Roberto breathed. Lydia drew closer to him. It had become obvious in the last few days how much Lydia cared for Roberto. "I'm sorry, but being a girl and not a man made it very difficult for me." Gloria's eyes were watering. She could hardly go on with the letter. Lydia gripped Roberto's arm tightly. "I think you understand, and I hope and pray to God that you will forgive me, for truly, I did the best I could."

Gloria stopped. She could read no more. She turned to Roberto with tears in her eyes. "Oh, all you men are the same! And this sister of yours is so brave, and I don't care if all your money is lost. You better love her. I mean it!" She gave the letter to her sister. "Lydia, you finish it. I can't." And she began crying.

Lydia took the letter, brushed back her hair, and read on, and Esperanza said that their mother had given birth to a boy, a big healthy boy, and for him, Roberto, to please send some money for food. Immediately.

Roberto began to laugh. Gloria saw, and her eyes went large, and she jumped up. "Why do you laugh? You think her request is silly? You think women have a chance in Mexico?"

Roberto stopped laughing and eyed her. "No, I don't think my mother's request is silly. It's stupid! And impossible. Hell, I'm broke. Why did she have another child?"

"It takes two to have a child. Don't you dare blame her!"

"I didn't blame her."

"Yes, you did. You and your backward double standards are always blaming us women for everything."

Roberto paused ... then he glanced around at all of them. All were eyeing him strangely, except Lydia. He looked at her. "I sent them everything." And he began to laugh again, but he couldn't. So he stopped and went off alone.

He walked along inside the tall wire fence that enclosed the camp, and once he was far away, he gripped the fence and fell down crying. The night was approaching and the moon went behind the clouds. The summer was gone, the fall was ending, and winter was beginning. Someone spoke. He turned. It was Lydia. "Here," she said. "You forgot your letter."

He nodded.

"I finished reading it. Do you want me to tell you what else your sister said?"

"Yes. Please."

"Well ... " And she began to read in the dying light of the day, and Esperanza went on to say that she didn't want him, Roberto, to come home. To trust her judgment. That they, the family, were safe because the next oldest boy of their family was only twelve. That this stupid feud would surely die out if he and Aguilar didn't come home. That not even Pedro, who was now with the Reyes brothers, who had killed their father, dared intimidate or hurt a boy of twelve.

"Pedro?" said Roberto. And the word, "Pedro" rang in his head. He paused ... then, after a moment, Roberto trembled, his whole body shaking. Then it all passed, and he was cool and calm, as an icy smooth feeling came up into his gut. He stood up. He was set, and all of his present being was now *a la prueba*, at that place, that spot, where this needed cultural act was already committed, and the proof of this act of life, was now death. For birth a man cannot choose, but at death, the other side of the coin, man can choose, and gain. In style. So that makes death the best gift each man, individually, can give to himself. Alone. Privately. And well. And honor, this woman, will be upheld. Now and forever.

He swallowed. He turned and looked at Lydia full in the face, and she didn't shy away. She returned his look, and their eyes held, boy and girl, transcending, becoming man and woman. He reached for her hand. Her hand reached for his. And they touched. Breathing and looking and growing all warm inside. Time passed. Then someone was calling them to dinner. They, becoming self-conscious, smiled to each other and then went to the calling. For it was set. No words had been spoken, but it was as set as the mountain code of ethics unto death. As set as the idea that each girl brings her virginity to the bridal bed in proof of blood. As set as acts already committed in one's destiny. Religion, tradition, and life were all one and the same as they flowed in the veins and back to one's heart.

BOOK THREE

Now the volcano stood fifteen hundred feet, and it no longer gushed fire and lava. It only smoked ... giving witness as all other mountains to-be-spoken-to. Then man spoke, and the volcanic mountain moved.

Chávez was in jail and the Teamsters brought out old contracts, claiming to have had these contracts with growers for years. The judge told Chávez he must call his people off. His boycott was illegal, the workers had the Teamsters as their union.

But Chávez only laughed in the judge's face, stood up tall and said, "I've always been against violence. I'm a man of peace. But I say . . . boycott the hell out of them and their sweetheart contracts!" He was taken to jail.

Mrs. Kennedy, the widowed wife of Robert Kennedy, came through a crowd of name-cursing people to see Chávez. A Mass was held. The Salinas Valley was up in arms. At one point the growers claimed to be losing more than two hundred thousand dollars a day.

For the first time in years, illegal Mexicans were returning to Mexico on their own by the thousands. The whole U.S. of A. seemed to be afire, and California, which brags about moving more money in one year in the agribusiness than all it moved in the gold-rush years, was the main battleground. It was war . . . money, the American god, was at stake.

CHAPTER ONE

Gloria was crying. She was terrified and didn't want Roberto to go. Roberto said nothing. He was learning how to handle the U.S. .45 automatic that Marcos had gotten him in Sacramento.

"Please," said Gloria, "don't go. Surely your sister who lives there knows best, and she asked you not to come."

Roberto looked at Gloria, saw the desire in her eyes, but didn't know what to say, so he said, "You don't understand, and no words I say could ever make you understand."

"But Lydia does! Is that what you're saying?"

He breathed. "What I have with her, you leave out of this. Anyway, no, I don't believe she understands either, but at least she doesn't insult me with all this questioning."

"Oh, Roberto, listen to your own words. Listen to what you just said. You think I insult you because I ask you to question your system of values."

"Look," he said, feeling pushed at, "I don't understand you. All I know is that if I go down there all confused like you ... I'll get killed. I've got to go down there prepared, committed, and ready to act. Not hesitant with talk and thinking."

"Then, you really are going to take vengeance and endanger your sister and mother and ... Oh! I'm going to tell my father. I'll make them not let you go."

She jumped up to go to her father. Her father was with Luis and Aguilar. She asked them to stop Roberto. The men glanced at one another. Then Aguilar spoke first. He said Roberto was doing the right thing, and that he, Aguilar, would be going with him. So for her not to worry.

"Pedro has to be killed."

Luis wrinkled up his forehead and said, "I just don't know. It all seems so complicated. But certainly Roberto has to get his family out of that pueblo."

"Father," said Gloria. "I love him! Please, don't let him go!"

Her father drew her close and told her that Roberto was a man, and a man had to protect his home, and for her not to worry. He was no fool. He was strong and had a good head. He'd proved it this year in the fields and, *con el favor de Dios*, he'd return.

"No, he won't!" said Gloria. "Lydia will probably follow him down there, she's so stupid!"

"What?" asked her father. Truly astonished.

"You heard me," said Gloria, and she jumped up, calling them a bunch of backward beasts and saying that she hated them all for the way they stuck together and that she hated Roberto most of all. She would never marry a Mexican. And she ran off to Mr. Davis' house. Mrs. Davis was gone once more, and Gloria was keeping house for Mr. Davis after school.

Lydia was watching Roberto take the .45 apart, put it back together, and practice loading clips and taking quick aim.

"Roberto," she said.

He glanced up. She was wearing a rose-colored dress. He'd never seen her in a dress before. She looked very nice. Her long brown legs and long brown arms looked strong and shapely and healthy. And her waist, and her hips, and her breasts, and her face and teeth and those plump high cheeks that made her face look like a little rabbit's were so very lovely.

"I got you a present," she said.

He smiled. She was handing him a tiny square box. He took the box. He opened it. It contained a round medal and a silver chain.

"Saint Christopher," she said. "He'll protect you."

And, for the rest of his life, Roberto would never be able to explain it, but at that moment, in that simple gift, coming from one so young, so brave and forward, he was overwhelmed with ancient good feelings. He stood up, and they embraced for the first time, then kissed, and kissed again. His ears heard her say, "I love you. May I put Saint Christopher about your neck?" And he was breathtaken. So many happy feelings were rushing into him. He waited, not saying anything. He couldn't. He was so choked up. He sat down and extended the box to her. She took the medal and put it around his neck. Bending close, putting her breasts to his face, warm and good. She fastened the chain and stepped back. She smiled. He breathed, smelling her freshly soaped body. She sensed that, and kissed him, then began to dance. Laughing and turning. He moved to join her, but he dropped his .45. A loud heavy thud. He stopped. He looked down at the gun, then, after a moment, he picked it up, realizing his future once again, and so he went back to putting the big square weapon in his pants and practiced drawing it. Walking around in circles and trying to get used to the gun's feeling. He adjusted it a few times, and little by little it began to come out easily. She went away. He never noticed. He was completely absorbed with his loaded .45 against his groin. Feeling big, heavy, and awkward, as his body, step by step, grew more accustomed to its cold flat metal.

Two days later Roberto and Aguilar each carried loaded .45's by their groins, and they were ready to go south. So Roberto, asked Lydia's father if he would allow Lydia to walk in privacy with him for a little while. Quickly Lydia said yes, of course. Mr. Sánchez saw and nodded, and then said, "You wouldn't be asking her to go with you, would you?"

Roberto grew nervous. "Of course not. How could a man in my position ask such an outrageous thing?"

Mr. Sánchez nodded. "Good. I didn't think you were a man who took responsibility lightly. Yes, you may walk alone with my daughter. But not too far. I want you in seeing distance."

"Of course," said Roberto.

Cautiously they began walking off together, but then she took his hand and pulled him along in a brave defiant manner. They stopped under a tree by the heavy wire fence. They talked, saying nothing. They were that happy. Then he asked her the real question. He asked her to open her mouth so he could see her teeth. She laughed. She hit him playfully. And her dark eyes danced, twinkling like stars, and her face flushed red as she opened her mouth and smiled wide, happy, and healthy. He studied her teeth and nodded his approval, and she, knowing what this ceremony of the teeth meant, stuck out her tongue and slugged him in the stomach. He doubled over.

"There!" she said. "Can your stomach take that? Eh? My teeth are all in order, but how can a girl know if you, the man, can survive a lifetime of marriage with a woman with such teeth?"

He smiled and said, "Well, you know how it is with us mountain people. We're all healthy, so when we take a liking to a girl from the valley, we've got to check her teeth. After all, valley people have bad teeth and pass it on to the children. But you have no problems." He touched the loose ends of her long black hair. "Our children will be of the finest health. But please, no more joking. I would like for us to come to really know each other."

She blushed crimson, then coquettishly said, "Have you asked my father?"

He shook his head.

"Then how am I to know you're honorable?" And she touched his hip ever so lightly.

He felt the touch of her hand, brushing past his hip, and his heart leaped with love and wanting, but then, suddenly, fear came into him and he stopped ... feeling her touch but also feeling the .45 against his groin. "When I return, I'll ask. Honorably. To ask now, before I do what I am about to do, would be rash." He played with her hair quietly. Feeling it through his fingertips and bringing it to his lips, he kissed her hair. He was so uptight he was afraid ... for her, for himself, for the future. He stepped back. Quickly. And he was all alone.

And now, as he and Aguilar traveled south to Mexico on the bus, Roberto fingered the lock of Lydia's hair. She had cut off six inches of hair, tied a pink ribbon around it, and said she'd wait as he'd asked, and not follow him, but only for as long as it took that hair to grow back. And for him to hurry, for her health was excellent, her hair grew quickly, and her desires were strong.

He and Aguilar were soon in Mexicali, across the line, and trying to decide whether to take the bus or the train to Guadalajara. They were concerned about the inspection stops, the cost, the time element, but most of all the inspections, for they were carrying guns, and guns, especially .45's, were illegal. They finally decided to go by bus. It was more expensive but twice as fast. It took only forty-some hours on a straight-through first-class *camión*, and there were only two or three inspection stops. They bought bus tickets. The price was less than eighteen American dollars. From Stockton to Calexico had been $17.78 plus tax. And these Mexican tickets would take them more than fifteen hundred miles into Mexico, almost three times as far as their American tickets had taken them.

They boarded the first-class bus. It was advertised as air--conditioned. They went toward the back and sat down by the emergency exit. The bus was hot. The air-conditioning didn't work. They began traveling fast. There were two drivers on the *camión*. They took turns, one driving while the other slept. They were both fat with wide butts. Roberto looked out his window and said nothing. He'd been very quiet since he'd gotten the letter, and then, after buying the gun, he'd become completely distant. Like all alone. Somewhere else. And heavy. Only Lydia and her laughter had drawn him away from this heavy feeling.

Aguilar brought out a small bottle of mezcal with a worm in it. The worm was fat and short, and it lay at the bottom of the bottle. At the top of the bottle, tied around the mouth, was a small red sack. Aguilar opened the sack, poured a little of its white-brown salt-chile on the back of his hand, and offered the sack to Roberto. Roberto saw, breathed, and did the same. Aguilar tipped the bottle, sipping and causing the fat brown worm to float up and down in the bottle. He exhaled, smacked his lips, licked the mixture of salt and chile, and sighed in a good hot feeling of relief. Roberto followed him, and the worm came down near his mouth but then bounced back down in the bottle. Aguilar watched and truly knew what the worm meant in the mezcal. The fat worm came from the agave plant, a type of cactus, and the worm was charcoaled and put in the bottle for flavoring, and the worm was the highest joke of the Mexican people. It showed the comedy of life. It showed to one, with each sip, what one truly would come to ... a worm. Nothing more. After death, no matter how expensively one was buried, one still went to the worms.

Aguilar nodded. A quiet smile. Pedro, or he, Aguilar, would soon be with the worms. He coughed. He had worked on a spray rig for a few weeks and he was once again coughing badly. It only seemed to take a little exposure to chemicals and it was all reactivated in him. He brought out a big red handkerchief. Between coughs he glanced at this boy, Roberto, who sat so upright beside him. If only he had had a son. He sighed deeply. He began to speak. But his words were stopped in a convulsion of coughing.

The bus stopped. They were at Sonorita. The main inspection stop. Juan Aguilar never got to say what he had to say. They all had to get out of the bus and have their luggage searched. Aguilar watched the federal inspectors in uniform and tried to figure their money and the price he should bribe them with. He and Roberto got way back in the line. He wanted the inspectors to tire, get bored, and then he'd offer them just a little. For, if he offered too large a *mordida*, they'd get suspicious. When their turn came, Aguilar offered the inspector an American cigarette. The inspector stopped, looked at Aguilar, and smiled. Aguilar lit the inspector's cigarette. The short fat inspector thanked Aguilar and asked if he, a gentleman, had any more American cigarettes? Could he spare a few packs? Aguilar acted like it hurt, like it pinched him close, but then he smiled and gave the man two packs. The inspector said fine, thank you, and that was that. Aguilar and Roberto went back on the *camión*, and two more times they were inspected before they got to Guadalajara.

At Guadalajara they boarded a country bus and went southeast on the road that went to Lake Chapala, Zamora, Morelia, and ultimately to Mexico City. But they didn't go that far. They were on a country bus, and it stopped off at all the small towns, and they got off before reaching Morelia. Near Caropan. They tried to hire a truck to take them into the mountains. They found one which would take them by the tourist places, around the experimental ground, and to the first river crossing. They made the deal. They boarded the truck, and Roberto looked out at the country. They were now past the tourist places and going up the valley toward his home, but he felt nothing. *Nada.* No joy. All was deadly still within him. But then, when they went by the experimental grounds with the wire gates and uniformed guards and he saw the big round buildings like balloons of bright colors on the hill with a forest of posts and lights and lines; he felt a chill go up and down his spine. It all seemed so unreal. Then, to add to his feeling, here by the road, which now turned from blacktop to dirt, was a team of oxen with men working them. Oxen, here at the foot of this hill of super-modern experiments? Was this possible? And Roberto paused ... feeling anger. What was all this? A joke?

At the bridge the truck driver stopped. He would not cross. That bridge was old and more than a hundred feet long and had only two old wood beams for each tire to ride on—like the rails of a train—and he wouldn't cross. The *barranca* it bridged was bottomless. Roberto spat at the bridge. Another joke, and he was sick of jokes. What was all this? Hell, he'd been to a world where there were freeways and cars, rich fields and plenty of water, lots of work and unlimited money, and here, his people were like from another century. Oxen working alongside a mountain of power. A bridge that a truck driver was afraid to cross. He yelled and kicked at the bridge and walked on one of the twelve-by-twelve beams as down below the river twisted and roared and he saw ... the river was a weird green plastic-like color. And over there was a pipe pouring out thick green fluid. He raged. What were they doing? Poisoning his people? He crossed the bridge quickly.

And that evening he and Aguilar came walking into town along the road lined by rich mesquite trees. Three bottles of tequila in two days were under their belts, and all they'd eaten were the charcoaled worms; they were hungry. Starved! And in much need of Pedro's blood. The noseless bastard whom Roberto had failed to kill, because he, Roberto, was a good guy, and the bastard had come home and avenged himself on his father.

They came walking into town and stopped ... the pueblo had lights. Electric lights. No kidding. There were lights in the plaza. Naked light bulbs up on four-by-four posts on each corner of the plaza, and over there, the Holy Catholic Church was all lit up. Lights were everywhere about the holy sacred church. Roberto and Aguilar looked at each other, said nothing, and went on, and over there on the other side of the plaza was another lit-up building. It was the cantina. Of course, naturally! All the lights should go to the church and the cantina. Then they heard music playing loudly. Good music. Not local *mariachis*.

"Well," said Aguilar, "it looks like they have electricity here, and now they have a music box." He laughed. He brought out a cigar and struck a big Mexican match. "How do you feel?"

Roberto unbuttoned his Levi's jacket. He was the first *norteño* ever to return without a fancy suede jacket. Also he wore no holster for his .45 automatic. He carried his .45 in his pants, handle up over his wide belt, pitched at an angle so he could cross-draw with his right hand.

"Nervous," said Roberto. "Very, very nervous." He opened and closed his right hand.

"Well, that could be bad, but ... " Aguilar smoked his cigar. " ... knowing you, I believe it will prove to be good. Remember, Pedro is mine." And Juan smiled that smile that he had smiled at the attorneys before the mob had killed them.

But this time Roberto didn't tremble. He was there, all present, in this same time and place, all *a la prueba*, and that was that, so he said, "No, *compadre*, Pedro is mine."

"Oh?" said Aguilar. "You think so?"

"No, I don't think so ... I know."

"Oh," said Aguilar, using an entirely different type of "oh." "Well, then, that being the case, allow me to talk to him privately before you take him. He is an old friend of mine. Truly, I owe him this. I want to explain to him why he must die."

"Okay," said Roberto.

"Good," said Aguilar.

And so they walked by the church, across the plaza, and to the cantina. One man, tall and wearing a suede jacket, and a big Texan hat, a *tejana.* And the other man, nineteen years old, wearing a cheap Mexican hat and dressed in pure Levi's. They both wore western boots. They both walked straight and upright but so easy-like. Aguilar walked in the front door. He stood there. Boss. Solid. And terrible. Men saw him, saw his cigar and gun, and the gun was already cocked, just waiting in its holster. Some men smiled, some said hello, and other men stood up quickly to go out the back door.

Pedro was not to be seen.

The back door slammed shut. Moving men stopped in their tracks. And there stood a young man dressed in dark new Levi's, and in his hand was a .45 automatic. Cocked and ready. Then those who knew him saw it was Roberto. But he was bigger, he had put on weight around the neck, and his eyes were not the eyes of the boy Roberto.

"*¡Hola!*" yelled Aguilar. Eyes turned back to him. Pedro was nowhere in the room, and none of the Reyes brothers were in the place either. "How are you all? Eh? Let's have a drink. I buy! And then you can tell me where the rest of my old friends are. Pedro, my oldest and best friend, I haven't seen him in almost a year. And the Reyes brothers, where are they all?" One old man began to leave. "Hey! You can't leave!" The man froze. Carved in motion. "Don't you know the way to treat a long-lost friend who's just offered to buy you a drink?" Aguilar came forward, laughing. "You drink. You toast to friendship, honor and respect." Aguilar, the eagle trainer, as his name meant, was now up close to the old man. The man was dressed in white peasant clothes made of coarse cotton sack. He was terrified. Aguilar, the eagle boss, put his arm around him. "Come and drink, *amigo.*"

"Please," pleaded the old man. "I don't wish to get involved."

"Involved?" asked Aguilar very grandly. "Involved in what?"

"I swear!" yelled the old man. "I don't know nothing, and I get confused with that! Please, I wish to go home.."

Roberto heard the man and put his gun away in his belt. This old man was as poor and humble-looking as his father had been.

"*¡Camaradas!*" said Roberto, and came in, walking away from the back door. "You all know me. You all know I've been an honest workman all my life. Come, please, and join us in a drink, but . . . if you don't wish to, then go. You are free men to do whatever you wish."

Men raced to the doors. Roberto was astonished. He'd spoken so sincerely, and yet here they were rushing past him in escape. Moments later he and Aguilar were all alone. Aguilar was turning over the tables to see how they were made. Finally he found an old one made of heavy oak, and he said, "Boy, you are going to get us killed yet. First you bite off his nose and let him live, and now you send the whole town to warn him so they can become his men."

"His men? But these people hardly know him. He was not born here. I was. They are my people."

"Your people, bull! You've gone north, you've returned with health and money. You are the big bad stranger now."

"Me? A bad stranger? That can't be."

"Bullshit! These small towns, I swear, they're only good for vacationing in. They're so full of fear and jealousy that they're diseased and get worse every year. Help me move this table." They took the table to the wall near the back door, and they sat down with their backs to the wall. Now they were good, and Aguilar brought out a pack of cards and called for the bartender to bring down two beers. He smoked and dealt and said, "Give them electricity, cars, planes, but these backward people are the same. They stay here ... scared. Holding on to their ancestors' assholes! Sucking prejudice and stupidity! Your turn. Deal the cards."

And so the die was cast. The town had gone to warn Pedro and to stick by his side. For whatever he had done, he, Pedro, still lived here and he was one of them now, in the present, and he needed help. These were *norteños*, men of the U.S., and their guns were new, well-oiled, and they were a foreign element to their little pueblo.

That night Pedro didn't come to the cantina, so Aguilar and Roberto—sipping beer very carefully so they would not get drunk—had the barman close the place down and fix them something to eat. First came *menudo*, then *frijoles* and some *carne asada* and tortillas, then a Mexican brandy and coffee. Roberto stood up. He wanted to go home and see his mother and family. Aguilar said no.

"You'd never make it home. They'd ambush you in the dark."

"Think so?" And Roberto wandered over toward the front door. This was his hometown. Aguilar was exaggerating. "I think everyone's in bed asleep."

"Keep away from that door," said Aguilar. "The lights ... "

But Aguilar didn't get to finish his words. Fire flashed. A white form ran in the trees across the street in the plaza. A *retrocarga* roared. Roberto dropped, drawing his .45, as pebbles from the homemade shotgun rang everywhere.

"Turn off the lights," yelled Aguilar.

The bartender turned off the lights. Moments passed. More moments passed. All was quiet. Aguilar told the barman to get them some blankets so they could sleep there. The bartender-owner didn't like it. Aguilar told him not to be afraid. Tomorrow he could tell the town he had been forced to give them shelter. The barman nodded, gave them blankets, and went home. Aguilar told Roberto to help him set tables by the doors.

This would be a long night ... the town was set.

The mountain feud was *a la prueba.*

Unto death.

Code of the mountains. Mexican style. And honor, she, this most precious of virgins, would be kept alive by him, *a lo macho.*

In Mexico, Chávez was a hero to the students and intellectuals, but to most of the workers he was not well thought of. Not only was he stopping so many Mexicans from earning money in los Estados Unidos *so they could bring it home to Mexico—where a strong middle class was arising because of these tens of millions of dollars—but also he was not* un macho. *No, he didn't drink or swear or have beautiful women pulling at his pants. And any man who didn't have these qualities of* bravura *was not to be respected a lo macho but instead to be ridiculed and pushed off the sidewalk of life. For to be a real man was to be a* macho *with tanates, and an hombre with tanates can be killed but never defeated. For he is his own god. Here. On earth.*

So Chávez, who talked softly and didn't drink, who preached nonviolence, and had no women pulling at his pants but instead had a lady, a female, as his second in charge, was not very well thought of in many parts of Mexico. No, he was ridiculed, despised, and pushed into that realm of other great men who'd been despised and ridiculed—Lincoln, Juárez, Kennedy, King. And, of course, your own true-self, if you've been good enough to have developed enemies. Especially spiritual ones. For no man or woman is worth their salt here on earth unless they have people who despise them and, hence, have proven to the world that he or she, indeed, stands for something. Down deep inside and real.

CHAPTER TWO

Nothing more happened that night, and the next day, with the sun high and women and children up and about, Roberto and Aguilar came out of the cantina. It was daylight now, and the chances of ambush were very far between. For the mountain code is like an honorable duel, and an ambush happens only at night. For in the day there would be witnesses, and witnesses would tell the truth and the dishonorable ambushers would be ridiculed and shamed out of town.

Now it was daylight, and Pedro and the Reyes brothers would have to present themselves face-to-face, and so Aguilar felt good, solid, and boss, and he and Roberto now walked the streets upright, out in the open for all to see, and all eyes watched. Everyone knew everything. And in some eyes there was fear, in others there was admiration, and in the children's eyes there was wonder.

Aguilar bought some candy and gave it to a group of playing children. The children were as cautious as deer at hunting season.

Roberto swallowed. And shook his head. This was all no good, and yet ... he had to do what he was about. At home Roberto found his mother with his brother of twelve, Juanito, who'd had his head cut open, the result of a rock fight with the youngest of the Reyes brothers. Roberto watched quietly as his mother attended to Juanito's wound. Then he asked about his father's death. Esperanza told him that three of the Reyes brothers, along with Pedro, had pressured his father into betting big money at a cock fight. Then they had lost but wouldn't pay his father, and their father, wanting to be a man of ethics, had bought a gun and tried to make them pay so he could keep face among men of honor. But he had been scared. So he had gotten very drunk before going after them, and they had then laughed at him, joked at him, ridiculed him, and when he had drawn his gun and shot and missed, they killed him.

Pedro alone had shot him five times right in the face. He, Pedro, was a no-nosed monster. It made one's hair stand on end just to see him.

Roberto nodded, and after a while his wild heart went calm. So still it hardly beat. His decision was made; and Pedro was dead. Dead and buried. He breathed ... and petted the one-eyed horse.

Esperanza was filling him in on the town's news. Since the town had electricity, once a week a big truck came to the corrals of Don Carlos Villanueva—Esperanza never called him Don Skinny—and put up a big white canvas. Then, as the night came on they'd let people inside the corral for a few *centavos*, and showed movies, and the people would all sit down on the ground or on a blanket and watch.

"Oh! There's such a lot of world out there! I've seen newsreels of Europe, of Spain, of Mexico City, and yes, one of the United States."

Then she told Roberto that some families had radios now. Not many families, but a few. That their own father had bought one even before the electricity came in, but then he'd sold it at a ridiculous loss before they'd even heard it once. She stopped talking. She hung her head.

"Oh, God!" she finally said. "You sent us so much money, and things were truly going well. Papá was working, helping, and not drinking ... " She began crying huge tears. Roberto stopped petting the horse and looked at his sister. " ... then came that Pedro, and he began baiting Papá. And poor Papá was so afraid that he began to drink. Getting real drunk and then coming home and beating us. Then he would order me to write you another letter, a letter that we were going to buy a ranch and that he was not drinking.

"Once, when I stood up to him and called him a coward and said he could have no more money, he began to beat me as he had never done before. Truly, I still have the marks. Look." She lifted her dress. Roberto looked but didn't really want to. He'd never seen his sister's body before. Brothers and sisters, fathers and daughters, were never to see each other after the proper age of eleven. He blushed. She talked on. "But you know ... the blows didn't hurt so much. I just closed my mind and held so mad that I felt nothing, and then screamed so loudly and asked him why. 'Why are you not a man, Papá? Ah?' And he stopped in fright." She lowered her dress, and she laughed. "Like a bad little boy he looked for a moment." She ceased her laughter. "Then he began to cry ... disgustingly. The poor, poor man, rest his soul. But I can feel no compassion, I must confess. I was sick of him. Truly sick of him and all this *machismo*. Do you see what I mean? Ah? Do you understand? Truly, our father asked for it. He was as much to blame as they." She drew close to her brother. "Roberto," she said, "I don't want you proving your manhood to the town. You are above that. I want you to think of the future, and I want you to leave. Now. Today. You don't need to avenge our father. You need to take Juanito and leave immediately."

Roberto continued to pet the one-eyed horse. The horse had been his father's. And Pedro had shot his father five times in the face, and it had been his, Roberto's, fault. He should have killed Pedro that day in the desert, and he had not done so, and ... custom was destiny, and yes, he'd see destiny done this time. Truly. As all was written in the stars above. He'd failed, and he'd make it right now.

"Roberto, you're not listening."

"I can't listen to you," he said.

"Yes, you can," she ordered. "You've got two legs, you can leave right now."

"Look," he said. "I'm a man, not a woman, and I must do what a man knows he must do."

"Oh?" And it was one of the finest of 'ohs.' "And a man, what must he do? Eh? Do as all other men do?"

"Esperanza, no more. You are a woman and don't understand. You're all mixed up with books. Like Gloria, the older sister I told you about." He tapped his gut. "The real truth is here. Swelling up, reaching to the heart from Papa, from our grandfather, from our great-grandfather, and it must not be forgotten." He swallowed.

"Ha! I spit on those words. Leave our ancestry out of it. And I say you lie!" Roberto flinched. He eyed his sister. He hadn't lied. And how could he leave his ancient bloodlines out of it? She was being too high and untrue. She and Gloria were so much alike. No wonder he instinctively felt more trust with Lydia. "I saw you go against custom and throw out your *compadre*. I saw you become a foreman and not ever lower yourself to this small town's gossip and rumor. I say you are a conceited liar and have come home to prove your own manhood and not accept the fact ... " Roberto raised his hand to slap his sister. She screamed. "Go ahead and slap me! I'm not afraid. I'm willing to admit the truth. Our father was a coward! We were sired by a nothing! Hit me! Hit me! I'll not shut up! For truly, in my heart, I do believe ... " And he lowered his hand and walked away. Heavy. Confused. Very divided. And ... the phrase, "For truly, in my heart, I do believe" rang in his mind, and he suddenly recalled in a flash, like a picture, the girl on the van at the strike in the U.S. and ... and ... and he breathed ... not knowing. Not knowing. And this state of not knowing hung heavy. There ... all alone. As ancient territorial warnings arose in his veins, and for a split-instant he knew in his mind that his sister was indeed correct, and yet ... in his pounding heart ran a blood of ancient custom, and he knew to the bone of his soul that Pedro had to die. Die! Yes.

But from the distance, his sister continued yelling, "You fool! You are no better than they. All you men are so stupid and stubborn! Always needing to prove your *machismo*! I swear, I'm not staying. I'm leaving myself. I'm going to go to Guadalajara and work to get money so I can go to Tijuana and pay an agency to get me work in *los Estados Unidos*.

"In La Jolla. There, even a servant lives clean and decent and makes big money. I know all about it, and I've made up my mind. I'm going! And I'd rather die than marry a Mexican!"

He looked at her, and she was going off to the house in long swift movements. He shook his head. These girls nowadays were such outspoken bitches. They were not like the good girls of his mother's day. They were so demanding and stubborn. He breathed deeply. He had to get back to his thinking about the situation at hand. He couldn't allow his sister to confuse him. He went back to the one-eyed horse and began to pet him. Later, all-together once again, he went to the house, and Aguilar was under the lean-to of the kitchen, smoking a cigar, and talking to his mother. Dinner was almost ready. Roberto called Aguilar to please come with him to a respectful distance away from the women. He had to talk privately. Aguilar saw the boy's eyes and came away.

"Aguilar," said Roberto. "I got a plan. How much money you got?"

"Enough."

Roberto nodded. "Okay, then let us have a horse race. Let us go to Don Carlos and get him to set up his famous mare against the champion Charro Diablo. There's always been bad blood between the Reyes and my old boss. And with a horse race, Pedro and the Reyes will—"

"—have to come to us. Not us go to them." Aguilar smiled. Happily. "Good thinking. Let us go now. Before dark. Quickly. We'll get the word going, and by tomorrow—" Aguilar smoked, thumbs in his gunbelt, and he rocked back and forth on the balls of his western boots. "—We'll have the sweet blood of revenge for the sauce of the horse race. Let's go. We don't want to be out after dark."

And so they went afoot out to Don Skinny's place, and all the while Aguilar talked with *gusto*, but Roberto couldn't join Aguilar's happiness. In his mind he was with his sister and Gloria and Lydia, and he felt heavy in his heart. All alone. And very divided, and he got to hating this division within himself.

Chávez was out of jail for the time being, and time, the Father, was ticking on in his weird cancerous way and saying, "There is a time to live and a time to die, there is a time for peace and a time for war; there is a time to create, protest, and go off to jail happily." You know, all that Biblical stuff. So to make it short, there is and will always be plenty of time for everything as we all go dancing, singing, reaching into our own timelessness. Or . . . how was your shit this morning? Did you eat good stuff for the makings?

Why not? You really are what you eat. You really are what you think. You really are what music you listen to, what vision you have, what value you give yourself. So do it, take in good stuff and shit out your own self, true hero.

CHAPTER THREE

The die was cast. The time was appointed. The duel of horses was tomorrow, at sunrise, and so now there would be no more ambushes. Everyone knew about the duel of horses, and no one would allow a Reyes, or Pedro, to cheat them out of the pleasure of a first-rate show unto death.

Now it was the late afternoon, and Roberto and Aguilar were with *el Don*, Señor Villanueva, and they were out in the stable of his great mare, La Niña Linda. The stall was well built. No wind or rain touched this beautiful bay mare. She was the most expensive and prized possession of *el Don*. He had brought her from Arizona. She was of the finest quarterhorse blood, and he, Villanueva, would sacrifice much to keep her housed like a jewel. So, like a ruby in a velvet jewel box, he kept her stalled. He now petted her and checked her feet and felt her legs and petted her strongly muscled rump and said, "We will win the race." He breathed. "The Charro Diablo is a magnificent stud, but they overfeed him and breed too many mares with him." He turned to Roberto and Aguilar and to the old man, Antonio, the owner of the farting mule. "And my Niña Linda has never had a stud, and her innocence will put her mind and soul entirely on the racing." He smiled and looked at the mare's huge dark eyes. She was nervous. He calmly stroked her. "She is a fine young lady of the highest breeding, and in her soul . . . she is a winner, and later, when I start breeding her, she'll give colts as these mountainous lands have never seen." He kissed her. "Won't you, my lovely daughter?"

She snorted. Calmly. Lovingly. And he, *el Don*, then gave orders to his wrangler not to feed her much. Keep her stomach light. And spend the night here by the stall talking to her kindly.

The wrangler, a true lover of horses, said, "Of course. Nowhere on earth would I rather be this night."

El Don and the others went out of the horse stall, by *el Don*'s house, which was a good big house but ... it was not as good inside as the mare's stall. Villanueva and Roberto and Aguilar mounted horses. Not great ones, but not bad ones either. And Antonio mounted his white mule and they rode toward town two kilometers away. And a short distance from *el Don*'s house they came across his old Chevy. In the last rain the Chevy had got stuck in this rut and *el Don* had simply left the car there. They stopped by the car. The horses sniffed at it cautiously. *El Don* said, "Cars, I was foolish to have brought one out here. A thing should be kept with its own. A car needs good roads." He reached in his breast pocket. "Here, care for a cigar?" Aguilar took one. Roberto nodded and took one also. "Tell me, Roberto, after this thing is over, will you return to the United States?"

Roberto nodded. "Yes. I think so."

"Oh," said *el Don*, moving his horse away from the dead vehicle, "you think you've seen so much, learned so much, that you cannot return home to your village?"

Roberto moved his horse and began to speak when Villanueva cut him short.

"Listen!" said his old boss in a commanding tone. "How are we to progress, here in your homeland, if the best of you keep going north? Ah, you answer that. But no, not to me, to yourself. And while you think that over, keep in mind that in the last year some of us townsmen have organized and brought in electricity. And we now have plans of tractors and machinery, but where are our best young men to encourage us, to give us a real sense of the future? Ah, you tell me." And he spurned his horse away into a graceful canter.

The evening was spent in talking, drinking, and arguing out the details of the duel. This evening was a time that the village had been awaiting for years. This evening, all men who had the spirit of God would not labor. All men would do time of leisure and give witness to the setting sun and the approach of the mystic night. This evening no women would be among men. Roberto and his group were now entering the town and Villanueva was ready to deposit his bet. Aguilar had put up half of the money, five hundred American dollars. The Reyes, a powerful but not too rich family, had been trying to make this race with *el Don* for more than two years, but he had always declined. Very politely. Always saying that the time would come. Now the time had come, and Pablo, the eldest of the Reyes, had sent word to *el Don* that his family would bet a hillside of land on their Charro Diablo. *El Don* had sent word that they should meet at the cantina across from the plaza to work out the details. In public. Before men of honor. Pablo agreed and Villanueva now rode into town with Aguilar at his side and Antonio and Roberto behind. Roberto was silent. He was thinking of *el Don*'s words, of the words of the three young women who were so influencing his life. Hell, all these men were talking of the duel of horses, and the money, and the code of honor, and no one mentioned the blood, the vengeance, the deaths that were to come. Roberto rubbed his head. His head truly pained, and in that split-moment of pain, he saw why men kept the realities away by calling them justice and honor. His bowels moved. He didn't want to play these games. He wanted to kill quickly and get the hell out of town. How could *el Don* be so naïve as to ask him to stay? Aguilar was right. These small towns were only good for vacationing.

They were in town now. There were many horses tied up under trees in the plaza. They dismounted and went into the cantina, and there was Pablo, and he was stout and dressed in a *charro* outfit. He had one brother with him. The one called Jesús. And Jesús was lean and lanky, and he owned several deaths, but not all justly. He was a man of ill-fame. He was dull in the eyes and crazy enough to do anything Pablo asked of him. Roberto blinked nervously, and his jaws quivered. Were these the ones who had killed his father? Where was Pedro? Oh, these Reyes were doing this game of customs very well. Pedro and the murderers had probably been left at home. There would be no blood this evening. Just talk and drinking and *gusto a lo pendejo*.

Quickly, all the men in the bar took note, but did not shy away. Now they too were prepared inside their very souls, and so they either moved aside, or over by the Reyes, or saluted Villanueva, Roberto, Aguilar, and Antonio, and moved close. They were set, and the village was alive. The ancient beast of man had arisen, and tonight was a time of fiesta. Tomorrow would be the time for *un desmadre a todo dar para gallos de estaca! ¡Con tanates a la prueba!*

And so, in this spirit, *el Don* offered to buy drinks, and men moved up quickly and soon the cantina was alive with laughter and *gusto* and ... death—the father—was here close to life, the mother, as each man's very soul trembled with an almost religious longing of fulfillment.

Soon Roberto and his group were not alone. It seemed the town respected Roberto's gesture of the horse race, and many were coming over to his side. He was not like his father. He was an open soul of a man. He was *un macho.* Sure, they hated his gringo money and his gringo ways, but hell, they could forgive him, for he had caused the creation of this horse race. He was respectful of old customs. He'd included everyone in his rightful want of vengeance. So of course, they'd back him. He was not like his father.

Roberto swallowed. He knew they were trying to compliment him, but if another son-of-a-bitch said something bad about his father, he didn't know if he could take it. But many more things were said, and he took them.

Then it was daybreak, and the first rosy light of dawn began combing, like fingers, into the valley.

Villanueva drank his last drink, shook hands with Pablo, the boss of his enemies, and said, "I'm going home to eat and get my Niña Linda. I'll meet you at the *carril* in an hour."

Roberto and many others accompanied him outside. He mounted his horse, and Antonio mounted his white mule. *El Don* then looked at Roberto for a long, long time.

"*Hijo,*" he said to Roberto, "after this is all over, do you think you'll still be leaving?"

Roberto licked his lips, thought, and then said, "Yes."

"Oh, well, it's probably best. If I were young, I'd most likely do the same." He breathed, looking across the plaza toward the church and the rosy sky of the dawn. "These towns, these customs of ours ... " He shook his head. "In my head I realize they are stupid, but in my heart I still see them as beautiful." He licked his lips. He was tipsy, but he held himself well. Mounted on his horse and wearing a large sombrero like a *charro.* "But these codes are our way, and even though I've traveled and seen better, I still live here, in my gut, the soul." He glanced at Aguilar. "*Amigo,* you know what I mean? The soul, that is life."

Aguilar removed his cigar. "Yes. It is."

El Don started to smile but began to cough.

Antonio came up on his white mule. "Let's go home and rest for the race." *El Don* turned his horse as told. Antonio called to Roberto and Aguilar as he moved off. "You two had best get home too. This is a heavy time." He spurred his mule, and the mule farted and galloped off, hooves echoing on cobblestones.

"Well," said Roberto, "should we go home and eat?"

Aguilar began to answer, but someone yelled.

"Oh, no!" It was Pablo. "Come and drink. We're not old like those two. Come! We'll stay drinking and talking and get to know each other ... " He smiled. "I would like to know this man Aguilar better. I would like to know what kind of man it is that shoots boys!" He, Pablo, was at the door of the cantina, and he had a bottle in his hand. Jesús, of lightning speed, was to his side in the shade, and his body was a dark, meaningful shadow. "Come! We drink! Man-to-man, *¡a lo macho!*"

Roberto looked at Aguilar, and Aguilar was not moving, and he, Roberto, felt sickish pain in his gut. Then, all at once, he knew why Aguilar was not moving and why Jesús was in the shadows. There were footsteps running lightly on the cobblestones in the plaza behind him. He stood still, knowing these steps were for him. It had to be Pedro. So he turned. Jacket open, .45 waiting. Then he saw his sister, Esperanza, and his whole world moved. No woman should be here. He rushed at his sister.

"What are you doing here?" he demanded. "This is no place for a woman. Get home!"

"No!" she yelled, and she held her ground.

Men laughed. The Reyes began sing-songing sounds of ridicule.

Roberto gripped his sister and tried escorting her back across the plaza toward the church, but it wasn't easy. She was putting up a struggle, until, suddenly, she froze. Eyes huge.

Roberto stopped. He saw her looking over his shoulder in awful fear. And he knew. He could feel it. So, slowly, he pushed Esperanza away and then turned, and there was Pedro, and he was on horseback. Under a dark tree. With two other Reyes, and he was smiling. And when he laughed, one could see through his torn-out nose and into his very skull.

Roberto swallowed, then glanced around and saw that men were coming from everywhere, and they were as happy and nervous as men at a cock fight.

Roberto took up ground.

Esperanza screamed, rushing in front of her brother.

Pedro laughed and calmly swung his far leg over the saddle horn, and now he was one well-built Indian ready to leap, but, oh, his face looked monstrous.

Roberto tried to knock his sister aside. She wouldn't let herself be knocked away. Men were laughing. Pablo and the other Reyes moved over by Pedro. Roberto still couldn't handle his sister. Pedro's monstrous face was gleeful. But ... then came Aguilar.

And he, Juan Aguilar, took up ground in front of Roberto and Esperanza, and he was boss. Terrible.

People quieted down, and Roberto, desperately, now slapped his sister. Hard. And threw her away.

"*Amigo*," Aguilar was saying to Pedro as Roberto came up by him. "I've been looking for you. Where have you been?" Pedro smiled, and his no-nosed face twisted in an awful mess. "Ah? Is this the way to treat a *compadre*?"

"Oh," said Pedro, "maybe not. But I've been busy. You know how it is." He shrugged, glancing at Roberto and then over to Esperanza, who was being held by two men. He laughed. "But I'm here now. So ... surely, we can make up for any lost time." He turned, whirling to the ground, and he was upright. Solid. And all lethal Indian. Hearts stopped, and one could see that he was armed with gun and knife in the traditional style. "How do you want it? Eh? I don't give a shit. All I know is I want that boy's face!" He spat. He raged. Mad in the eyes. And he looked insane.

"No!" screamed Esperanza. But Roberto wasn't hearing her or anyone else. He was all here. Undivided and complete.

"With you or without you," Pedro was saying to Aguilar. "But I was hoping you'd be with me ... .I'd hate to have to kill a dear old friend." The battleground was now cleared. Esperanza and the horses were moved away. "Eh, *compadre*? My dear friend of so many years of struggling north ... are you going to step away so this boy and I can get on with it?" He drew his knife. "I'm going to skin him alive. That knife fight of Empalme is going to seem like child's play. Give him your knife. Now! *¡Pronto!*"

Esperanza was down on her knees. Begging to God.

"No," said Aguilar, and smoked his cigar. Calmly. "No knives. This is not a game. This is not a sport of bravery. This is an ethical thing of right and wrong." He took a step toward Pedro. The Reyes brothers held their ground. They really were with Pedro.

Pedro roared. "Step aside! I want his face!"

"*Amigo*," said Aguilar, "*por favor*, you two can go at it afterward. But first, you and I must talk privately."

"No," said Roberto from behind Aguilar. "There is no need for you two to talk first." He moved to the side away from Aguilar. His jacket was open. His gun was ready. All eyes were upon him. "I will not fight him."

Pedro was in a crouched position, ready to go *a la prueba* with his knife, and his no-nosed face was a sight to see. He bellowed. "Why not? Are you a coward like your father!"

Roberto held.

Pedro laughed. "A filthy coward!" He glanced at Esperanza. "And your sister is a whore!"

Roberto flinched. Trembling still like a hummingbird in midair. But he did not move.

Pedro roared with *gusto.* "Your father deserved to die! He was a coward and his balls were so diseased that all he sired were whores and cowards!"

Roberto stepped forward. "Listen, you thing, I will not be provoked! For to kill you would be the kindest act a man could do. You want to live! You're a monster. Ugly in face and soul. So I will not kill you. I want you to live and hate yourself to damnation!"

Aguilar rolled his cigar about in his mouth, withholding a smile, and stepped away. Good tactics, he figured. The finest of revenge. Roberto was going to make this man crawl and truly understand why he must die.

Pedro screamed. "You are gutless! You are a woman! And your sister *es una puta! ¡Putísima!* The greatest of whores!" He spat, twisting his face in an ugly, awful mess.

Roberto jerked upright. And all around one could hear whispering. People were asking if Pedro was not indeed right? Was Roberto a woman? For how could any real man allow someone to speak like this of the women in his household and not fight?

Roberto held. Heavy. And said, "*¡Hacerle caso a pendejos es engrandecerlos!* I will not lower myself to fight you!"

Esperanza ceased crying. Her brother's words. My God, her brother was being great. But not all agreed with her. Someone laughed.

Pedro looked around. Smiling. Proudly. He had been more than a little afraid of this boy, but now ... oh, this was good. He bellowed! And Aguilar held in wait for Roberto to do it now.

"*¡Chinga tu madre!*" yelled Pedro, and he went on and on shouting insults.

"I will not be provoked," began Roberto, but did not finish his words aloud. People were laughing, and the Reyes brothers were laughing the loudest, and Pedro kept cursing all the women of his household, but he, Roberto, strange as it seemed, was not here, but over there. Facing death, the father.

Aguilar, throwing his cigar away, stepped forward to be counted. Boss. And terrible. "I say, shut up! Now! Or die where you stand!"

"No," said Roberto, moving in front of Aguilar. "This is my fight."

"Well, then, kill him!"

Roberto looked at Juan, saw his eyes, and all at once had the feeling that this strangeness had something to do with the cock fight, the knife fight, the not killing of the already dying cock. He held, not knowing why. And he heard the people all about him laughing, joking, ridiculing, and beginning to go back to Pedro's side. And then one of them said that indeed Roberto was like his father, and Roberto looked at this man and then he knew. Yes. Indeed, in his very soul he knew that he was like his father.

"Listen!" he said. "Yes, I'm like my father. Exactly! And I now know!" His hands were fists, and his knuckles were white. His face was pure power. "He was no coward! He was simply better than all this stupid proof of balls, but ... he didn't know it. So he lived, and died, believing himself a coward. A barfly! A nothing! When he should have died knowing he was one hell of a man." His eyes were watering. "And I'll tell you this ... I'm strong. I'm fast. And I'm capable of killing ten Pedros, but I will not be provoked!

"Look at me! See my eyes! And each man here knows to the root of his soul that I mean what I say! "I'm so much man, here, in my guts, that I can say to all of you ... good-bye."

And he turned. Turned his back on a man who was *a la prueba.* Completely. And such a thing had never been done in honor, in pride, in the strutting walk of a *gallo de estaca,* and mouths fell open, and Pedro froze, not believing, stunned ... as Roberto turned to his sister to walk away.

Pedro screamed! Lunging like a madman with knife in hand. And Aguilar shoved his gun in Pedro's oncoming no-nosed face and fired. Blowing his face into bloody nightness.

Roberto whirled, gun drawn, and pushed Esperanza to the ground. The Reyes were firing. Then Aguilar was hit. And among all this shooting and screaming, came a "*¡Viva México! ¡Gringos cabrones!*" And there came a horse and rider. From the side. Jesús. And he was rushing upon Aguilar with machete in hand.

Roberto fired at Jesús. He hit the horse, and the horse reared, whirling down with death as Jesús swung his machete, cutting Aguilar's stomach open. The horse collapsed, kicking in his own death, and Aguilar, holding in his intestines, squirmed behind the horse's body. Roberto was at Juan's side. Putting two bullets through Jesús' head. The Reyes were going every which way. Everyone was shooting. Esperanza took cover with Roberto and Aguilar behind the fallen horse. The horse began to smell of burning hair as bullets struck it.

Suddenly two .45's burst out. Shooting so fast and numerous they sounded like a machine gun. All men were awed in silence, and there stood *el Don.* Two guns shooting to the heavens, and behind him were thirty men with *retrocargas.* It was the local *forestales* once again, and they were *a toda madre.*

"Enough!" *el Don* commanded. "*¡Basta!*"

Men began lowering their guns. *El Don* lowered his .45's and began to speak. "When are we going to learn? *¡Estos son desmadres de pendejos!*"

Some *forestales* were now escorting the remaining Reyes out into the open. Pablo was with Jesús. He needed no escorting. This had been his favorite brother.

Esperanza and Roberto were with Aguilar. Juan was no longer trying to hold in his intestines. He was straining to speak.

"Roberto," he said, " ... my money. Take it." He coughed, and blood came up from his mouth. " ... my mother." He took Roberto's hand. His eyes narrowed, and his hand was sweating. ." ..my mother. I never bought her ... after all these trips north." And his eyes went huge. Transfixed. He squeezed Roberto's hand. "*¡Júramelo!* You understand!"

Roberto nodded. "*Te lo juro.* I understand."

And his eyes relaxed, looking out over Roberto's shoulder, and stayed there. And Aguilar was dead.

El Don told Pablo to tell his brothers to turn in their weapons. The fight was over for today. Justice had been done. Aguilar, who had killed Pablo's two young brothers last year, was dead. Pedro, who had caused the death of Roberto's father, was dead. And about Jesús, oh, well, he'd always loved *el grito,* and he'd got his gut-true cry of a *charro*-god on horseback. So it was enough. They'd get their weapons back a few days after the respectful funerals. Bloods had to unboil.

Pablo, after a moment, told his brothers to turn in their weapons. After all, they had more at home.

"Oh, no," said *el Don* with *forestales* all around him, "I said, it has been enough." He turned to his group. "Don't you agree?" They agreed. "And you, Roberto, turn in yours and Aguilar's." Roberto obeyed. Giving both .45's.

Then Roberto and his sister loaded Aguilar in a wagon, which Antonio had brought up, and they went home. They'd have to hold the services for Juan quickly and get out of town. *El Don* could not keep back Pablo and his brothers back for very long.

Late that afternoon, after their family goods were loaded in a wagon, Roberto went around back to get the one-eyed horse, and he stopped. The sun was going down, and over there, across the valley, was the mountainside to which he'd taken the *bueyes* every evening. He looked at this distance for a long while. This mountain, with all its hidden valleys of grass and water, was truly a good place. He nodded in self-agreement and quit petting the one-eyed horse and began to walk out of his backyard and into the open valley. Breathing, smelling, feeling.

Oh, the evening breeze of this valley was so rich one could almost taste it. He stopped walking. He reached down and took up a handful of soil. He smelled it, and in that smell he was suddenly taken back to that day of his childhood when his father had returned home all excited. And said that no, their valley had not turned evil. That a man in town, Don Carlos Villanueva, had discovered that the blackness in their valley was good, that it was volcanic ashes, and that when plowed under, it enriched the earth. They'd eaten well that night. And they'd had good crops after that for many years. But then the bad years started.

Roberto breathed, remembering, and tossed his handful of earth up a little at first, and then up high with all his might. Hell, life could still be made good down here in this valley. Why not? The gringos had done it with lesser valleys. And shit, those incredible gringos weren't so incredible. They couldn't even do their own labor out in the hot sun. They'd turned soft. He laughed at his own thinking. He took up another handful of soil. He smiled. He squeezed the handful of soil. Hard. He'd learned a lot up north. He could, if he wished, do a lot of good down here. He kicked the earth, feeling good in self—a true-self hero—and threw the fistful of soil up to the sky, giving *un grito*, a man's cry of good gut feeling.